About the author

I am someone who is curious by nature, I enjoy researching and thinking about hypotheticals. I am a history enthusiast, who likes to understand how things work in life. I like to spend my spare time watching biographies, documentaries, the news and funny videos.

ALTERNATE REALM: THE HERALD
AWAKENED

George Maccall

ALTERNATE REALM: THE HERALD
AWAKENED

Vanguard Press

A CIP catalogue record for this title is
available from the British Library.

ISBN 978-1-80016-696-7

*Vanguard Press is an imprint of
Pegasus Elliot Mackenzie Publishers Ltd.*
www.pegasuspublishers.com

First Published in 2023

**Vanguard Press
Sheraton House Castle Park
Cambridge England**

Printed & Bound in Great Britain

Dedication

To all who enjoy reading historic fiction, and are not bothered by historic inaccuracy, because the story was not trying to be historically accurate, despite my best efforts to make it so. Please don't expect the details to be perfect and hope you will enjoy my work.

Acknowledgements

No amount of thanks can be enough for the fellas who provided me with support and brutally honest feedback — Scot from the gym, Hidde and Derek (the Dutch boys), Jacob from la la-land, Mum and Lallida (hope I spelt it right).

Special thanks to: Half-life, Assassins Creed, League of Legends, Thanos from Avengers and the very informative YouTube channels; Biographics, Kings and Generals and HistoryMarche.

A man finds himself walking in a graveyard, mist and fog in the air. He feels pain in his belly, as though something had punctured him there. He keeps walking, oblivious to what led him to the graveyard. He delves into his memory, hoping to remember something, but to no avail. He happens upon a paved cobblestone path, situated in the middle of the site. He decides to follow the path, hoping it will lead him somewhere. He struggles to move forward while on foot, almost giving up from the pain. He was on the brink of capitulating to the pain, just then he began hearing the voice of a little girl singing in the distance. The agony and exhaustion dulled his sense of direction, making him unable to discern the voice's origin.

'The stranger comes, the stranger goes. He's still perplexed, as to where he goes. He finds himself, among the souls. But yet he longs, to know who calls.'

Intrigued by the mysterious voice, he felt curious enough to investigate. He first tried to focus on his breathing, feeling overwhelmed and discombobulated. He pressed on, forcing himself to walk, in search of the person behind the voice. Moments later, he was able to see a tree emerge from the fog, just up ahead. The voice grew louder with every step he came closer to the tree. This prompted him to walk faster, once the tree was in full view. It was then he spotted a little girl, scraping the tree with a stick. He slows down as he walked towards her. Once he was close enough, he stopped a few paces away from her, to catch his breath. He leaned forward, both hands planted on his knees trying to breathe. He was desperately hoping the pain would dissipate. He kept gazing at her as she scraped away at the tree. She spoke before he had a chance to say a word,

'Greetings, Hannibal!' She spoke to him with a calming voice.

Hannibal saw a glimpse from past, which did not make much sense to him. He remembered standing on an ice lake. More importantly, he was worried as to why he forgot his own name. He was trying to speak, but the heavy panting prevented him from saying anything.

'What is it that you seek, Hannibal?' She turned facing him.

Hannibal's pain abruptly faded, giving him much-needed relief. He felt exhausted, so he gently collapsed to the ground to help him catch his breath.

'Why am I here?' he asked her, whilst gasping for air.

'You are the one who wanted to be here.'

Her response surprised him, but he kept asking eager to find out.

'Why is that?'

'Your journey to free yourself from a curse led you here. But now that you're here, you must make a choice.'

Hannibal raised himself to sit up against the tree. He asked for clarification.

'What choice?'

The little girl approached him, extending out her arm. Hannibal nervously grabbed her hand, unsure of what would happen. Suddenly, everything around him vanished, including the little girl. He was left in a black void. He found himself suspended over nothing, which looked daunting. He closed his eyes, in an attempt to focus on his breathing. When he opened his eyes, he found himself in the village where he was born, not far from Carthage. He saw himself walking with his father, dressed like a military levies. He followed them to see what happened to him. He was looking around, wondering why no one was able to see him. The child's voice emerged from the void, explaining.

'This is when you were a child, by your father's side, heading off to fight Rome during the second Punic War.'

'I don't understand! What happened to me? How did I end up here?'

The child continued. 'Along the way, you travelled to Hispania, where Hannibal Barca's army was stationed. Your father died a natural death along the way. This put you in a precarious position, among the other recruits. You felt scared, going at it alone. You no longer wanted to fight in the war. So later that night, you deserted the army, hiding out in a nearby forest. The army was informed by a local, so they sent scouts to capture you. When they eventually found you, you managed to evade the scouts, hoping to escape the capital punishment. You went deeper into the forest. When they continued to give chase, you panicked. This caused you to flee and you managed to escape the pursuit. This led you to run into a cave, where you stumbled on your way in, falling deeper into the cave. The fall did not kill you, but the impact knocked you out. The cave was home to the most powerful relic on earth, the

Hourglass. Your body touched the relic, preserving your youth. You then woke up a century later when Rome had conquered Hispania. You did not know it then, but the Hourglass was a cursed relic that has powers, of which you gained. You picked up the relic, bringing it into your possession, which allows you entry into an alternate realm, even after death. You were captured by the Romans, because you were mistaken for a local criminal who was wanted by the Republic. You were sentenced to live with the gladiators, as a captured slave in Capua. Eventually you regained your freedom, when the slave uprising broke out, led by Spartacus. You killed a Roman militia man and took his clothes in one of the battles. You then escaped to join the Romans as one of the survivors. You were sent back to Hispania because Pompey was quelling a rebellion. You came into the service of the local Praetor. You confided in him, showing him the relic. He confiscated the Hourglass from you, hoping to use it to bargain with his creditors; he also thought that by having you killed, he might be able to use it for his own purposes. You were imprisoned and killed in a cell. That is when your journey began.'

Hannibal was able to see these incidents, as she described what happened. He did not recognise or know the person who took the Hourglass from him. He was looking around in the cell, where he was held captive, before he was executed. The voice of a woman from behind called him.

'Hannibal.'

He turned around to see a majestic-looking woman, with an ominous smile, staring at him with a piercing look.

'Who are you?' he asked.

'I am here to help you, Hannibal,' replied the mysterious woman. 'I am the Spider Queen, and I can offer you your life back, if you are willing to accept the consequences.'

My life back? Is that even possible? he thought, then asked her, 'What consequences?'

Another woman to his right interrupted, urging him, with a calm voice, 'Don't listen to her, Hannibal! Walk away! Return to the realm of the dead. Returning from the dead is not without consequences. It is a burden so great that you will wish for death, but you won't find it.'

Hannibal now found himself in a difficult position because he did not understand what was said to him.

He asked her, 'And who are you?'

'I am Lady Justice. And you must listen to me. You will be making a great mistake.'

The Spider Queen interrupted Lady Justice, to divert Hannibal's attention away from her.

'The only mistake to be made, is not trying in the first place.'

Lady Justice urged him once more. 'You are walking into oblivion, should you make the wrong choice.'

Hannibal could not stop thinking about his killer, who was weighing heavily on his mind and pride. The notion of being deceived and betrayed, was not something he could forgo, especially when it was a person of status. He also found the opportunity of being brought back to life very appealing, which would allow him to exact revenge.

Hannibal asked the Spider Queen, 'What are the consequences?'

She quietly laughed, followed by a vague explanation. 'You see Hannibal; it is part of the bargain that the consequences remain unforeseen. That is the steep price one must pay to be brought back to life.'

He gulped before responding. 'Fair enough. How can I retrieve the Hourglass from my killer?'

Lady Justice asked Hannibal, 'Are you sure you want to do this?' She then stepped closer to Hannibal, cautioning him. 'Time and death are not phenomena to be meddled with.'

Deep down in his heart, Hannibal knew that she was right. He acknowledged that it was a serious warning, but he did not fully grasp the severity of it, nor his situation. The temptation of revenge was too great to pass up. Because he felt it his duty to exact revenge, an eye for an eye. At this point, he had already made his mind up.

Hannibal again turned to the Spider Queen and said, 'I wish to return from the dead. I want to confront my killer and find the Hourglass.'

'And do you wish to bind yourself to those terms, as the price for your life back?' she asked him, being coy.

He firmly stated, 'I do.'

A wider smile crept onto the Spider Queen's face. She snarled at him, 'Of course you do.' She then started laughing hysterically as she faded away.

The deranged laughter frightened Hannibal. He turned to Lady Justice with his arm outstretched, seeking her help.

She regrettably informed him, 'I am sorry Hannibal; you already made your choice. What has been done cannot be undone.' Then she too faded away.

Hannibal's despair left him wondering. *What have I done?*

The last thought that lurked in his head was that of regret. He was not fully aware of what his decision really meant, because he had no idea what he had gotten himself into. Even though it took a while for him to reach that conclusion, he acknowledged that it did not matter. His thoughts accompanied him, as he fell unconscious once more. He had reached the bottom of the pity pit of the abyss, or so it seemed.

Hannibal found himself in a safe and quiet place. He knew he was not awake; rather, it was him floating in his own thoughts. The utopia that everyone drifts off to when they are troubled. The noises in his head had vanished, leaving him contemplating and reflecting on his actions. Wishful thinking interfered, as a form of blissful mercy, helping him cope with his choices moving forward. The only problem was that he now had to relive his actions to remember what happened.

Over the horizon, he could see a stranger. He could not make out who it was. The stranger distracted Hannibal from his thoughts. Despite wanting to remain in this quiet void, he wanted to commence his journey.

The Child appeared before him, blocking out the stranger. Hannibal put his head down because he was ashamed and afraid. He did not know what to say at this point. He was hoping the child would provide him with answers.

She told him, 'He cannot harm you yet. The man you see on the horizon, that is. But when the time comes, you two will meet again.' She sat down next to him. 'The powers of the Hourglass were absorbed by your body because you were in contact with it for just over a hundred years. But they activate after death.'

Hannibal was listening to the words, but still he understood nothing.

She continued, 'The accord you made with the Spider Queen has unique terms, since it involves you taking back your Hourglass and finding your killer. You see, when you agreed to her offer, you stated that you wanted back the Hourglass, and you also agreed to exact revenge on the Praetor.'

He mumbled to himself, as though he had lost his sanity for a moment. Then he said,

'How will I find him? He would have used the power of the Hourglass for his own gain; it is a lost cause.'

The Child smiled reassuring him. 'The Praetor cannot use the Hourglass because he did not follow the rules of possession. only the one whom receives or finds the relic can use its powers. The Praetor confiscated the relic from you; therefore, he cannot use it.'

This cheered Hannibal up somewhat, so he asked, 'What about my journey? Where will it leave me?'

The Child answered, 'The curse will take you back to Phoenicia. Right when the Persian King Cyrus conquered the region. He will find you at the ancient city of Sidon. You will find your way from then onwards.'

'Why Phoenicia?'

'Well, you see Hannibal, not everything will make sense.'

The Child then bid him farewell, parting ways.

Despite the vague answer, his thoughts faded away, as she departed. This is where he began to feel the dream fade out into reality. Right after, he was able to hear voices. Hannibal woke up in a crowded prison. A Persian soldier opened the cell, walking in. He was followed by King Cyrus.

The king addressed the prisoners.

'I came here to liberate you all, as I am in need of able-bodied volunteers, as levies for my army.' After looking around the prison, the king asked, 'Which of you would like to volunteer?'

Hannibal stepped forward.

'I would like to volunteer.'

The experience thus far felt unreal, he could not actually believe his eyes. The king approached Hannibal smiling, as he presented his hand to greet him. The king then added, 'Welcome to the Achaemenid Empire. What is your name boy?'

'Hannibal, your majesty.'

'Seeing that you are the first to volunteer. I will summon you later today, as I like to inspect all the troops myself. I would like to present you with a token of my appreciation, for being so brave, for being the very first man to come forward.'

'Yes, of course great king,' replied a shaken Hannibal.

Later that day, Hannibal was indeed summoned by the king to his quarters. Hannibal entered the king's chamber, being warmly greeted by him again. He then sat down with him at the table.

The king spoke gently and diplomatically. 'I had a vision. That I would find a wanderer in the prison, upon entering Sidon. Seeing that you were supposed to be in my army, I appreciate your enthusiasm to join, but I also understand that you have somewhere else to be. Come the morrow, you will be escorted onto a merchant ship to be on your way.'

Hannibal felt butterflies in his stomach, surprised by what he heard.

He then hesitantly replied, 'I don't know what to say, but thank you, great King'

The king replied with an inquisitive look on his face, 'I am a servant of the light, and I know that strange occurrences are ill omens. Whatever your motives are, I care not for them. I will host you until you reach the Greek city states. By then, you must make yourself scarce.' The king presented him with a parting gift, stating, 'This is something given to me by a very strange merchant, on my way to Sidon. I would like you to have it. A reward for your commitment, as promised. Think of it as a strange item for a strange young man.'

It was a shrinking sack, but Hannibal did not know it yet. The king wanted Hannibal gone for good. Hannibal nodded in agreement, then left the king's quarters. He then took to the streets, to roam the local bazaar. He was scouring for provisions, seeking only what he needed for his journey. While looking around the city, he noticed how similar the buildings looked to the ones in Carthage. Even the language spoken in the city was similar to his Punic mother tongue. He found it strange hearing it again, especially since he only recalled speaking Latin, in his past life. After a while, wandering about in the bazaar, he found a blacksmith's workshop. He spoke with the blacksmith, asking to buy a falcata sword. The blacksmith responded in his Persian tongue. Hannibal was surprised to find himself able to understand the man, despite having never spoken the language. He reached into the sack, hoping to find something to barter for the weapon. When he dipped his hand to reach rummage for something, his hands bumped into objects that made a rustling sound. He was able to hear the clink of coins. He then pulled out a few coins, only to realise that they were Persian gold coins. The discovery left him ecstatic, and grateful to the king. Still astonished by the coins, because he had never seen gold before, he paid the smith. The blacksmith gave him a newly forged sword, with a leather sheath. Hannibal smiled in appreciation, then moved on. He did not know how he understood the local tongue, but he felt elated.

He kept walking around in the bazaar, until he happened upon a crowd. The crowd surrounded two poets, who were challenging each other in a strange poetry duel. One was from Arabia, the other was Persian. He was impressed by their improvised display of poetry. He was not someone who would usually enjoy poetry, but it was quite the spectacle. After a while, the crowd had dispersed, when the poets concluded their verbal duel. Afterwards, Hannibal was able to find a vacant rooftop, overlooking the harbour and the sea castle. The scene reminded him of a time when his father took him fishing. He remembered how he helped his father gather the fish into a woven basket, afterwards they sold some of them at the local market. He had another memory of how his friends embarrassed him in the presence of the girl he adored. He then tried to remember the Praetor who stole the Hourglass, but instead he was met with a blank of darkness, which greatly irritated him.

The following day, Hannibal woke up to a sunny morning. He climbed down from the roof, to head towards the harbour. Upon arrival, he found a Persian royal representative, flanked by two guards, waiting for him. The king had sent them to escort him to a merchant ship bound for Athens. Hannibal understood what was happening, so he followed them. After a short distance, he was instructed to board a certain merchant ship. He was also given provisions that would last him the voyage. He then boarded the ship, remaining on the upper deck, while the ship was still at anchor. He wanted to take in the view of the city and the harbour, for as long as possible, before the ship departed for Athens. Once the crew, travellers and goods were on board, the ship disembarked into the open sea. The duration of his journey was not very fruitful, as he spent his time switching between the upper and lower decks. The time was spent on self-reflecting on everything that had happened. He kept focusing on his memories, specifically trying to remember the Praetor's identity, but nothing would come of it.

On the last night of the voyage, the Spider Queen came to him in a dream. They were on the top deck alone, gazing upon the full moon in the clear night sky.

She said, 'You must be wondering to yourself what is this place? Why have I been brought to the past? The truth of the matter is simple. Ever since the Hourglass came into your possession, it has given you some powers, and a chance to acquire more powers on your pursuit to seek what you came back for. To unlock these other powers, you need time to know what they are, and how to use them.'

Hannibal was unable to process the reality of his predicament, but he appreciated the irony of needing time to learn. In his mind, he could not comprehend what was being said, because what was said, made no sense whatsoever. He was frustrated with the nature of his journey because knowledge is exactly what he required to progress through his journey. The only problem was that he would have to wait. But he continued listening.

'Along your journey, you must avoid sentinels and seekers, people like the Persian king, Cyrus. They are the ones who can see you for who you are. They can harm you, and possibly even end your journey. What this means for you is that you will die, but death will send you straight to Hades, where you will continue to suffer for eternity. The very curse you seek to break is also an entirely different form of eternal hell. Think of them as your enemy, the type of enemy you must avoid, rather than fight. Along the way, you will be able to discover your true potential. Reaching your true proportions.'

The dream was about to come to an end, when her voice spoke to Hannibal saying, 'The ability to understand other tongues is one of the many powers you now possess.'

Come the morning, the ship had reached its destination, arriving to a vibrant Athens. The harbour was full of merchants who had travelled from all corners of the Mediterranean. Hannibal disembarked the ship, heading inside the city. The guards at the gates were completely oblivious to Hannibal, as he walked past them into the city. He was still amazed by the fact that no one noticed his presence, wherever he went. He found it convenient, making his journey simple, because that is what he needed to evolve and progress.

Hannibal loved everything about Athens. The citizens' attire, the sophisticated culture, the buildings and infrastructure. He liked the forums and how organised everything was. His eyes could not leave the many sights of the city. He took his time to discover the wonders of Athens, street by street. The city reminded him of his past life when he lived in Capua. When the sun began to set over the horizon, he decided to retire, after such an eventful day. He was drawn to a villa that caught his eye, so he climbed to the rooftop, to have a full view of the city. He dropped all his belongings on the ground, placing the shrinking sack against the wall to lean on it. The night brought about a beautiful solace to the city. Hannibal snuck inside the house, to fetch something to wrap himself with. Once back on the roof, he lay down and gazed upon the clear night sky. The silence helped him delve into his thoughts; he was thinking about what to do the following day, which helped him smoothly transition into a deep sleep.

He had a vision, where he saw himself at an amphitheatre. It was an open structure, with many arched rows, overlooking the main platform. The rows were filled with Greek citizens, who were captivated by a charismatic orator. He did not know why he was there or where this place was. Suddenly, the clouds above the theatre turned dark grey, blocking out the sun. Hannibal got scared, not knowing what was happening, being petrified by the clouds. He heard the voice of a woman calling him. This prompted him to look around, but he saw nothing, however he did notice that the audience had disappeared. He then looked back down at the platform, where he saw a woman wearing a toga. She looked immaculate, with black hair, and a unique blank expression. The woman told Hannibal,

'Come to Delphi.'

Hannibal woke up from his sleep, to find the sun rising. He knew he had to travel to that amphitheatre, but he did not know where it was. He stood up to admire the city from the roof, he found that it looked different in the daytime. He found it majestic, realising that this was where the wealthy families of Athens lived. He then sat back down, leaning against the wall, reflecting on the vision, whilst admiring the scenery. The morning quiet was interrupted by the inhabitants of the house speaking with one another. He tried to ignore it at first, but his curiosity got the better of him. He crawled over to the roof side, above one of the windows to the house, eavesdropping on their conversation. He overheard the woman urging her husband to visit the amphitheatre at Epidaurus. Hannibal squinted in concentration, as he listened to the conversation. The discovery made his stomach turn because this coincidence was far too uncanny. He also realised that if he followed the family, they would act as a guide to help him reach the city. He scrambled to pack everything into the sack, which made the garment shrink into the sack. Hannibal recoiled at the sight. He slowly pulled the garment out of the sack, which made it go back to its original size. After pausing to ponder, he smiled having made the accidental discovery. He placed it back into the sack, then hastily climbed down from the roof.

The family made their way to the front of the house, with the servants following closely behind. They loaded the family's belongings onto the awaiting wagon. A few servants accompanied the family, while the others stayed behind. Hannibal followed the family in the wagon, as they made their way through the streets. Along the way, he found an idle white horse standing nearby with no apparent rider, so he approached the animal and mounted it. It was a pleasant surprise to him that the horse did not resist him. He continued to follow the wagon, until they had departed the city, through one of the main gates.

Hannibal enjoyed the scenery along the main road. He would occasionally break off from the wagon to forage for food, from nearby farms and groves. He would also stop by the roadside wells, to drink and allow the horse to drink as well. He would spend the night, sleeping near the family with his horse. He used this time on the road to enjoy mother nature's beauty and thought of little else.

After many days of travelling on the main road to Epidaurus, he saw the small city from afar. He left the wagon, to make his way into the city. He had this gripping fear in his stomach, as he approached the city; it was the nerves of anticipation. The horse stopped at a small apple tree to eat. He dismounted the animal to let it rest after an arduous journey. Hannibal collapsed on the grass, feeling exhausted, and falling unconscious into a deep sleep.

He had another vision, where he saw himself standing on the frozen lake. All the surroundings were covered in frost. The night sky was illuminated by a long stretch of green light, flowing smoothly, in a river like motion. There were no cold winds, only a calm atmosphere, which helped put him at ease. He started to walk forward in a slow pace, with his eyes fixed gazing upon the light in the sky. He then slipped on the ice, falling to the ground. He found the tundra terrain fascinating because he had never seen a place so white. He tried to stand up, but lost his balance, causing him to fall on his back, slowly sliding in one direction. Although strange, the feeling was exhilarating. He carefully stood up once again and tried to slide on his feet. Once he gained momentum, he kept sliding up and down the ice. He was filled with glee, because moving fast while upright felt great. After a while, he tried to stop sliding, but he ended up falling again. He lay down on the ice, facing the sky, admiring the miraculous light. He did not care why he was in this strange place, because it was majestic. Despite his initial thought, deep down he was wondering why he was there. He understood that it held significance, because he recalled being here once before, but he didn't know when or why.

The Aurora light in the sky started to move out of sight, escaping as though it were a snake, slithering away. This mildly irritated him, because he had never seen something so beautiful, like the Aurora. His experience was cut short when he started hearing the child, who was singing a lullaby. He rose to his feet, whilst looking in the direction of the voice. He saw the little girl emerge from the darkness, slowly making her way towards him. The vision came to an end, when she told him,

'The Oracle is what you seek, Hannibal.'

He woke up to his horse licking his face. Hannibal slowly moved the horse's face away from his own. He opened his eyes, seeing a calm night sky, much like the one in the vision. He stood up, and started strolling through the city, enjoying the quiet, in the dead of night. He was looking for the amphitheatre, hoping to find a way out of the city into the open fields. He kept walking for most of the night, until he found a neat slab stone path that led outside the city. Hannibal followed the path, which eventually led him directly to the amphitheatre.

Hannibal approached the entrance to the structure. It was the same place he'd seen in his previous vision. Only now, it was lit by torches, which he found odd. He saw a group of actors rehearsing a play, so he climbed down the steps, to sit in the front row. He was watching them closely. He realised that the actress in the middle looked and dressed like the woman in the vision. The other actors around her were on their knees, with their palms clinched together, asking her questions. He concluded that the one in the middle must be the Oracle. The actors began to walk back, starting over. The two actors were speaking to one another, about travelling to Delphi to visit the Oracle. This had confirmed to him his thoughts about the woman he saw.

He heard a voice calling him, from his right. When he looked over, he saw the Spider Queen sitting in the front row, not too far from him. He found this strange, because she never appears in reality. She spoke to Hannibal, whilst watching the rehearsal.

'This is not reality, Hannibal. You are still asleep.' This had come as a surprise to him; he felt perplexed. She continued, 'Have you given any thought as to how you will unlock your powers?'

'Yes, of course,' he eagerly replied.

'The Greeks believed that Hercules was a demigod. He wanted to prove he was a deity. So, he took it upon himself to embark upon twelve labours. In the end, he prevailed, proving himself strong, capable and worthy.'

'Is that what I have to do?' he asked her. He then remarked, 'Because it sounds like a punishment.'

'Don't be facetious, Hannibal. The salient point is that for you to unlock your powers, you must endure through several trials of your own. You were warned that there will be consequences when you chose this path. You see, there is a greater purpose at work, you will know why in time. But one thing is for certain, experience will be your greatest teacher.'

Hannibal looked to the sky, simply replying, 'I don't know, but we'll see about that.'

The Spider Queen continued. 'You will not be left clueless this time.'

Hannibal looked down at the theatre and saw a cloud had replaced the actors.

'To unlock your powers, you must; fight the most cunning swordsman who ever lived. Then you must learn the secrets to the art of war, walk a path of two deserts, speak with spirits, discover the city floating above water. You must learn to fly, commit regicide against a tyrant, a warmonger and a savage; help one rebel and betray another.'

First, he saw a warrior dressed in strange and colourful armour. Then he saw a man mocked by an emperor. He then saw snowy mountains and a desert. He then saw many teepees on a plain, with smoke leaving through their tops. After that he saw a fleet of canoes, with strange-looking people, rowing the narrow boats. He saw a man in a beautiful city; writing in a language he had never seen before. Afterwards, he saw three kings, one wearing chainmail armour, another on horseback and the last in Hellenic armour. Finally, he recognised Spartacus and saw another man with blue paint on his face.

'Is there a particular reason for these specific quests?' he curiously enquired, seeking clarification.

She taunted him, suggesting, 'Wrong question, Hannibal.'

He nodded, then asked again, 'How will I find all these people and places? Because I'm guessing the execution is the difficult part?'

'To find the tasks alone is a challenge within itself. To execute those tasks is another challenge entirely. You will be crossing paths with sentinels, whom you must avoid throughout those endeavours. The odds alone, would leave one wondering, can you emerge unscathed or even alive?' She turned to Hannibal. 'After all, the entire journey is a riddle to be solved.'

In an attempt to spite her, he sarcastically replied, 'It somehow sounds doable.'

'So be it!'

Before she could leave, he quickly asked her, 'What about the Hourglass, and the man who stole it from me?'

She taunted him one last time before departing.

'I have a feeling, that you are more than capable of using the powers of deduction to find both.' She then stood up and began to walk away, bringing the vision to an end.

Hannibal awoke to a beautiful morning, this time in reality. He made his way to the theatre. Once there, he climbed down the steps to sit in the front row. He spent the day watching the talent, one after the other, performing before the audience. He enjoyed the plays of past heroes, and the poems of passionate poets. He listened intently to the words of wisdom, from gifted orators and philosophers, despite lacking the context behind the acts and performances. He admired the genius design of the structure, and how it allowed the voices to echo. The design only amplified the magnitude of the performances, making them so alive. Despite the incredible experience, he eventually grew tired and hungry, compelling him to leave. He made his way back to the apple tree, where he had left his horse to rest. He picked as many apples from the tree as needed, placing them in the shrinking sack. He made his way back into the city to find a well to drink from. As he was searching through the shrinking sack, he found a hollow animal skin in the sack. He filled it with water, to use on the road to Delphi.

He mounted his horse, then commenced his journey to seek the Oracle. He was worried about how he was going to reach Delphi, since there was no guide for him to follow. He kept travelling on the road, hoping to find any sign, to direct him. In his mind, he was overthinking the problem, when suddenly he fell faint while on horseback, losing consciousness. He found these occurrences very irritating, but they served their purpose.

Hannibal found himself in another dream. He saw the little girl in the void. He asked her, 'How do I find my way to the Oracle at Delphi?'

'The next time you wake up you will be at Delphi.'

'How does the horse know which way to go?' he wondered aloud.

'Don't you have more pressing concerns to worry about?'

Hannibal found all of this very difficult to comprehend.

'When I saw the stranger on the horizon, you said that he could not harm me for then. What did you mean by that?'

'He is someone you must face; he is and represents your fears and doubts. He is part of the greater riddle to your journey.'

'What?'

'There are two strangers, the one whom you seek, and the one you must defeat. The Praetor's identity being the first, fear and doubt being the second.'

Hannibal felt frustrated to the point of anger. He was angry with himself, angry with his choices. He knew that there was some sort of lesson behind the labours, but his naïve self could not fathom the wisdom, as it sounded ridiculous to him. This felt like a punishment, as he initially thought. He felt conflicted about the Spider Queen because on the one hand she was humiliating him, and on the other hand she was offering a helping hand, but in a vague way. He felt lost and overwhelmed by the influx of thoughts. This also created more questions for him, that loomed over his journey, moving forward. The more he kept thinking, the less things made sense. Clarity was no more, instead, he would need to find focus. He decided to stop thinking altogether. He decided to worry about Delphi for now, then worry about the rest later.

Hannibal woke up to a sunny morning, right outside the temple of Apollo. Not knowing how his horse brought him there. He still could not understand how everything had come to pass; the world was not making ever less sense by the day. He did however, appreciate all the support he had received thus far. He fell off the horse when he tried to dismount, with the sack falling on his head. Out of exhaustion, he started laughing, but the laughter was cut short, by him coughing from the dust. He slowly rose to his feet. He reached into the shrinking sack to fetch an apple, to satisfy his hunger. He leaned back on his horse, eating the apple whilst looking at the temple. He watched the people going in and out, one after the other. He also noticed how everyone that entered the temple had food, farm animals and sacks stuffed with coin offerings on their way in.

Come the night, he decided it was time to enter the temple, so he could finally visit the Oracle in peace. The moment he entered the temple, he felt a calm atmosphere inside. He slowly made his way to the Oracle's chamber. Once inside, he began hallucinating and hearing whispers. He fell to his hands and knees because he lost his balance. He started shaking his head, thinking it was exhaustion. He then got up from the temple floor, and continued walking, wandering about in the chamber.

'I am here!' He called out, looking around.

The Oracle replied, 'Greetings, Hannibal.'

He started looking around, but saw no one, only a voice in the chamber with him. The Oracle then appeared before him, slowly coming into view. Suddenly, the chamber was being devoured by a white void.

She continued, 'What does the wanderer seek?'

Hannibal was too distracted at first, looking around him, as though the earth had been consumed by the void. Hannibal looked down at the void for a while, he liked the look of it, but it still felt odd standing on nothing. He was also thinking about what he wanted to ask. Being overwhelmed by an ocean of questions. He looked up at the Oracle, who was staring at him with a blank expression. He took a short breath, followed with a sigh of dread, he then asked, 'Who is the Stranger?'

'Only by unmasking your stranger, will help you learn their identity,' she cryptically remarked.

He remembered the man who stole the Hourglass, which prompted him to ask her, 'How can I find the Praetor?'

'You will learn about him, in the company of a poet, author and actor.'

Hannibal was extremely confused.

'I don't understand?'

She promised him, 'You will find him eventually, but that is something that will take time.'

Frustrated, Hannibal understood that he had to be specific, to help him narrow his search. He turned away walking back and forth, he then continued.

'How did he die?'

'He was stabbed by the conspirators.'

Satisfied with the answer, he asked again, 'When did he die?'

'He died during the Ides of March.'

'What year did he meet his demise?'

'That is for you to find out.'

Hannibal acknowledged this limitation, then asked, 'I saw myself on a frozen ground; where was I? And what significance does that place hold in my journey?'

'The vision you saw was in the land of the Norsemen, called Norway. You saw yourself on the ice lake, because you will be in search of the Black Rose, and it is of paramount importance to your journey.'

'Black Rose?' He thought aloud, then asked her, 'What purpose does the Black Rose serve?'

'The Black Rose is a token that one gives to an entity, to save them from harm, to be released from duty or it can be used to break one's curse, but it cannot be used for both. They are near impossible to find without an entity's guidance and can only be found in the most extreme weather conditions.'

'Are there other kinds of tokens?'

'There is the White Rose. They can only be found under the secret lake, in the highlands of Caledonia. They are used to task someone with a quest. The person to whom you give a white rose cannot harm you, because they are marked, by means of the White Token or otherwise, that puts you out of reach of their harm. The other purpose being a task of servitude, makes one obliged to serve you, when presented with the White Token.'

Hannibal was relieved to have some answers. He understood that this knowledge will help him later in his journey. His presence at the ice lake now made sense, but he still had to find it.

'I have heard the term Wanderer before. What is a Wanderer?'

'A Wanderer is someone who is lost in time, and therefore untraceable, unless marked by a hex or recognised.'

Hannibal had a parting query; he asked her, 'I have nine labours to complete. How will I know where to begin?'

She instructed him, 'Head to Sparta.'

The Oracle then began to fade away.

This concluded the interaction, taking Hannibal out of the hallucination. He then took his time, to recollect his thoughts, trying to understand what he had to do next. He now understood part of the end goal, to his journey, but the knowledge gathered was not useful for his current predicament. His thoughts were interrupted by the roaring of his stomach, so he decided to eat. He made his way into the storage chamber, where all the offerings where kept, and helped himself to bread, olives, fruits, and a handful of coins. He began eating on his way out of the temple. Once he was outside, he was enjoying the sight of the clear sky, being illuminated by the full moon. It dawned on him that the entire visit and the hallucination had lasted for a moment. He saw his horse slowly walking towards him, so he fetched the apples from the sack, and hand fed the horse. He then poured water from his animal skin into the horse's mouth. His eyes were starting to feel heavy, so he walked his horse under a nearby tree, where both horse and rider retired for the night.

Hannibal saw the Spider Queen in his dream; this time she did not approach him. She seemed too preoccupied with something else. Her back was turned towards him, as if she was not aware of his presence. Hannibal got up from the ground, he immediately noticed the black void, this was different, as they always met wherever Hannibal was, in his past dreams. Hannibal approached her with concern, he briefly paused to try to see what she was doing, but then continued moving towards her.

'Why are we in this place?' he asked her, whilst looking at the void.

'Your mind is at ease; we are in your thoughts, which are nothing,' she replied with disinterest.

Hannibal did not notice he really was at ease. The fact that he was not aware of his own mental state worried him.

'You worry about worrying, and you are anxious about everything.'

Hannibal looked down at his hands, but noticed how tense his entire body was, he was even holding his breath. He closed his eyes, took a deep breath to relax his muscles. He then started to slowly lay back down on the void, continuing his slow breathing. His eyes remained closed, because he hoped she would go away as her presence made him anxious. The only problem was, she had the answers he was looking for. He reluctantly asked her,

'How do I begin my journey? How will I know how to find the quests?'

'Every journey starts with a single step.'

Hannibal laughed as he thought about what she said.

She continued. 'For instance, you not taking matters seriously, or considering the gravity of your situation.'

He mockingly asked, 'What is gravity?'

She abruptly turned around, aggressively grabbing him by his clothes, lifted him up, then pushed him off the edge of the void. He was scared and panicked as he fell, which made him scream at the top of his lunges, thinking that he was about to die. During the fall, he was able to feel a strange transformation happening. Whatever it was, he no longer felt human, which was alarming. He tried to move his limbs and it felt like he began to glide on air. He looked at his body and saw that he had transformed into a crow. He then turned around and started to fly around the void. She seized him mid-flight, which made him transform back to his human self.

'That was gravity, and the gravity of your situation will lead you to discover things about yourself you did not know.' She then let go of him.

Hannibal was very frightened by what happened. He asked her,

'How was that possible? How did I turn into a crow?'

'You will be able to fly, Hannibal. But first you must learn to walk.'

In a twisted way, she now seemed more approachable, which made him feel at ease about her. But there was something about her that made his stomach tense in her presence. Despite his mixed feelings, Hannibal understood her point. He accepted the harsh reality, that he ought to change his ways, that of thought and demeanour, if he wanted to get far in his journey.

'Since every journey starts with a single step, you will walk all the way to Sparta.'

'You can't be serious?'

'Just do as you are told, or there will be consequences.'

She then disappeared before the dream could end, leaving him alone in the void, for a while longer. He was too shaken to think about nothing at all. He had learned his first lesson. Hannibal spent the following morning piecing together every bit of knowledge he had acquired. He made the decision to start taking matters seriously because he wanted to change. He decided to visit the Oracle one last time, before he departed for Sparta.

He entered the temple, but this time he did not collapse to the ground when he started hallucinating. He made his way into the oracle's chamber and decided to wait instead of calling out. Nothing happened, so he kept on waiting. After the day was over, the white void consumed the chamber, followed by the Oracle fading into view.

'What does Hannibal seek?' Her voice echoed throughout the chamber.

'I was thinking about the labours, and I think they may exist within the same century. Is that true?'

'No. They take place in different centuries and different places.'

'How will I know which century to find them in? So that I can wait for the quests.'

'Why wait when you can time travel and teleport?'

'Time travel?' He was bewildered. 'Teleport? What is teleporting?'

'Teleportation is the instant travel from one location to another. Time travel is obviously travelling through time. If one possesses the Hourglass, one can do both. If you possess any other relic, you can still teleport and time travel, but there are certain limitations. Non-Hourglass relics can still time travel freely, however you will need to be present at a monument, to teleport to another monument.'

'Is there a relic that I can find, in the near future or somewhere in this region?' he felt a knot in his stomach, realising that he lost a very valuable relic, in the Hourglass.

'Yes. There is the knot of Gordium, also known as the Gordian Knot. You will find it in Anatolia when Alexander, son of Phillip, marches on Persia.'

He felt relieved, knowing that there was renewed hope, with this new relic, but he still had to find it.

'I will know this... how, exactly?'

'When the Greek city states become weak, Phillip of Macedon will impose his hegemony over Greece.'

'Why must I go to Sparta? What awaits me there?'

'Sparta has a warrior culture. There you will learn wrestling and other necessary martial skills. You must remain there until you meet King Leonidas. Then you must depart to the Island of Crete. Where you will learn marksmanship. The death of King Phillip will be your signal to leave the island. Only then will you be free to go about your journey.' The Oracle then disappeared shortly after.

Hannibal left the temple, but before he did, he took as many offerings as he would need, to make the journey to Sparta. After much-needed reflection on future endeavours, he took a deep breath and whistled for his horse to come to him. He then shrunk him into the sack. He did not want to use him to travel to Sparta. His plan was to walk in the direction where the sun sets over the horizon. The first phase of the march passed well. The walking felt very slow, but he was able to soldier on, covering good distances. He often had a strong urge to release the horse when his legs grew tired. The only thing preventing him from failing this task, was the strong sense of commitment to the endeavour. During the first night, he noticed the Aurora in the sky and was it guiding him. It would serve as a sky mark to follow, because it was easy for him to still remember the direction he had to walk the following morning. The pleasant sight of nature all around him made the walk bearable and rewarding. After weeks of trekking, he had finally reached the city. He was happy to see it appear in the distance. Overcome with joy, he collapsed to the ground losing consciousness. The first task was now complete. He felt very proud of his accomplishment, but he was beyond exhausted.

He was able to hear the Spider Queen's voice speak to him,

'Well done, Hannibal. You have travelled a great distance, but you will not find rest here. Welcome to Sparta.'

There it was again, her sinister voice chiming through. Reminding him why he should be worried and weary of her.

A day later, Hannibal awoke to a man dragging him by his feet, to the fighting grounds. He slowly rose to his feet. He was being scolded by the man, who spoke to him in Greek. Hannibal understood that he was mistaken for a runaway slave. Thinking quickly, he put his head down in shame. He was dragged onto the fighting pit, where he was beaten by the new recruits. This was a harsh welcome he did not anticipate. He spent the night in a cell, battered and bruised and in a lot of pain. The voice in his head wondering, *What have I done to myself. What have I done to deserve this?*

The following day, Hannibal was released from captivity to serve as a slave for one of the training commanders. He would follow him around, fetch items for him, clean his room and serve him food. He would be remanded to eat in the corner, like a dog. During midday, he would be placed in the fighting pit and the recruits would beat him again. He would try to beg them to stop, but this only encouraged them to keep going. When he gave up, he would begin crying, while they mocked and laughed at him. This was his state for many months. Eventually they grew bored with beating him, so they resorted to belittling him instead.

One day, the Spartan youth were instructed to line up in battle formations. The commander stood at the centre, with a loud voice, exclaiming,

'You run, so that you can chase the enemy on the battlefield. You lift rocks, so that you become strong enough to wield the shield and spear. You wrestle, to be able to wrestle your opponent to the ground, or if you are disarmed or lose your weapon. Never forget the lessons you learn here, because you live, breathe and fight for the Glory of Sparta; nothing else matters.'

These speeches were constantly drummed into the minds of the recruits, so that they may never lose sight or focus of what they do. More importantly, so that they always remember their duty towards Sparta. Hannibal did not care much for Sparta, but he liked the spirit of camaraderie that existed between the men, as well as how the speeches applied to him in his own way. It served as a reminder, to maintain focus on the end goal in sight, and to carry that reminder with him, for what lies ahead. His journey had only begun, but he had a great many more steps before it would be over.

At times, Hannibal would become complacent, and this is when the beatings would resume. It reached a point where he was being hit by anyone that saw him and yelled at every time he was in sight. To avoid mistreatment and punishment, he became very disciplined, ensuring he remained out of sight, and never forgot his place among them. One night, when he was alone, he began crying, as the experience had broken his spirit. He felt like it was better to die than be alive. Many years had passed. He became numb to the abuse, but he learned how to live with it and avoid it at times.

Being a slave, living among the Spartans, and serving the commanders, he found himself privy to their confidential conversations. The fact that he looked hopeless and broken, was to his advantage. Because he was not perceived as a threat, they lowered their guard around him. He hated the fact that he did not have it in him to fight back or be defiant. By overhearing their many conversations, he learned a lot about the way they think. Why they did things the way they do. He was also able to develop his cunning skills, such as stealing, lurking or sneaking around, eavesdropping and infiltrating without leaving a trace behind. To get back at his abusers, he would often place one commander's items, in the other man's quarters to incite fights among them. Whenever there was a feud between two soldiers, he would destroy or damage one man's belongings, to make it look as though the other had done so.

One day, a new group of Spartan youth recruits were marched into the camp. Hannibal was getting ready to serve as usual. This time, he saw the king present at the camp. The commander shouted for Hannibal to come at once. He firmly told him,

'This here is Leonidas, show him to his quarters and get him ready in his new armour!'

Hannibal was happy beyond belief, because this marked the end of this dreadful experience. He did as he was told and made sure not to incur the wrath of the commanders. Come the night, he was allowed to sleep in a small room instead of the cell, due to his good behaviour. At first, he waited until there were no movements around his room, to decide when to flee. Moments later, he heard loud laughter, and soldiers speaking in a crude manner to one another. From his experience with them, he knew that they were drunk. When he snuck up to them, he realised that they were incoherently drunk. The perfect opportunity had finally presented itself to him, because all the guards that usually were on patrol, had joined in on the festive drinking. Hannibal released the horse and quickly rode out of Sparta, before anyone had a chance to spot him.

After the long journey back, Hannibal was glad to see Athens once more. He wanted to see the houses, walk through the streets of the wealthy families. He knew exactly which rooftop to spend the night on. It gave him some breathing room, from the madness of Sparta. He tried to recalled memories from his former life, in the hopes of remembering something. He was thinking about his past life. He was also thinking about the future at the same time. He still had not reached the villa, while his thoughts were racing through his mind. He managed to make it to the rooftop, before sundown.

The night had descended upon the city, bringing with it a blissful silence. He noticed that the house was too quiet, indicating that it was empty. He was curious enough to investigate so he went in. Once inside, there were a few servants, looking after the place. He went into the family's chamber, where the husband and wife slept. Being in the house, surrounded by comforts and luxuries was a rare feeling for him. He realised that there was no one stopping him from using the bed. Whenever a servant would pass by, this triggered him to hide, but he was quick to realise that they could not see him. When he lay down on the bed, facing the ceiling, this made him cry and laugh from happiness. He was finally safe from Sparta and her Spartans. Thinking back on his experience, he realised that although it was a terrible journey, it taught him many things including toughening him up. It also gave him the essential skills he would need for survival, after having survived that particular ordeal. Eventually, exhaustion got the better of him, making him fall into a very deep slumber.

The following morning, he woke up, not recalling much of what happened the night before. Despite the comfortable stay he had at the house, he knew it was time to move on. He wanted to stay another day, but the sooner he headed to the island of Crete, the sooner he would be able to leave this chapter behind him. He searched the house for provisions, to last him the journey. He was able to find a large storage room, containing everything he would need. He helped himself, by stuffing anything he could get his hands on, filling up the shrinking sack. He went up on the roof, to see the view of the city one last time. He remembered his first night there, as if it was yesterday. With that memory fresh in mind, he left for the harbour immediately.

He was wondering what awaited him in Crete, and how long his stay on the island would last. He was trying to imagine what the island looked like, not knowing what to expect. After he had made his way to the harbour, he stopped for a moment, to watch the ships. He was seeking a merchant ship heading out of the Aegean Sea. He was listening for merchants calling out for ships, leaving for or passing by Crete. He saw a bronze-skinned merchant, who was wearing Hellenic style clothing. He knew that this merchant may have come from Africa. He approached the man to greet him,

'Good day Captain. Where will you make port?'

The merchant looked at Hannibal with a welcoming smile, replying,

'And good day to you. The ship departs for Egypt.'

'Will you pass by Crete?' he asked, sounding unsure.

'Yes, we will. We also have an important traveller heading there.'

'Really? Who is it?'

'The great philosopher, Plato.'

Hannibal only replied by saying, 'Thank you.'

Hannibal paid the fare, then boarded the ship. He did not know what this Plato looked like, but he was guessing that he would be a man debating other sailors and travellers. He was looking around the deck scanning every face, crate, barrel even the ropes and the sails. He did not find Plato, so he moved to the front of the ship, to observe the scenery. When he moved past the sails, he saw a man wearing a distinct toga. He knew he had found Plato because his clothes looked different from the other sailors.

Hannibal stood next to him, leaning forward against the ship's rails.

'Excuse me, but are you Plato?'

'I must be.'

Hannibal wanted to know more about him. He asked, 'What is a philosopher?'

'A philosopher is someone who questions the many things in life.'

'And what do you do as a philosopher?' Not noticing his curtness.

'I see people; I question their behaviour; I know things and above all, I teach them how to do the same.'

'Can you teach me?'

'I understand that you would not have time for lessons at the moment. Because there is somewhere else you ought to be.'

'How do you know that?'

'I know things because I am a Sage.'

Hannibal was surprised to hear that. He asked him, 'What's a Sage?'

'A Sage is someone who has rare knowledge of things. But I fear that if I stay here to answer your questions, I will miss my class.' Plato turned around to leave.

Hannibal gently shouted, 'Wait! How can I find you?'

The thinking giant turned and answered Hannibal.

'You will not find me, because we won't meet again in Greece. But we will meet again, elsewhere.'

Hannibal was confused by his statement, so he asked him, 'What does that mean?'

Plato smiled, hinting at him with a vague answer. 'The mind is a powerful tool, when used well.'

He then left Hannibal to think about what was said. Hannibal's eyes followed Plato as he disembarked the ship. He was looking forward to this strange meeting. He had a good feeling about him because he had never met someone like Plato before.

Once the ship left the harbour, Hannibal felt anxious about Crete. He had always found travel uneasy and he was always worried about new locations. He preferred the stability of staying in one place, rather than living like a nomad. To keep his mind off the travel, his memory prompted the vision of the frozen lake. So for the remainder of the voyage he spent it fantasising over the frozen lake in Norway. All he had to do, was find it, but he knew it wouldn't be simple. He was aware that he would require the guidance of an entity, but that too wouldn't come easy. His mind moved on to deciding what to do when he would reach Crete. The only sensible thing he could think of was to focus on his martial skills, by learning new ones at the island and keeping the old ones sharp. This reminded him of his eventual appointment with the stranger, since he was foretold they will meet in the future. So with a new purpose in mind, he had all the inspiration he would need to keep him occupied on the island.

The final day of the journey, saw the ship approaching the island, which was being unravelled by the sun rising over the horizon. Hannibal climbed to the upper deck to see Crete, eager to be on land again, after a long time at sea. He was among the sailors waiting for the ship to get closer, as the distance grew shorter. When the ship was close enough, he was able to see the scenery, which exceeded his expectations. The moment the ship anchored, Hannibal was the first to disembark, eager to discover the island for himself.

The moment his foot touched the ground, he felt a rush, filled with anxious anticipation. It was the good kind of anxious anticipation. What he saw was very different from the scene in the mainland. Green landscape, filled with mountains and hills, as far as the eye could see. Even though Crete was an island, he felt free, despite being confined to this plot of land. He would be able to enjoy a peaceful existence; after enduring a lengthy period of hardship. He found that Crete was an open place, unburdened by walls, with a healthy small population, unlike Athens or Sparta. He liked this place more than the mainland, being surrounded by nature. Here he was free to think, live life at a snail's pace, away from a city's distractions. This is where the healing begins.

Heading into the city, he began to experience light hallucinations. But this time, he was able to hear the voices of two inhabitants. He was taken by surprise, because this was something he did not know he was capable of. When the hallucination began to dissipate, he was still able to hear the voices, but the ability began to gradually fade. Taking advantage of the new ability before it faded completely, he began to follow the voices, until he found them. They were two Cretan soldiers talking about heading back to their camp. Hannibal quickly released the horse.

'Good boy,' he told it. 'One day we shall ride into battle together.'

The horse neighed as Hannibal spoke. He smiled as he continued patting the horse. He then mounted the beast and began following the soldiers back to their camp. Once they arrived there, Hannibal toured the camp, to see how the Cretans lived. The military camp was very different to what he saw in Sparta. There were many tents, targets and projectile weapons. It was in a walled-off compound, surrounded by vegetation. The camp environment was different, more relaxed, but discipline was present among the Cretans. They did not wear the same type of heavy armour as the Spartans. Their attire was more that of a levy than a soldier. It became apparent to him that no one noticed his presence, which was a welcome change. When the sun set, Hannibal found himself a tent to sleep in for the night. Whilst waiting for nightfall, he lay outside by his tent, gazing at the sky. He ended up falling asleep because he was very tired.

In his dream he was looking up at the sky. He was able to see the Aurora illuminating the sky. It spoke prophesising,

'Look westward: a son of Macedon will lead the way.'

Hannibal wanted to ask the voice, but he did not know if he would be given a response. Instead, he heard a familiar voice, the voice of the little girl speaking to him,

'It is a voice of guidance and warning.'

When he looked up, he saw the child. Once he was reassured that it was a dream, he put his head back to the ground. He then turned his gaze back to the sky.

She continued, 'The one whom you seek, is Alexander — son of Phillip.'

Thinking back on his labours, he remembered the art of war, he asked her, 'What is the art of war and how will I find it? Not sure if that makes any sense.' He subconsciously spoke to her, as his mind was fixated on the Aurora.

'Seek a warrior Sage known to history as Sun Tzu.'

The dream was interrupted by the horse licking his face, he woke up to the dawn of a new day. He got himself up to his feet, with his eyes still half shut. He was leaning against the horse, still trying to wake up. He heard the Cretans preparing their equipment to train for the day.

Hannibal went over to the troops and helped himself to a leather brace and a hunting bow. He also took a spare levy's outfit. He then inserted himself among the troops, to be able to train with them. Hannibal was surprised when they thought he was a Cretan mercenary, and therefore accepted among them without question. This gave him a sense of belonging.

He was trained to use a bow, javelin, sling, as well as sword and spear. He participated in the wrestling when the men challenged each other. Familiarity with the essential martial skills gave him the credibility of being a soldier, which is why he was accepted without any doubt, since he interacted with them first. At first, he was not able to master the use of ranged weapons right away, not for a long time. Even under pressure, it was apparent to the Cretans that he required further training, so he was placed among the poor performers. He joined the Cretans during hunts, he joined them during the annual runs around the island, which was always intense. Hannibal relished in this new place he now called home.

Years had passed, and he was thriving on the island. He began spending time learning to use his listening ability to practice eavesdropping on merchants, sailors, bureaucrats, intellectuals, tradesmen, farmers and anyone of interest. He was surprised at how easy it was to perfect using that ability, in a short time. During that time, he also decided to name his horse Flavius. It was a name he recalled hearing many times in his former life. The horse instantly took a liking to its new name. After having to endure the countless frustrating sessions of learning to use the ranged weapons, he was finally able to demonstrate that he was capable of using the bow, sling and javelin properly. What really stood what was his incredible accuracy in using the bow. Hannibal was very proud of his new accomplishments.

One day, news had spread like wildfire throughout the Aegean Sea, about an imminent Persian invasion into the mainland. This made Hannibal worried because he this was likely to have an impact on his future, especially since this could involve him leaving a place he really liked and now had a special bond with. When he learned that the Spartans were heading to stop the Persian advance, he was annoyed at the news. When he heard that they were annihilated at Thermopylae, he was very delighted to hear about it. But eventually the Persians were forced out of the mainland, by a combined mighty allied effort. This gave him the reassurance that his stay was not over yet.

He went to sleep that night, wishing for time to pass quicker, in hopes of being able to leave the island. In his dream, he found himself at the graveyard, but he was alone. Walking past the giant tree, he found Plato sitting on a boulder. He was happy to see him again and could hardly believe his eyes. He initiated the conversation asking the Sage,

'Is this what you meant by "we will meet in my mind"?'

'That's not what I said, but I see you caught on to what I meant by it.'

'If I'm being honest, I had no idea what you meant.'

'But we got there in the end.'

'So... Can you teach me what you now? Now that we have the time.'

'Very well… you have waited long enough for this moment, and your patience shall be reward.'

'Last time we spoke, you said that you question things, people, and life. I have a problem with an entity, and I also have many questions, but can't seem to find the answers I'm looking for.'

Plato gestured for Hannibal to sit beside him. He told him,

'In instances such as these, you must ask yourself the right question. Then followed by another question, until you find the answer. That is why you question what you know. Call it critical thinking, because you have to think critically about your situation and what you know, to arrive at the right conclusion, or the one you might be looking for.'

'It sounds simple enough, but how do I even begin?'

'What is your concern with her?'

'I feel very uneasy around her, she scares me. She mocks me but wants to help me at the same time. I don't know what to make of her.' Hannibal noticed that in Plato's company, he is began to speak more eloquently.

'Do you trust your instinct?'

'Always.'

'And what is your instinct telling you?'

'It feels like she wants something, because no one has ever helped me for nothing in return.'

'Is she receiving anything in return?'

This helped Hannibal find a different locked away part of his mind. He began to think and see things differently, just from this interaction with Plato. After pondering for a while, he answered, 'I don't know. I feel that she wants something but can't quite place it.'

'That is how you question things.'

'Thank you. I really appreciate this. I didn't know such a simple thing could be so liberating.'

'I find that the most effective ideas are the simplest ones.'

This had brought an end to the dream. Hannibal made it a habit to learn more about the art of the mind, seeing Plato nearly every dream. He learned how to speak properly, think critically, and analysing facts. He had a knack for becoming a thinker and found it easy to understand what was being said. He was able to distinguish between fact and rumours, when analysing claims and conversations. He enjoyed learning allegories and the fine way of speaking effectively. Plato taught him that words have meaning, and therefore if utilised correctly could have a great impact. He was also taught that by asking yourself questions using advanced language, can help clarify many obstacles and help one find their answers. Hannibal also frequently interacted with his horse, which cheered him up, and helped him heal the mental wounds he suffered in Sparta. He would often pat him, rub the beast's neck, and speak with him, as though they were best friends. Being around Flavius made a world of difference to Hannibal, and drastically improved his mental state. It was a very unusual form of cathartic therapy that he had discovered.

Many years passed by, and news of a new Macedonian king named Phillip who was the talk of the century. He was making unprecedented progress by conquering his Greek neighbours, which was unheard of. Eventually, rumours began spreading of a Macedonian invasion eastward, into Persian territory. These events would encourage serious debate among the locals. They wanted to join the fight, being stuck on the island, with little else to do. Macedon had always been looked down upon, with contempt, by their Hellenic neighbours. The rise of Macedon, brought about an overhaul of military reforms, which gave it the ability to subjugate the Greek city states. The name brought chills down Hannibal's spine, because this spelt the end of his comfortable stay on the island, but he knew this day was coming. This new revelation made him frequent the harbour more than ever before. Because he found the harbour to be an excellent source of learning about world news. He would shadow couriers, spy on diplomats and politicians, because they were the ones that held such rare knowledge of transpiring events. After the conquest of Greece was concluded, King Phillip did not live long enough to see his new dominion; he was assassinated under mysterious circumstances.

One afternoon, Hannibal walked Flavius to the city. He was observing the populace going about their daily lives. Hannibal kept roaming the marketplaces and the forums, listening to the noises of the city. Listening to every conversation that was taking place. He came across a conversation between a mercenary company master, and a Macedonian emissary.

We will need archers, slingers, and javelin men.
I see, is there a war coming?

Haven't you heard? There is a new king now.
Who?
King Alexander, son of Phillip.

I see... How many men do you seek? And when will you depart Crete?

We will need four-thousand Cretan warriors, your most skilled ones. We will be departing in the next full moon.

The voices vanished when Hannibal stopped using his ability. To make his way back to the mainland, all he had to do was insert himself among the Cretan mercenaries. When the full moon was upon them, the time had come for the company to leave Crete heading to the mainland, to Macedon. Hannibal was able to make his way onto one of the transport vessels. Once onboard, he noticed one of the Macedonian captains staring in his direction. This put him in an awkward position because the ship was already departing. When the man walked in his direction, Hannibal had a feeling that he might be one of those people that he had to avoid, rather than fight. He began to blend in with crowds, and moving between them, until he successfully, made his way down to the lower deck. There, he hid among the cargo, which was uncomfortable, but necessary to evade detection. He would sleep during the day and use the night to discover more hiding spots and how to manoeuvre his way around the ship undetected, should the man continue to look for him. This continued throughout the whole journey, until they made it back to Macedon. The final night of the journey, Hannibal was visited by the Spider Queen, in his dream. She began by greeting him,

'Hello, Hannibal. We meet again,' she spoke in an uncharacteristic ordinary tone, but the sound of her voice still made him anxious. 'How many decades has it been since we last spoke?'

Hoping to avoid her questions, he replied, 'I don't know.'

'Has it ever occurred to you what awaits at the end of these labours?'

Hannibal had been wondering about that the whole time, of what the purpose was behind the labours, but he pretended to be paying little attention, watching the waves on the surface of the water. She went on, 'the labours are quests to be completed, so that one can become the Herald.'

'The Herald?' asked Hannibal as he muttered to himself. He was visibly worried and left him wondering as to why this is being brought up now, right before the final stretch of the voyage.

'Yes. The Herald is a very powerful entity, which will bind itself with the successful host, once the quests are completed, and of course, once the Herald has been claimed.'

'Why am I being told about this now?' he asked her, unsure of the arbitrary timing.

'There will come a time when you must know about this. Since you seem to be in the full swing of things, so to speak. I wanted to share this with you, for when the time comes, so that you are ready to properly embrace your journey. The Herald will allow you to do marvellous things, because the Herald will allow you to unlock and

59

discover more powers than you thought were possible. More importantly, the Herald will allow you to exact revenge, and not have to worry about Sentinels, Sages and Seekers who will be getting in your way. But this is merely an introduction, something to bear in mind when as you progress with your journey.'

'So you are telling me, that I am doing all of this just to become the Herald?'

'I can tell you this. No one has ever gotten this far before you. Because it is a fool's errand to even try. And anyone who has tried, had failed miserably.'

He didn't know what to think after learning that, he asked her, 'What can the Herald do exactly?'

'There are many things, he who is the Herald can do. The only way to find out, is to carry on.' She then began walking away.

'By the way, what are Seekers and Sentinels?' he asked her in a hurry, as she was leaving.

'You will find out very soon.'

She then faded away, bringing the dream to an end. Hannibal abruptly woke up, puzzled by what he had learned. He began to hear a voice speaking loudly,

'Welcome to Thessalonica. This will be your stay for a few days, to rest before heading to Pella, so that you can present yourselves before the king there.'

Whilst Hannibal was contemplating what to do next, because he woke up late, thus missing his chance to disguise himself among the Cretans. He began to creep up to the upper deck. Once he was there, he came face to face with the Macedonian captain, whom he was avoiding the entire voyage. The captain shouted,

'Spy! Seize him!'

Hannibal immediately jumped off the ship, onto the wharf, the moment he saw the Macedonian. He then released Flavius, and began riding away, deep into the city. It took some time, but word had spread about a Persian spy, disguised as a Cretan levy. Hannibal kept riding around in the city, until he came upon a slum hiding himself for the time being.

He first began to watch the city patrol to see which parts of the city had greater concentrations of guards. Anyone who was dressed like a levy or was wearing a hood was being apprehended. It became obvious to him that he would need to somehow change his attire. He quietly lurked around in the slum, hoping to find an unsuspecting person to swop clothes with. He found a beggar, who was glad to trade for his Cretan outfit, in return for the beggar's own impoverished clothes. Right before contemplating his escape, he used his listening ability to learn about the situation. He discovered that the search had greatly intensified, because the Cretan mercenaries had gotten involved. The search for him involved the troops heading into the slum as well. Hannibal asked the beggar if he could stay the night in his shack, giving him food and coin to convince him, the man agreed, thus he was safe for the night.

The following day, a mouse walked by his shrinking sack, and he was watching as the sack shrank the creature. This caused him to wonder if the same could be done to a human. He experimented on a child, from the slums, and to his surprise it worked. This new discovery gave him an unprecedented advantage, on how he could deal with the guards, should he be compromised. He waited until nightfall to make the attempt. There were two guards patrolling a secluded area. He was listening to them converse. To his luck, they both needed to stop to relieve themselves, so he stopped using his ability and began sneaking around them. He had his sack ready to shrink them if they turned around. This was one of the tensest moments for him to undergo. Once he was out of view, he was able to breathe a sigh of relief. He then spent the first hour, trying to find a vantage point that gave a view of the main road leading out of the city. He took refuge in an awkward rock formation away from the road, overlooking the flat terrain.

The next morning, the Cretans marched out, making their way to Pella. Hannibal followed them from a safe distance, until they reached the city during the night, days later. He did not wish to risk being confronted by any Sentinels or Seekers, so he used the cover of darkness to head South, to Delphi. He maintained a state of alertness, the entire way to Thebes. Once he arrived at Delphi, he was relieved to have undergone an uneventful trip. The same day he arrived in the valley, he decided to wait for nightfall before visiting the Oracle. In the interim, he found himself a bush to sleep in, still afraid of being followed or spotted by a potential Macedonian scout, sent after him.

Much like his journey on the road, he had a peaceful sleep, and was able to wake up at midnight. He was admiring the night-time scenery, while making his way to the temple. It reminded him of the first time he was in the valley. The place had a majestic atmosphere and a calming feeling to it, during the night. Once he entered the temple, he was able to hear whispers. The voices gradually intensified; with every step he approached the chamber. Once inside, he was in an instant state of hallucination. He was able to see the Oracle appear before his eyes, just like the first time. She spoke to him,

'Greetings Hannibal. What does the Wanderer seek?'

'I recently heard the words Sentinel and Seeker. What are they?'

'Sentinels are prominent people, like Alexander. Seekers are lesser and more insignificant people, like the captain you encountered. Both can spot you as a Wanderer, and as a result are able to kill you.'

Hannibal was curious about the young monarch, and wanted to know more, 'What type of monarch is Alexander?'

'That is a matter of perspective?'

He wanted to know about a potential relic encounter, suspecting that Alexander will be involved, so he asked her, 'Does he find or interact with a relic?'

'After the battle of the River Granicus, he will travel to the city of Gordium, where he will be invited to untie the knot.'

'How does he interact with it?'

'He destroys the relic by cutting it in half.'

'Would I still be able to use it?'

'No. Therefore you will have to wait for a very long time, until you find another one.'

'How does it end for the Macedonian king?'

'Poisoned by his enemy.'

He had a feeling that there was more to the Aurora's advice, than to simply follow the son of Macedon. His instinct was telling him to stick with Alexander, but that would be too risky. He did not know why, so he decided to follow him at a distance, but the threat of the seekers would always be present.

'Is Alexander surrounded by Seekers or Sentinels?'

'He is indeed, and there are many of them.'

'There is one other thing I need to know about. Where might I find Sun Tzu?'

'You will find him in the Far East, in a place called middle kingdom.'

Hannibal expressed his appreciation by telling her, 'Much gratitude.'

He nodded his head, acknowledging the Oracle, before leaving the chamber, ending the visit.

He took a few offerings to last him the journey back. A portion for the horse and the rest for himself, he then went on his way. He allowed a day to pass, to give Flavius time to rest. Once the day had passed, he travelled back to Pella. He was consumed by different thoughts, the entire way back. He tried to picture the knot, imagining what it would look like. He also realised that following the young monarch around, will help him better understand who he is, because he figured that being mentioned by the Aurora is no small thing, and maybe there was more to it. He decided to stalk Alexander, to see if he was more than a guide. But first he needed to get his hands on the relic first, before Alexander gets to it.

Surprisingly, his journey on the road was relatively brief because he was able to arrive back at Pella earlier than he had anticipated. He remained on high alert, avoiding Macedonian guards and troops, who might have been looking for him. He decided to rest in the slums of the city, waiting for the army to march out.

Hannibal began stalking Alexander, eager to learn about him. When Alexander met the Hoplites, he noticed that Alexander knew most of his men by name, which he found impressive. Alexander had a good rapport with his men, almost like a father and son relationship. He always liked to address his men with words of wisdom and inspiration. In turn, his men were swayed by the words, enchanted by his charisma. Hannibal was in awe of what he saw, because he had never seen anyone who was this charismatic and effective. He noted that the young king chose his words carefully, leading him to believe that he must have had a mentor like Plato. His men looked at him as a divine figure, to the point of worshipping him, if he ordered them to do so. He also recognised the approach, because it was very similar to Plato's style of rhetoric and manner of speech. Despite being so young, he was a very intelligent young man, who could gravitate everyone's attention towards him. The only issue that remained was his gut instinct, regarding how Alexander might be a person of interest for his quests. He chose to disregard his instinct momentarily, being convinced that Alexander was innocuous.

During the weeks that followed, he watched as Alexander drilled his troops, personally overseeing their training. They marched up many hills, undergoing many mock trails of uphill fighting. They also trained to avoid carts charging at them, by lying down, allowing them to harmlessly pass over them. Hannibal found this bizarre and nonsensical, because there was no need for the troops to avoid carts in an open field. After their training was complete, the army was ordered to march north, against the Thracians. Hannibal kept a safe distance, but a close eye on the army.

When they arrived in Thrace, he saw the Macedonians charge up the hill. The Thracians responded by pushing carts downhill, to break their formations. This is when the Hoplites lay down, avoiding the carts. Hannibal was shocked by what he saw. It was like Alexander himself was an Oracle.

It must have been scouts or spies' information that led to this discovery, he thought.

After the Macedonian army was victorious in Thrace, they returned to their homeland to celebrate in triumph. This had earned Alexander legitimacy in leadership, strategy and battle tactics. Next, he announced his intention to campaign east, against the mighty Persian empire. He claimed that he wanted to finish the work of Leonidas and the Athenians, from centuries past. This endeavour would prove expensive and would require extensive funding for such a colossal task. He spent the next period raising a professional army, capable of confronting the Persian giant. He focused on poets and orators to motivate the populace to work hard, and to raise morale. Reliable weapons and armour had to be procured for the campaign. He spent months carefully planning the logistical demands for the coming war. Once all preparations were met, he addressed the empire, starting with his troops.

'Centuries ago, our ancestors fought off the belligerent Persians, when their king sought to subjugate our people. Despite facing the odds, the eastern giant still proved to be a menace, interfering in the Peloponnese affair, after their defeat. They look down upon us with great contempt, thinking themselves superior. As long as they remain the hegemon, their eyes will always look westward, ready to strike back whenever they please. Even now they still loom over us, the same way an elephant towers over an ant. It is about time we meet them in a show of force, to let them know that we are no longer the downtrodden. It is time to reveal our true strength to the world and assume our rightful place as the regional hegemon. Together we will witness the fall of an empire and let another rise in its stead.'

Alexander's speech received overwhelmingly support. Seeing their reaction, he knew that they shared his sentiments, and that the time was right to strike. He also knew that word would have reached the Persians, expecting them to be ready to halt his advance at Anatolia. Hannibal was very impressed by Alexander's silver tongue and display of authority. He watched the army march out of the city, on the main road. All the citizens gathered to wish the troops good fortune and be present for the farewell. The event marked a day of pride for the city and the new empire.

After a lengthy march out of the mainland, the army was able to cross over into Anatolia unopposed. This surprised both Hannibal and Alexander, but the army pressed on. The Persians were advised by Greek mercenaries to implement a scorched earth policy, drawing the Macedonians away from their line of supplies, deep into enemy territory. The aim of this ploy was to deprive Alexander from foraging or living off the land. In typical Persian fashion of distrusting the Greek mercenaries, they disregarded their advice. They chose to face Alexander at the River Granicus.

On the day of battle, the Persians deployed their forces on the opposite side of the river. They were waiting to catch the Greeks during the crossing, when they try to ford the river. Hannibal positioned himself off to the side, curious to see what Alexander would do in response. The Persians seemed to be very relaxed, labouring under the false assumption that they were in a superior position. They believed that they would secure a quick victory over the Hellenic forces. They failed to notice that Alexander's Hoplites were wielding sarissa pikes, twice the length of a spear, giving them a reach advantage. This was one of the many innovative efforts undertaken by Alexander's reform of the Macedonian army. To everyone's surprise, Alexander ordered his entire phalanx line to cross the river. The Persians were both confused and delighted because they wanted to crush the young upstart monarch. In their eyes, they saw an arrogant boy king who knew nothing of what he did. After the Persian infantry clashed with their Macedonian counterpart, they quickly found themselves on the back foot, being repulsed by the phalanx. Alexander's modernisation efforts of the Macedonian army were now proving to be highly effective. Their training prepared them for fighting in all types of terrain, which is why they were able to push back the Persians with relative ease. The Persians didn't fare any better on the flanks, with their cavalry being decimated by Alexander's elite companion cavalry. The day ended with a spectacular Macedonian victory, forcing the Persians into a humiliating defeat. Against all odds, the young upstart was able to upset the balance of power in the new empire's favour.

After witnessing Alexander's brilliance in battle, Hannibal realised that he was an exceedingly intelligent young warrior. At one point in the battle, a soldier managed to save Alexander from certain death. Hannibal recognised that even if he wished to approach him, the young king would be heavily guarded. He followed the Macedonian column to Gordium, where he was told the relic will be. The army arrived in the ancient city, unopposed and welcomed as liberators. One of the city's bureaucrats invited Alexander to solve the tangled knot of Gordium, as an honoured guest. Luckily for Hannibal, the young king insisted that he would see it for himself the following day. This gave Hannibal the chance to look for it before

Alexander destroyed it. Hannibal spoke with Flavius as he dismounted, saying,

'I don't suppose you would know where it is. Would you, Flavius?'

The horse had its head down, Hannibal understood that Flavius was tired. So he shrunk him into the sack to rest. Hannibal then proceeded to roam the streets, looking for a ruin or a temple that housed the relic. He travelled many roads throughout the city but came up empty-handed. He stopped for a moment to catch his breath. He looked down facing the ground, rubbing his eyes for a moment. He was beginning to feel sleepy. When he opened his eyes again, he saw the reflection of the Aurora in a water puddle. Hannibal looked up and saw that it really is the Aurora in the sky. He noticed that it was pointing to a certain direction in the city, so he began to follow the direction. After some time of walking around, he was able to find the ruin he was looking for. He saw that it was guarded by some hoplites. The very seekers whom he was hoping to avoid, were now standing between him and the relic.

Seeing the Hoplites made him restless. this unexpected discovery forced him to stay up all night. He would lurk about to study the structure, to spot possible points of entry. The place was filled with seekers, which complicated matters for him. He could not fight them off, nor fight his way to the relic. Sneaking into the ruin was not a possibility either. He spent the night thinking about what to do. He recalled shrinking the boy from the slum, back in Thessalonica, affording him an option. He figured that he would only need to shrink the guards around the relic, to avoid the others noticing the absence of their comrades. The most difficult part was sneaking into the ruin undetected.

Once he had planned out what to do in his head, he decided to get on with it. There was a strong sense of fear and rush coursing through his mind, body, and stomach. Despite the enormous pressure, he was able to time his movements well and quick enough, to slip in completely unnoticed. He began shrinking the guards, in abrupt successions. In fact, he was able to do it so fast, that no one even realised that guards were missing. He quickly grabbed the relic, and vanished out of there quickly, like a ghost. Once he made it back onto the street, he rushed to a quiet corner of the city, where he took his time to inspect the relic.

While he was in deep thought, he heard a voice, firmly shouting at him.

'It's you again! Hand over the relic, thief!'

Hannibal quickly turned around and saw the same seeker, who had confronted him at the harbour. His heart sank to his stomach; he felt his entire chest flare up with fear. He was startled by being spotted and caught off guard, unexpectedly. The seeker began charging at him. This is when Hannibal very firmly squeezed the knot. To his dismay, nothing happened, which made him close his eyes awaiting the fatal strike to kill him. After much waiting, there was silence. His entire body was still tensed from the encounter, but he began to slowly open his eyes. It looked as though the seeker had vanished into thin air.

After realising he was safe, he collapsed to the ground. His instinct had reversed time by a full day. He lied on the floor to catch his breath from this harrowing experience. He was shaking and breathing so heavily that he felt as though his chest was about to explode.

Hannibal took his time to recollect his thoughts, after the fact. He dragged himself to a nearby alley, leaning against a wall. This eased his transition into sleep, after struggling to calm himself. In his dream, Hannibal saw the Spider Queen approaching him. A bewildered Hannibal asked,

'How did I make him vanish yesterday?'

'You made the hour reverse, by a day prior to the incident. But it was your instinct that did the work. The boy king is now on his way to the city and will arrive at midday, just as he did the day before.'

Hannibal was happy with what he heard. He took a moment to allow the thought to sink into his mind. He had a sharp pain in his stomach, the type someone experiences having faced a fatal incident. He was told about time travel, but the realisation sets into consciousness differently once experienced.

'Was it really the relic, or did I see that in my dream? Because if it is a dream, then everything makes sense.'

She reassured him, 'Your instinct made the hour reverse. That took place in reality but you are now asleep.'

Hannibal changed the subject, 'About the Herald, you said that he has abilities. What are they? I'm curious to learn more.'

The Spider Queen scoffed at the question, she told him, 'When the time comes, you will learn more about the Herald. Until such time, try to keep yourself alive.'

Hannibal awoke from the dream, quickly working on disposing the shrunken guards, in one of the tents in the camp once they fell asleep. He travelled with Alexander's army, because he did not wish to risk time travelling, and losing Alexander in the process. He made sure to avoid being near the boy king, or any of the Sentinels and Seekers, who constantly surrounded him.

The second confrontation Alexander led against King Darius was in Syria, near a city named Issus. It was another battle that saw either side staring down the other, separated by a river. Much Like the Granicus, both sides engaged the other, hoping to brute force their way to victory. On one flank, the Persians were able to get the better of the Macedonian cavalry. On the other flank, the companion cavalry were able to push back the Persians. After a brutal struggle, it became clear that the Persians were not able to hold back the Macedonians forever. Eventually the companion cavalry was able to break the stalemate. Alexander managed to achieve a stunning victory, snatching it away from the jaws of defeat. Hannibal was very impressed by the young king's bravery and leadership.

Alexander then resumed his conquest south, breaching any city that did not submit to his army. When he arrived in Egypt, the young king was greeted as a hero and a saviour. Relishing the many titles bestowed upon him by his new subjects, Alexander did not shy away from proclaiming himself to be great. Around this time, the young monarch received a peace offer from King Darius, offering his daughter's hand in marriage and half the Persian empire. Alexander was not interested in a truce, nor was he interested in half the empire, he wanted it all. Hannibal was astonished to hear Alexander mention to his generals that he wanted to conquer the known world.

Throughout the campaign, Hannibal saw the gradual shift of Alexander's character. He saw him turn from a beloved king to a tyrant who cared little for others' opinions. The Greeks were also beginning to see him as out of touch with his roots, someone who was infatuated by the Persians and their way of life. He noticed how his subordinates began to loathe Alexander's decrees and behaviour towards the Persians. In one campaign, he slew the soldier that saved his life at the Granicus. Then again, when he secretly ordered the death of Parmenion, his most trusted general, right after he murdered his son. His megalomania for conquest was made more apparent, when his troops refused to cross the Indus valley with him, threatening to mutiny if he pressed on. Hatred towards the young king grew by the day. Despite Alexander's neglect of his generals and inner circle, he was still a revered icon in the eyes of the majority. This was made obvious when he addressed his men, in his famous speech after their mutiny, stating,

'What I am about to say isn't meant to stop you from returning home. As far as I came, you can go wherever you wish. But I want you to know how you have behaved towards me, and how I have treated you. I'll begin, as is right, with my father, Phillip. When he found you, you were mere peasants, wearing hides, tending a few sheep on the mountain slopes, and you could barely defend them from raiders. Under him, you began living in cities, with good laws and customs. And he turned you from slaves into rulers over those very barbarians who used to plunder your lands. This is what my father did for you. Great enough, but small compared to what you've gained from me! I crossed the Hellespont, defeating the satraps of the great King Darius, and made you rulers over Asia Minor. The rest of the land surrendered willingly, making their wealth yours. The great cities of the east all belong to you. The wealth of Lydia, the treasures of Persia and the jewels of India, and the outer seas. You were once the downtrodden, then I promised you the world, and now you have it. You are generals and captains. What have I held back for myself, apart from this purple cloak and diadem? Nothing. No man can point to my riches. And what would I do with them anyway? I eat what you eat. I get no more rest than you. Who among you believes he's worked harder for me than I have for him?! Come on! If you've got scars, strip and show them to me! I'll show you mine. My body is covered in scars from every weapon you can think of. All for the sake of your lives, your glory, and your wealth. And yet here I am, leading you, as conqueror of land and sea. We've celebrated our weddings together. I've paid off your debts, without asking how you got them. Those who have perished, were buried with full honours. I have sent back some of you who've been wounded or crippled, or have grown old, to be welcomed back home

as heroes. But since you all wish to go, then all of you —
go! When you get home, tell them how you abandoned
him, leaving him under the protection of the foreigners
you'd conquered. Perhaps this report of yours will seem
glorious in the eyes of men, and worthy in the eyes of the
Gods. Be gone!'

After the speech, the troops begged for forgiveness,
leading to an emotional reconciliation between the king
and his army. This gave him the opportunity to plan further
future conquests. Seeing that the rift was now made
apparent, he had two options, either wait for something to
happen, or make it happen. Hannibal was grateful for fate
having handed him his very first quest. He wanted to catch
the unsuspecting monarch in a moment of weakness.

Having followed Alexander's campaign closely, he
had a very good understanding of the region. He wished to
attempt teleportation for the first time. He wished to visit
Egypt, a place infamous for its poisons, which would also
help him take out Alexander. He had to travel from Darius'
palace to the Pyramids of Giza, this was his assumption
since they were special places. He was both nervous and
excited, because it was something he was looking forward
to. He had no idea what to expect or if teleportation would
work. He looked to the sky with his eyes closed, tightly
squeezing the knot. When he opened his eyes, he saw
himself atop the biggest pyramid, overlooking the
landscape the view was incredible, words could not
describe what he was looking at. He began staring at the
giant rocks that formed the great pyramid. He could not
understand why everyone was in awe at the sights of the

structures. He found them too ugly, but he did appreciate the view from above. At that exact moment, he understood that monuments and wonders were the gateway for teleportation. Allowing a relic holder to teleport to and from these locations, which included prominent cities. Even though he was told about this, he now understood the notion, after having gone through it. He spent a year learning about poisons in Egypt. After he learned the essentials, he decided to head to Syria. Hannibal looked up to the sky, as the knot started glowing in his grasp. He then teleported to the sea castle at Sidon, the city where his journey began.

Hannibal was wrestling with a two ideas, because he was not sure about the method of carrying out the deed. He thought about assassinating Alexander with a blade, but it would be too great a risk. Hannibal decided to poison the king's drink, as that was the most logical and common way for an influential figure to die in antiquity. That way, no one would suspect anything.

He spent his time there, observing the locals go about their daily lives. He found it intriguing, watching other people live their lives. There was a young couple that would often meet in secret, to spend time with one another. He never understood how other men were able to successfully interact with women. He did not believe he was superior to them, but he never understood how they were able to talk to women. This unlocked a glimpse into his past life, of how he tried to approach a girl he adored in his village, but failed miserably. He was also mocked by the other kids. He would also spend time watching merchants and sailors negotiating and trading. He was able to learn so much from these significant interactions, by simply listening to how they dealt with one another. These observations taught him so much about the art of negotiation, and how to conduct yourself appropriately. He realised that he had the ability to decipher what each party wanted from the other. It turned into a game, where he would analyse the situation and try to predict the outcome. He did not always correctly predict the outcome, but he did correctly analyse what each person wanted from their interactions. After listening to so many conversations, he became so well versed in reading what people really want. It was easy for him to learn matters of wit and strategy, because he was fascinated by them.

He applied this knowledge to see if he could uncover what the Spider Queen wanted. He was aware that she was trying to help him, in a roundabout way to become the Herald. However, he was still unable to decipher why.

One day, Hannibal came across a woman that wove and sewed clothes. He would observe how she worked for hours every day. He would try to mimic what she did, to perfect the trade of sewing cloth and other materials together. He decided to buy fabric, threads and cloth to sew them into a hood and cloak. The hood was several outer pieces of black cloth, bound with an inner layer of soft fabric, sewn together using a black thread. The cape to the cloak was a very dark blackish-blue piece of fabric, which was fraying at the bottom edges, giving him the appearance of a ghost. The cloak reached his knees because he did not wish to fall by stepping on it. It took him several attempts to finish his design. When he finished the cloak, he tried it on. He was pleased with it, because it had a crude shape to it, fitting him perfectly. Not long after this, he heard news of a massive celebration, taking place in Babylon, for Alexander and his men. This was the opportunity he was waiting for. To strike him when he would be drunk and incoherent. He teleported from the sea castle at Sidon, back to Babylon.

When the festivities began at night, Hannibal waited until everyone had celebrated late into the night. Alexander was too drunk to realise what was happening around him. Hannibal quickly approached him, pouring the poison into his chalice, without anyone noting his presence. By the time he was done, he quickly slipped away into the dark. The king innocently gulped from his chalice. Days later, Hannibal was lying in wait, hiding near the king's chambers, until the king had succumbed to the poison. In that moment, he experienced a hallucination, like the one with the Oracle, where everything turned into the white void. Alexander rose to his feet, asking him,

'Who are you?'

Hannibal shook his head, responding, 'It doesn't matter. It had to be done.'

'You shall be hunted down to the ends of the earth for what you did!' shouted the boy.

'No matter how loud you shout; no one can hear you from here.'

Alexander put his head down in defeat, realising Hannibal was right.

'At least history will remember me for all my great deeds. No one will remember you.'

Hannibal responded in admiration. 'You are quite the gifted silver tongue. A very moving speech it was, the one you gave after the Opis mutiny. A masterful manipulation so good that even I almost believed it. But unfortunately for you, I knew exactly what you were doing. But nonetheless, well said.'

'But it worked for me. I needed them, the silver shields, the companions, and all the rest of them.'

'Well, it looks like destiny had other plans.'

'No matter. I am the first piece of the quest. The other one is, Attila, king of the Huns.'

'If it's all the same to you. I never really liked you, but history will remember you as one of the greatest generals. I hope we never meet again.'

Alexander remarked, 'Be gone, stranger.' This brought the hallucination to an end.

Hannibal decided to stay, curious to see the fate of Alexander's empire. He knew that Alexander left no heirs of age, to inherit his empire. He wanted to see if Alexander really was loved by his generals and bureaucrats. However, what followed was something he would learn about power. Instead of banding together, his empire fragmented into many warring states, leading to a bloody civil war amongst his successors. The very troops who'd fought under Alexander's banner together were now fighting each other. Ptolemy, Antigonus, Antipater, and the emerging victor in the war, Seleucus, ushering in the Seleucid empire. Alexander's tomb was seized by one of the generals, who secreted Alexander's corpse away. Alexander was lost in the annals of history, despite his great feats. Although his accomplishments will go down in history, he lost himself and his empire along with it. This proved Hannibal's suspicions, that the king was not loved by everyone, because Alexander's policies were immediately reversed upon his death. Such was a tyrant's reward. Hannibal learned a valuable lesson from this experience, to trust his instinct.

After the civil war, Hannibal wanted to meet the child, to seek out the man in the Far East. So he travelled to the edge of the desert, where the vegetation met the sand. He was looking forward to meeting Sun Tzu. He waited until nightfall, to sleep. The child appeared in his dream on the first night, at the edge of the desert.

'Who does Hannibal seek?' asked the child as she played with a strange toy.

'Why is it that I only meet you in the strangest part of a land?'

'When someone is travelling in pursuit of adventure, for knowledge or gain of profit, they often have to travel across different lands.'

Hannibal acknowledged the wisdom, stating,

'Clever!' He continued, asking, 'Where can I find Sun Tzu?'

'You will find him at the royal court in the kingdom of Wu. Which is why when you awake from your slumber, time would have reversed to his time period.' The child then walked away, disappearing into the night.

Hannibal spent the rest of the dream staring at the night sky, which was devoid of the Aurora. Come the morning, when he awoke, he walked into the desert, hoping to find something to guide him east. To his luck, he found a merchant caravan travelling in his direction. He was relieved at the sight of humans treading the desert. When he approached the travellers, the leader of the caravan was instructing someone to give the lone Wanderer food and water. Hannibal was given dates and water. He was very appreciative for the role coincidence has played in his journey so far.

He felt lost because he had no clue what to do. More so because he hated travelling. A journey that saw him venture into unchartered territory always made him anxious. Hannibal was recognised as a Wanderer by the seeker leading the caravan, but it made little difference, because their culture obliged them to be hospitable with everyone. Hannibal enjoyed their hospitality. Up to this point in his journey, he had come across a handful of cultures and peoples, but none were like the people of Arabia. In no time, Hannibal found himself aboard a spice merchant ship, bound for the Indus valley. He was told that eventually the ship might make its way to the middle kingdom.

Aboard the ship, Hannibal enjoyed listening to the many stories of past heroes and elders, the travellers shared. He also liked listening to the poetry duels, which occurred among different tribal elders, to entertain travellers. At one point in the trip, he heard a piece of advice that had a profound impact upon him. When a traveller was seeking an elder's wisdom, the elder said,

'The powers that be, will always guide a man in pursuit of knowledge and self-betterment.' When the traveller asked for clarification, the elder responded, 'Things will materialise out of thin air, for those who are serious about their craft and are making a concerted effort to find what they are looking for.' It was not intended to be literal advice, but it felt literal to him, having experienced that for himself.

Hannibal was wondering if this was directed at him, indirectly, or perhaps another coincidence. Later in the voyage, another traveller came seeking the tribal elder's wisdom, regarding morality and doing what's right. The elder responded stating,

'Anything born out of malice, ill intent, deception, lies, or being insidious, will never manifest or see the light of day.' Much like the first traveller, the second one asked for elaboration. The elder responded, 'When something is done with nefarious intent, it will never last. Good things never die. Always take it upon yourself to do what is right.' The elder concluded by proclaiming, 'That is why one must always conduct oneself honourably and do the right thing, even when those around us do not do so.'

When the ship finally reached the Indus valley, Hannibal liked the valley's lush vegetation. He spent the entire trip on the upper deck admiring the scenery. He kept watching as every meander revealed the next breathtaking part of the valley. He remembered the greater half of the valley, from when Alexander invaded the region. He saw how the locals used the mighty Indian elephants to transport heavy goods and materials.

When the ship anchored in a local port, Hannibal disembarked to board another ship bound for the middle kingdom. He had no idea what the middle kingdom was, or what to expect upon his arrival. As the journey kept heading east, he saw different cultures and peoples, from the ones he saw in India and the Mediterranean. The buildings had pointed rooftops, with unique decorations that were beautiful in their own right. The locals adorned themselves with modest clothing. The farmers wore round pointy straw hats. The people had small eyes, something he had never seen before, but had a smooth physical appearance. Hannibal felt estranged in this place, he felt that he did not belong in this part of the world. He liked the ecosystem, as it looked miraculous and diverse. Despite his feeling uneasy and increasingly anxious, the region had an irresistible charm to it. That was the only aspect he enjoyed about the land. The shape of the leaves, the different trees and plants mixed together in the thicket, forming marvellous scenery. He decided to leave the ship and travel the rest of the way on foot, as he wanted to see the scenery for himself, up close in person.

He followed the stars at night, forming a line, leading him to the Wu kingdom. During the day, he would visit the different parts to the region he was in. He saw many rice paddy fields; he had never seen anything like them, in any other lands he'd previously visited. The roads where different from the ones back in Syria, Egypt, Greece, and Babylon. There were many statues and shrines everywhere he went, lit with candles and incense. He saw the locals pray and bow at these shrines. Hannibal eventually grew tired of the sights and released Flavius, to travel the rest of the way on horseback. When he finally reached the middle kingdom, he saw a distinct culture, that stood out from the ones in the region. Along the way, he often heard about the wars between the kingdoms, from the merchants on the road. He kept hearing the same names over and over: Wu, Yue, Chu, Zhou, Qin, Jin, Qi, and Song. The names at first were confusing, but the name Wu was the only one he was interested in. Weeks later, he heard about the rising tensions between the Wu and Chu kingdoms. The locals were constantly speaking to one another about this friction. Hannibal decided to follow a group of gossiping merchants to the royal court of Wu.

After days of travelling on the road to Wu, Hannibal set out to search for the imperial palace. Unsurprisingly, it was not difficult for him to find it, for it was distinguished by the decorations, walls, and the imperial guards surrounding it. Hannibal went past them and slept in one of the palace gardens. Even the ground felt more comfortable here. He fell into a deep sleep which lasted for days. When he woke up, he saw the emperor being escorted to the palace, followed by his guards and council. He followed them maintaining his distance, without anyone detecting his presence, but he exercised caution as many of them were Sentinels. Hannibal did not know what was taking place, but he wanted to get as close as possible to observe what was happening, before using his listening ability.

Once they entered the palace, the council was discussing the war with their neighbouring kingdom of Chu, and how to resolve the situation. Many who spoke, recommended diplomacy or political intrigue to resolve the matter. Most of the generals requested permission, to lead the entire Wu army against the Chu. A lone general stepped forward and requested to address the emperor. At first, he was looked upon with contempt, but the general persisted. The emperor and his council proceeded to mock and belittle the general, but for some reason, he maintained a calm demeanour, not bothered by their insults. This display of composure impressed Hannibal. He recalled seeing this very scene in the cloud. The general was finally allowed to speak.

'Great Emperor. I am Sun Tzu and I request the honour of leading the Wu army into battle against the Chu imperial forces.'

The emperor laughed with the council before responding, 'No one in this hall has ever heard of you. No one even knows of your accomplishments if you have any.'

Sun Tzu ignored their mockery, confidently replying, 'I can train and lead anyone. And I am willing to prove it to you, before your very eyes, and in the presence of this council.'

The entire court burst out laughing once again. Except the emperor, who had a stern look on his face, as he sharply stared at Sun Tzu.

'What makes you so certain that you can make such a claim, when our whole army does not even amount to a third of the Chu army?'

'Give me the chance to prove myself, and I will not disappoint.'

The emperor looked to his right and pointed.

'What about the concubines? Can you train them?' the emperor mockingly asked Sun Tzu.

Much to everyone's surprise, Sun Tzu replied, 'Yes I can.'

The shock and surprise on the emperor's face was reciprocated by his council, when they looked at each other in disbelief, silently muttering to one another. The concubines were ordered by the emperor to present themselves before him, and to obey Sun Tzu.

Sun Tzu stepped in front of the women addressing the court. 'Communication is central in leading forces on the battlefield.' He turned to the women, 'You two will the lead the rest of the women on my mark. Watch closely.'

After choosing two of the most senior concubines, he slowly showed them a sequence of sword moves, he wanted them to perform, when he gave the order. He then turned facing the members of the court once more explaining,

'If the instructions are not clear and nothing is done, the fault lies with the commander. If the orders are clear, and nothing is done, the fault then lies with the subordinate.'

Sun Tzu signalled to the drummers to sound the drums for the women to perform the sword sequence. The women began laughing and giggling among themselves, believing this to be amusing and flattering. Sun Tzu raised his hand signalling for the drums to stop. He was about to demonstrate to everyone how serious he was. He then approached the two concubines, with his sword unsheathed, then proceeded to decapitate them both. The other women immediately stopped laughing, and started quivering in fear, being in a state of shock, after witnessing what happened. This seized the attention of the emperor and his council. Sun Tzu then chose two other concubines, to replace them as the new commanders. Once again, he signalled the drummers to sound the order for the new commanders to lead the rest of the concubines in performing the sword sequence. This time every woman performed the sequence in synchrony, following the lead of the two commanders. The emperor's expression turned from disinterest to pure shock over what he saw. He then stood up ordering the concubines to stop, which prompted Sun Tzu to turn around facing the emperor and bowing to him.

'A man must apologise when he is at fault. As you have demonstrated today, before the entire court,' the emperor sat down and continued, 'You have proven to me that you are a man who is capable of doing the impossible. That is precisely what we need to defeat the Chu army. You have my permission to lead the army against the Chu forces. The heavens will recognise your accomplishments. You shall have a permanent place there and in history, should your campaign yield success. But I must also remind you that failure will lead to death. You may take your leave, to make your preparations.'

Sun Tzu once again bowed in respect and gratitude. He then left the palace to prepare the army for the upcoming war. Hannibal's heart dropped to his stomach after listening to and observing the entire situation. The intensity of what he heard made his stomach tense. He quickly followed Sun Tzu, who was heading to his private quarters. Hannibal waited for a while, after the Sage entered his home. He then knocked on the door, nervously waiting for the Sage.

Sun Tzu greeted him. 'Greetings, stranger. What is the purpose of your visit?'

He wanted to use a different approach with the Sage so as to not arouse his suspicion, so he asked him, 'I heard that you might be a man of war? Something about knowing the art of war.'

Sun Tzu believed that Hannibal was a spy. He replied, 'I am sorry, you have come to the wrong place,' then proceeded to shut the door.

Hannibal released that he had compromised himself, which meant that he might very well be hunted by the royal guards. He decided to lurk about and learn by observing and listening instead. This reminded him of the Thessalonica incident, but he would have to be a lot more careful, because he is easily identified as a foreigner. It never occurred to him that his appearance would immediately place him under suspicion.

Hannibal secretly followed the Sage, watching how he interacted with everyone. He used his ability to listen to

Sun Tzu's meetings with senior military members. Hannibal was very impressed by how thorough the Sage was. He had a holistic approach to everything he did as well as taking into consideration all potential problems. Hannibal made a mental note of everything the Sage said and did. In fact, he liked the Sage's methods so much so that he decided to adopt his strategic way of thinking. The Sage made plans to address intelligence, logistics, weapons, tactics and the strategy for the campaign.

Hannibal obsessively stalked Sun Tzu around, because he wanted to learn everything he could about him. This experience allowed Hannibal so much insight into his mindset, he temperament and how he addressed problems. He found him mind boggling in every measure of the word. He noticed how the Sage built rapport with everyone he interacted with, treating them with utmost respect. He was always inspiring those around him, encouraging them to contribute, seeking their counsel. He personally oversaw the troops during training, and often lectured them on the importance of unity, camaraderie and cohesion. He appointed leaders who were likeminded, because that made his command easier. He always resolved quarrels among the men, using pragmatism and diplomacy, avoiding punishment, unless it was deemed necessary. He built the men's morale, by giving them goals to strive for, with a heightened sense of purpose. He always explained everything he did, sharing his visions with those around him. He never discouraged those who questioned him, to raise their concerns, because if there was a problem no matter how small, he wanted to know about it. He became the fatherly figure, building an army so loyal, that they would throw themselves off the highest mountains for him.

Like Alexander, he constantly drilled his men, to adopt his style of warfare, and to implement his tactics. He instilled in them a stringent code of honour. Strict discipline was required, to ensure absolute adherence to his orders. He emphasised the importance of the coming war, stating,

'For out kingdom, this is a matter of survival and longevity. We cannot be the losing side, otherwise the generations to come, will suffer from our mistakes.' After a long pause, he concluded with his final remark, 'Think not of victory, for you will not have it, unless it is within your grasp.'

Hannibal noticed how Sun Tzu made great efforts in intelligence, sending many scouts and spies to survey the enemy's territory and report back. He wanted to know the lay of the land. He wanted to know the strength of his opponents. He wanted to know which ground was suitable for his strategy, and which parts to avoid. He wanted an overview of what the kingdom looked like, and what are the strategic places of interest. He explained to his generals that they could not take on the Chu forces, in a direct confrontation. He pointed out that a greater army has the disadvantage of slower mobility, which was something they could exploit. While the troops were training tirelessly, the scouts were able to report back with their findings. He included merchants and women in his clandestine efforts, because no one would suspect them, especially women. They were able to observe and gauge the readiness of the army and the public sentiment. Every aspect of life was a crucial piece of knowledge he leveraged, to make his decisions. Hannibal was fascinated by his dedication and brilliance.

A month later, Hannibal saw the army mobilising on the main road. Around the same time, word had reached Sun Tzu that the Wu ally bordering their enemy was under attack by the Chu forces. Hannibal followed the Sage closely, but maintained a safe distance, listening to everything he said, and observing everything he did. He was curious to see how he would react. He saw that Sun Tzu was calm as always, despite the change in circumstance. The general decided to get close enough to the Chu forces, so they can give chase, relieving the Wu ally.

Hannibal could not see how being chased by a mighty host, was a sound plan. He watched Sun Tzu taunt the Chu forces. The move was enough to provoke an intense pursuit by the Chu army. The general marched his army for days, until they reached a mountain. He then ordered half the army to hastily march to the Chu capital. Hannibal was left perplexed, thinking that the Sage had lost his mind, because splitting the army made them vulnerable against the enemy, who was hot on their tail. The following day, Hannibal watched as Sun Tzu addressed his men before the battle,

'Today we fight the giant, because once a giant falls, they do not recover. Each and every one of you shall be judged by the heavens, by what you do here today. The only way for us is forward. The mountain is at your back, and the Chu army will be bearing down on you. All our training has been preparing us for this moment. Today you prove your worth to me. Show the world what you're capable of.'

The entire Wu army roared with the fervour of battle fuelling the men's thirst for the coming fight. Hannibal was speechless by what he saw. It was as if they were a flame that was lit ablaze and was now spreading uncontrollably. He saw an army that was impervious to defeat. But even then, he could not understand how the general's plan was going to work.

Hannibal watched from the mountainside, able to oversee the battle from above. Later that day, the Chu army appeared on the horizon. The Wu forces assumed their positions, waiting for the enemy's advance. The Chu army deployed into their formations and started advancing to the Wu's position, as anticipated. The anxiety grew as the Chu forces kept drawing closer and closer narrowing the gap, but the Wu forces held their nerve and stood their ground. When they closed the distance, the Chu army eagerly charged the Wu forces, who were seemingly trapped against the mountain. It was their finest hour; the Wu stubbornly held their ground, despite being vastly outnumbered. Their vigour both in mind and body, inspired them to brutalise the enemy, fending off wave after wave of Chu forces. Sundown marked the end of the day's fighting, the Wu forces claimed an initial victory, which bolstered morale. Sun Tzu reminded them that they were not out of the storm yet.

The following morning, a rider informed the Chu forces that the second half of the Wu forces was marching on the capital. Forced between staying and saving the capital, the Chu general chose the latter. He gave the order for the army to prepare for a quick march, to save the capital. Hannibal was in disbelief when he saw that the Sage's plan had worked.

Days later, the Chu forces were surprised to encounter the second half of the Wu forces, waiting for them. Their commander realised what had happened, when he was told that the second Wu army was behind them. Being surrounded on all sides, the Chu fought in a desperate last stand, but their struggle was futile. The Wu army crushed their counterpart in a decisive battle. Hannibal was stunned to see how Sun Tzu was able to turn the tides, behind enemy lines, and against a larger foe. He recalled the Sage's words, when he stated,

When giants fall, there is no ascent. Because after the battle, Chu no longer had an army to defend its large dominion.

Sun Tzu was able to restrain his men from plundering, when they entered Ying, the capital of Chu. The emperor had to be present, to make the surrender official. This required half the army to return, to escort their emperor to Ying safely.

One night, Hannibal was shadow sparring inside the city walls, using his sword. When suddenly, the stranger appeared, emerging from the shadows. He was startled by his sudden appearance. He recalled seeing the enigmatic figure over the horizon when he was first with the child in the void. The stranger pulled his own sword and dashed at Hannibal striking him. Hannibal traded blows but was outmatched by the stranger. Despite having never properly used a sword, he was able to react to the attacks. He fought in a clumsy manner, whereby he constantly found himself on the back foot. Flavius quickly intervened, knocking the Stranger to the ground. Hannibal quickly stabbed him in the chest. The stranger evaporated like smoke, vanishing into thin air. He found this harrowing encounter terrifying. This pointed out the need to learn how to properly wield a sword, so that he can protect himself in future encounters.

In the morning, Hannibal went to the royal palace to continue following the Sage. He carefully stalked the unsuspecting general, because he felt there was more to learn from the Sage. The Sage had confidential disciples, whom he shared the art of war with, as they helped him compile the principles to the art of war. Hannibal was able to learn that the key to victory was knowing your enemy. This is accomplished through spies and informants. You only rely on those who share your vision and mindset. You have to know your own limits and capabilities, to use them to your advantage. You have to understand what your enemies' limitations and capabilities are, to know how to deal with them. A wise general knows when to act and when to wait for the right opportunity. Use deception to trick your enemy into fighting you, on your own terms, when you are at a disadvantage. A good general knows how to conduct himself, when dealing with his men. The silver lining to all the principles was the strange fact that; war must be avoided at all costs, because conflict creates more problems than it solves. He once heard Sun Tzu claim,

'The best way to fight, is by not fighting at all,' he explained to his disciples, 'If you can resolve a matter by sowing the seeds of conflict between your enemies, you avert disaster for yourself and those around you.' He paused then then made a statement, 'The more you can accomplish through diplomacy and intrigue, the better your chances are at preserving your kingdom. Prolonged conflicts drain empires.'

Sun Tzu also famously advised, 'Keep your enemies close, and your friends closer.' When asked about it, he explained, 'Keeping an eye on your enemy is obvious, but less worrisome, because you know of their malice towards you. Friends smile in your presence and profess to have your best interests at heart. But the greatest enemy to fear, is from within, because they are in a position to do the most harm.'

When the emperor arrived in Ying, the army and the bureaucrats celebrated the Wu forces' triumph over Chu. Hannibal was not interested in the festivities, so he found himself a quiet corner of the city, contemplating what comes next. In the first night, Hannibal was in his dream exploring the city, as it helped him think and clear his mind from distractions. He was piecing together the information he learned from the boy king. Attila the Hun would be his next target, but in the meantime he wanted seek out any quest that provided insight. Following Sun Tzu showed him a marvellous side to acquiring knowledge, because knowledge was a powerful weapon to possess. He was obsessed with how Sun Tzu was able to manipulate the Chu, leading them into a trap. His thoughts took an arbitrary turn, to thinking about the Herald. His mind was racing with different thoughts. The more he tried to focus on serious matters, the more overwhelmed he felt. He decided to stop thinking, closing his eyes, taking a deep breath, slowly facing up to the sky. He then faced straight ahead and opened his eyes. He was surprised to see the Spider Queen present before him, with a chilling smile on her face.

'Have you missed me?' she creepily asked.

He was startled by her presence. He responded, 'What? I mean, I forgot you even exist.' His heart began pounding.

'I do and I don't.' She started to slowly walk around him, then continued, 'There will come a time when you will question humanity.'

This comment threw Hannibal off, he asked her, 'I am afraid I don't understand.'

'It is something to keep in mind, or as they say in the future... Food for thought.'

'I will.' After a pause, he asked, 'Is this a good time to ask about the Herald's powers?'

She stopped at a well. She then gestured for Hannibal to come over. He looked at the surface of the water.

'Becoming the Herald means that you no longer are human, but you will still have a soul and body. The Herald is actually a smoke-like entity, you can see it. But unlike smoke, you will bleed and can very well be harmed.'

'Smoke-like?' Hannibal thought aloud, as he saw what the Herald looked like in the reflection on the surface.

'Yes, and to become like smoke, your journey to the spirit world will help you reach that form.'

He began to think about an ability he'd experienced but had not the chance to use it. He remembered the time in the void, where he was thrown off the edge, allowing him to feel the transformation into a crow. He asked her, 'How will I learn to fly? And discover the other abilities?'

'To learn how to fly, you must visit the first man to fly in history,' she then started walking away. Hannibal walked with her, as she explained, 'The Herald, has enhanced senses, with an incredibly keen instinct to help him survive. The Herald allows one to transform into their preferred spirit animal, understand every spoken tongue, phase through objects, speak with the dead, is able to use the elemental objects, clone himself and of course, manipulate time by slowing it down, temporarily of course.' After a pause, she remarked, 'The ability to hear others is a wonderful example of how you will unlock your powers, to becoming the Herald. There is also the matter of one's inner energy, but that is unrelated to the Herald. Something to discover for yourself later on.'

'Where on earth would the spirit realm exist?'

'That is for you to find out.'

'You mentioned inner energy. What is that?'

'It is the energy that exists within you and around you. Depending on your actions, you will manifest the one that reflects who you are. Mind, soul and body create an aura that reflects your energy. The different types of energy are: Rage; Chi; Transcendence; Mana; Exalted and the Gift.'

He was curious about the time manipulation ability, 'How does slowing down time work?'

'When you wake up, time would have passed. There will be a Sage who was invited by the emperor; he can help you learn about how time works.' She then turned around and walked away. Her voice echoed the words, 'Until next time.'

Hannibal woke up to a festival, different from the celebration he saw from the days past. Hannibal walked to the citadel to see what was happening, but was unable to enter, as all the pathways were blocked by dignitaries and visitors. He looked to the rooftops and decided to try to transform into a crow, but he was unable. He had an idea to throw himself from a height, so he found the nearest tree and climbed it. Once he was high enough, he jumped off, which helped him turn into a crow. This meant that the initial trigger to the transformation was falling. He was flying in place, happy to see that he could still transform. He quickly flew to the rooftop of the palace before the transformation ended. Once he landed on the rooftop, he lost his balance transforming back to his human form, falling off the roof into a shrub. Upon recovering from his fall, he observed the delegations and visitors mingle with one another in the garden. He tried to use his ability to pinpoint Sun Tzu's presence. This is when he felt a hand on his shoulder which startled him. When he turned around, he found himself faced with an old man. It took him sometime, awkwardly staring at him, before he regained composure.

'Who are you?' asked a shaken Hannibal.

'Kong Qui, but the Chinese call me Confucius,' replied the Sage, followed by quiet laughter. 'Come, let us walk away from the guests and the noise.'

Hannibal and the Sage walked around the gardens and conversed until nightfall.

'I was told that a Sage would help me understand time. Are you that Sage?'

'I must be,' he continued, 'Time is a curious thing. It is a notion that moves forward indefinitely, which can be recalled through memories, tales and records. Manipulate it, and the results shall be favourable or catastrophic, depending on your actions. The ability to slow down time, is achieved by piercing through the dimension of time. It is like catching a fly in mid-air. Time travel will help you build the sense of being able to feel for the dimension, and when you grasp it, you will have pierced the dimension. This can also be done by possessing five or mor relics, or the Hourglass itself.'

Hannibal asked a question related to manipulating history through time, 'What if a Sentinel was to have an untimely demise, diverging from their previous fate, does that remove them from time or the future entirely?' he asked, thinking about Alexander.

'No, they can be found in a different time in their life. If you wish to remove someone from the future or time, you must find their point of origin.'

'Point of origin? What is a point of origin?'

'The point of origin is when someone becomes a Sentinel. Time is a convoluted and complex dynamic concept. Make the wrong choice, and it will haunt you. The outcomes can be very unpredictable.' He then further expanded on this subject, explaining, 'There is an event known as the Time Lock. This can only be done by using the Hourglass. If one activates this event, this means that the past becomes fixed, and permanently out of reach for everyone, same goes for time travelling, but teleportation and manipulating time persist. This is a very dangerous event if the timeline of history is manipulated for the worst.'

The part that mentioned Time Lock had Hannibal visibly concerned, because it meant that if time was not handled properly, it might lead to the world's end. Hannibal wanted to change the subject, feeling very disturbed by what he heard, he asked him,

'When someone becomes the Herald, does time work the same way as it does now?'

'It does, but The Herald's actions preserve the past. Once you progress into the future, the past becomes fixed and therefore unchangeable. However, you can change the past if you do not alert sentinels and seekers or fumble an interaction with them, which is near impossible to do.'

'Let us assume the worst were to unfold; is there a way of undoing said catastrophe?'

'The only way there is to reset time, would be to meet the Roman Emperor Aurelian, and presents him with a white token or a relic.'

'Is that all there is to know about time?'

'Yes, simple rules, aren't they? Yet disastrous when done wrong.'

'Is time the same for a Sentinel and a Wanderer?'

'Yes and no, the difference is that a Sentinel will always live in their Time Loop, a Wanderer is free to explore. Remember Hannibal, a Wanderer is someone lost in time, which means there is no way of tracking them, especially if they become the Herald, however it is easy to find the Herald, because of its terrifying presence, and the fact that it is recognisable. They can send ripples throughout time, alerting guardians who can sense these things.' He added, ' There is one more thing to know about Sentinels or a Sages, is that if an interaction takes them outside their Time Loop, they will become a Rogue.'

'And what does that mean?'

'They change for better or worse.'

The Sage looked at Hannibal a final time, with both his hands planted on his shoulders.

'Always heed the Aurora's advice, for it is the voice of warning. And now, this is where I go off to meet the emperor. Good luck, Hannibal.' The Sage then turned around, heading back to the royal court.

Hannibal needed answers from the Oracle, but feeling too sleepy to travel, so he decided to head to the peasants' homes, to rest for the night. This journey had been exciting and overwhelming for him. He learned so much, in such a short span of time. He felt proud and content with having learned the secrets to the art of war. Simple and straight forward lessons and principles, yet very complicated in execution. He fell asleep, being drained from the day's events. Even in his sleep, he could not stop thinking about Sun Tzu, Confucius, the Herald, and the Spider Queen.

The following morning, he awoke from his sleep, feeling rejuvenated. He left the home, heading towards an alley. He was gazing at his surroundings, marvelling at the Chinese architecture, because it looked beautiful. Hannibal's gaze was interrupted when he saw a crow near him eating a dead pigeon. The crow then starting cawing at him. He was able to understand what the crow was conveying to him. He understood from the bird that crows and pigeons leave a trail, which he can follow. The trail looked like a visible scent, bearing the same colour as the Aurora. The bird then flew away, leaving the dead pigeon behind. Hannibal saw the trail behind the crow, as it flew away. He mustered all his inner strength, running in the same direction. Determined to follow the crow, he was able to transform himself, under the pressure of losing the bird. He followed the bird to a tower in the city, which was a large pigeon coop, housing homed pigeons. Before leaving the transformation, he tried to slow down to smooth his landing, but he was unable to. This led him to collide into a wall in the tower, losing consciousness.

He had a vision, where he saw himself in an empty city he had never seen before. It was unlike any city he had visited. The design and architecture looked distinct. Some of the buildings had words engraved into their stone. The calligraphy was meticulously and masterfully done. He took his time to explore the city, street by street. After some time had passed, he was able to see the vizier's palace. The sight alone was irresistible, and so he ran towards the structure. Once he was close enough to the building, he was able to hear a sound of music he never heard before. It was fast paced, and it captivated the ear. He rushed towards the gate, but the guards barred him from entering. Determined to see the festival, he flew to the top of the wall. What he saw left him at a loss for words. He saw a band of Avars dancing to the music. It was a very unusual dance, because the moves were very acrobatic, involving many rapid spinning motions, in constant successions. He was captivated by the spectacle for hours. The festivities abruptly ended, when the group and the audience in attendance all began looking to the sky, pointing at something. Hannibal turned around, and saw a man flying over the city, with a giant glider. He recognised the man who was flying, as he remembered seeing him in the cloud back at the amphitheatre. He tried to run after him but ended up falling off the wall. This prompted him to wake up, right before he hit the ground.

He leaned against the wall, breathing heavily, while trying to recover from the collision. A while later, he felt well enough to stand up. He made his way up the tower. He was looking at the many cages filled with pigeons. Whilst visually browsing he spotted a distinct pigeon out of the many. It had an aura that he was able to detect. It felt like being around a relic, only this one was a living creature. He gently grabbed the pigeon, stroking its head, which felt cathartic. He had the inkling to release the pigeon, curious to see if it would lead him to a monument, away from the city.

Hannibal followed the trail of the bird for a few days, arriving at a narrow rocky mountain, shaped like a giant pillar. The place was surrounded by trees and tall bamboo plants. He started climbing the mountain, slowly following the pigeon's trail. Once he had reached the top, he found the pigeon resting on a boulder. He picked the bird up, shrinking it into the sack. He then walked to the gate and started knocking on it with the wooden hammer placed outside. He waited for hours, but there was no reply, so he waited longer. This continued for hours, until a bald monk who seemed to be of senior rank opened the gate, with the help of his disciples.

Hannibal greeted the monk, but he was met with silence and a judgemental look. Hannibal was now visibly irritated by the monk's curtness, and cold welcome towards him. The monk gestured for Hannibal to follow him. He followed the monk into a large hall, housing a shrine. Upon entering, Hannibal felt the presence of an aura, that of a relic, but was unable to see anything. The monk presented him with a cup. The monk then started pouring warm water into the cup, until it overflowed. Hannibal thanked the monk, and was asking him to stop, but the monk kept pouring water into his cup.

The monk then stopped and instructed Hannibal, 'Drink.'

Hannibal was now weary of games and tricks. He asked in frustration, 'What are you doing?'

The monk once again instructed Hannibal, 'Drink.'

Not wishing to cause an altercation, Hannibal drank his fill.

'Why are you here?' asked the monk.

'Why does it matter?'

'I ask because people come here seeking guidance. What is it that you seek?'

'I don't think you can help me, old man.'

'Very well. Why do you come here if you do not intend to stay?'

'I don't know?'

'Then if your visit has no purpose here, you must make yourself scarce.'

'I will.' Hannibal shook his head in disapproval, as he made his way back to the courtyard.

Hannibal felt disappointed with this encounter, and chose to ignore it, as he had better thing to do, than argue with an old man. He closed his eyes and clinched his fists, grasping the knot. He teleported to the temple of Apollo. The teleportation made him feel ill because he was not supposed to teleport long distances. The exhaustion and side effects were so severe that he fell unconscious into a deep slumber. He had another vision, where he saw himself inside the secret valley. The beautiful, lush scenery was a pleasant sight to behold and he was instantly captivated. He heard multiple voices of women singing behind the trees. He proceeded to slowly follow the voices, curious to see who was singing. There was something bizarre about the voices, which made them echo in a strange and shallow manner. When he made his way around the trees, he noticed the day immediately fade into night. The valley suddenly had an eerie and secluded atmosphere. When he went past the trees, he was frightened and amazed to see a glowing lake. Upon careful examination of the water, he saw the singing women as they swam anti-clockwise. He stopped at a distance, with a range of emotions racing through him. He watched in confusion and amusement as he saw women, half-fish, half-human, and all with black hair, swimming just beneath the surface of the lake. They looked so majestic and enchanting, so much so, that he had a strong urge to join them. The only thing holding him back was that he was petrified by what he saw, literally being frozen in place.

'Who are you and what is this place?' asked Hannibal, looking stunned.

All the Mermaids slowly gathered at the edge of the lake, on the surface, led by the First Mermaid. She spoke to him,

'We are Demi-Guardians, Hannibal.' Their tone and manner of speaking was similar to that of the Spider Queen, but more enchanting.

Hannibal felt a chill up his spine.

He asked, 'What does that mean?'

'We are half-guardian, half-entity. We can take anyone to any body of water around the world, but unlike entities, we cannot grant wishes and requests.'

He sat down on the grass near the lake. He was still under the spell of disbelief, unable to come to grips with what he saw.

'Is this place real? Does it really exist?'

'This place is very real. You can venture to Caledonia, to see it for yourself.'

'And what makes this place so special?'

'This is where one acquires a white token.'

'The white rose,' he quietly remarked to himself.

'That would be the one,' replied the First Mermaid, she continued, 'You must know that one must pay a price to receive a white token.'

Hannibal looked past them, into the lake itself, curious to see what caused the glow. He was unable to see anything because his view was obstructed by the Mermaids gathered around the First Mermaid.

'What tribute would be considered a price to pay?' he asked her, as he continued to gaze into the lake.

'It is rather simple, we decide what price you pay.' The rest of the Mermaids started laughing.

Hannibal felt uneasy about her response. He changed the subject, asking,

'What about travelling through bodies of water? How does that work?'

'I am told that you possess a relic. A simple trade would be in order, for such an important transaction.'

'Is there another price to be paid?'

'You can always pay with your life.'

'Is that even possible for me? I am cursed with immortality.'

'Once that curse is broken, you will be recalled back here.'

'Would I die? Forever?'

'Of course. No one shall recall you after that,' answered the First Mermaid with a sarcastic tone. The Mermaids laughed again.

Hannibal pretended to be considering the offer. His interactions with entities has made him distrusting of them. He was unable to discern whether they were toying with him, or if they had no self-awareness. He knew he had to tread very carefully. Hannibal wanted to know whether they really wanted something from him, so he rose from the grass, commenting,

'I am not sure. You are asking too much of me, for little else in return. Especially since I have no guarantees that you will even honour your word.'

He turned away from them, with his head down, pretending to look defeated, and began to walk away.

'We understand that there is a certain world you wish to visit,' said the First Mermaid, hoping to grab his attention. She continued, 'We can arrange for you to reach the waters near the land that will take you there.'

Hannibal stopped when he heard that. He briefly smiled, realising his ploy had worked. He wanted to try something. He then quickly turned around looking curious and and feeling hopeful yet chose to act naïve and desperate.

He threw himself to the ground, asking her, 'Really? What do you want in return?'

'We can make it happen. We only ask for the knot in return.'

He turned away in despair, looking sad, he remarked, 'I understand, but I need it. Anything else I can do? Anything at all?'

'The next time you are here in person, we can discuss this further. You seem... conflicted and unsure.'

'What about the white token?'

'For that, you can either pay with your life, unless you wish to try your luck and help yourself to it at the bottom of the lake. Care to try?'

Hannibal wanted to see what happens if he interacted with the Mermaids. He was curious to know if he could interact with other objects in the vision. He was mostly curious to see what happened if he was able to get his hands on a white token. He stood up asking in a curious tone,

'Can you show me the white tokens?'

From his earlier conversation, he recalled that they like to taunt victims, he wanted to see if they would fall for his trick. They gestured for him to get closer, holding out their arms to grab onto him. He walked into the lake, where he was then slowly submerged. He focused his attention by looking down at the depths. The Mermaids lowered him to the bottom of the lake down to the rose bush. They then held him in place preventing him from reaching the surface. He started panicking when he was out of breath. He struggled to wrestle and wiggle from their grip. He grabbed onto the rose bush, trying to pull himself away from them. They began to laugh hysterically, looking upwards and at each other. He seized this exact moment to pluck a white rose from the bush. Right after this, he began to drift away from consciousness, as he watched them laughing in amusement. Hannibal then quickly woke up gasping for air, from the intensity of the vision. He looked at his hand and was very surprised to find that the rose really was there. He could not believe his eyes.

He felt disorientated after that ordeal, because it was so intense. He slowly pulled himself up and began heading inside the temple. He made his way, stumbling into the offerings chamber. He then started savagely devouring whatever he could get his hands on. He struggled to eat properly, as he was still shaken from the experience. After he filled his belly, he leaned against the wall taking his time to calm himself, because he was shaking uncontrollably, and still panting heavily. He spent hours staring at the wall opposite to him. He was trying to process what happened to him. When he had finally calmed down, he carefully examined the White Rose. He loved how it glowed in his hands. It looked so beautiful and majestic. He wondered if he would ever have to use it. More importantly, he wondered if the Mermaids knew about what he did. This experience taught him something he had suspected before, with the Spider Queen. He learned that entities cannot gauge how someone is feeling if they did not show it, but dealing with them is quite tricky. After he rested for a while, he slowly got up off the floor, by pushing against the wall. It was night-time so he decided to head into the Oracle's chamber. He found himself in the white void the moment he stepped inside.

'Hello Hannibal. What does the Wanderer seek?' the Oracle asked in her gentle, as she appeared.

'Where might I find the spirit world?'

'You will find it on the plains of the Americas, in the Dakota territory.'

'Where will I find the city above water?'

'The Demi-Guardians will help you get there.'

'What is the city above water called?'

'The one you seek is called, Tenochtitlan.'

'How can I find the secret lake?'

'You will find it in Caledonia, north of Britannia, but first you must make your way to the Stonehenge.'

'Stonehenge?'

'It is one of the seven wonders, a monument of great significance.'

'I saw a vision of dancing folks and the flying man. Where was that?'

'You saw the dancing Avars and the glider in Iberia.'

'Iberia? But it did not look like the Iberia I know.'

'You were in a different time period when it was called Andalusia.'

Hannibal looked to the side, squinting as he had come to a realisation that he might cross paths with the Praetor in Iberia. He also did not know which time period to travel to, to help him reach the peninsula. But a moment of epiphany hit him. He recalled that all he had to do was time travel to the second Punic War to find the peninsula, since Hannibal Barca marched his army there, before the war. He was also wondering whether he might find the Praetor there, should he attempt to search for him, since he was also killed by him there.

'Would it be possible to confront the Praetor, should I find him?'

'To do so, you must break up the Triumvirate. Any action before then is futile.'

'What does that have to do with anything?'

'He is protected, just like you are. In a shroud of anonymity, separating the pair of you from one another.'

'I don't understand.'

'It is not as simple as finding him, even if you came across the Praetor, you won't recognise each other. Besides, even if you both cross paths later in his life, he will be protected, surrounded by Sentinels.'

'How might I find him?'

'You will only find him when the time is right.'

He found it frustrating that he was unable to finish his quest, before finishing the labours. He was looking for any way of avoiding the labours, because he wanted to end the curse. It was hard to accept that there was no escaping his curse, so he carried on asking further questions,

'The man who was gliding over the city. What was his name?'

'The one you saw, was Abbas Ibn Firnas.'

'How can I find the time period of Abbas Ibn Firnas?'

'Keep time travelling, until you see the style of buildings have changed to what you saw in your vision, but if the Aurora is present, it will take you there.'

Why didn't I think of that? he thought.

'This is where we part ways, Hannibal.' She then promptly disappeared.

Hannibal left the void, but this time the hallucination did not affect him like it did before. His body seemed to have gotten used to it. He left the chamber heading into the hallway, where he suddenly collapsed to the ground falling unconscious. Long distance teleportation had taken a great toll on his body, and he still did not fully recover from it.

A week later, he awoke from his sleep. It was one of the most peaceful slumbers he had experienced in a while. He felt more rejuvenated than ever, by the much-needed sleep. He stood up and teleported straight to Carthage. He then time travelled to the first Punic War. He found that short distance teleportation seemed to be more forgiving.

He released Flavius and the pigeon, then rode out to his village. He felt home sick, to be back to a place he once called home. Hours later, he had arrived in the village. He saw the pigeon hovering over a house, so he dismounted to walk towards the pigeon's location. He remembered walking though the village before, from when he saw himself do so back at the graveyard. His memory was disrupted by Flavius, neighing with excitement as the horse interacted with his younger self.

'Father look, it's a white horse.'

'Leave it be son. We have to get back home. Your mother is waiting for the produce.'

Hannibal followed them with Flavius maintaining a small distance. Moments later, they all reached the family home. Hannibal was idle in place watching the strange family reunion.

'Shehrazal! We are home!' called out Hannibal's father to his mother.

'I am inside, Ashmoun!' responded Hannibal's mother.

Hannibal went inside, watching his family, with tears slowly rolling down his face.

'Father, can I go out and play with my friends?'

'Make sure you are back before sundown.'

When young Hannibal raced outside, he stepped aside, as he watched his younger self leave. Seeing this had warmed his heart.

'Welcome home son,' said his father while his mother smiled, both looking at him.

Hannibal was shocked to see them look at him and interact with him, because they did not seem to recognise him when he first entered the house.

'How can you both see me?'

'We are the only ones who can see you, son,' replied his mother.

He was at a loss for words. He began to walk towards them, wanting to embrace them both. They began to disappear, which made him panic.

'No!' he cried out, 'Don't leave me! Please, don't leave me!'

He broke down in tears. He missed them both terribly. After a while, he was able to bring himself to the bitter realisation that he must have relived a glimpse of his memories. It was hard to accept this bittersweet encounter, as a memory glimpse. He reluctantly wiped away his tears then proceeded to leave the house. He then time travelled to the second Punic War, where the officer had recruited him and his father for the war effort. Hannibal being a Wanderer, meant that both himself and his parents are wiped from time. He followed the party all the way to Hispania. The journey ended at New Carthage as it did the first time. The army made camp outside the city walls, ready to march the following day. Hannibal found himself a comfortable rooftop to spend the night atop of. He thought about what the next day might bring forth, and with that thought he fell asleep.

In the dream, the child explained to him that he was right about what he saw. They were indeed memories that he was reliving. The child also warned him about teleporting too many times in succession, especially long-distance teleportation, as it would harm his physical state, deteriorating his strength and causing him to experience exhaustion more frequently. This explained why he experienced fatigue and constant loss of consciousness. Before the dream concluded, he heard the voice of the Aurora stating,

Cordoba awaits.

He woke up the following morning, to a new city. Time had changed over to the Andalusian period. When he opened his eyes, he was delighted by the sight of a new city. He climbed down to the street, to travel to Cordoba. He released the pigeon into the air, then released Flavius to travel on horseback. The following days, saw Hannibal follow the trail of the pigeon until he reached Cordoba. When he finally made his way to the city, he could tell that there was something special about Cordoba. Words could not describe the beauty of the city. Even his vision could not recreate its incredible look. Hannibal marvelled at the many sights and could not contain himself. He visited the main attractions, particularly the ones he saw in his vision. He ignored the scent of the pigeon and decided to admire the architecture and design of the buildings, street by street. It felt like the buildings themselves were alive, and they were greeting Hannibal upon his arrival. By sundown, the darkness had enshrouded the city's beauty, lifting the mesmerising spell it had on him, allowing him to resume his search for the pigeon. He followed the scent until he found the bird resting above a house, right next to a workshop.

Hannibal approached the house to knock on the door, anticipating the Sage to welcome him. Instead, a young apprentice greeted him at the door. Hannibal entered to see Ibn Firnas writing in a strange language, which had beautiful calligraphy. He was writing while seated at a table, just as he saw him do in the vision. He was looking around and saw blueprints, papers, prototypes, and strange measuring instruments he had never seen. The young apprentice then invited Hannibal to sit down, while Ibn Firnas finished his work. Hannibal was presented with dates, fruit, and water. This kind of hospitality reminded him of the Arabian tribesman, whom he'd met in the desert and again aboard the ship bound for India. After he finished eating, he fell asleep waiting for the Sage. He slept the whole night, and by the time he woke up, it was dawn. When he was fully conscious, he heard a loud voice outside, so he went to investigate. He saw a grand building with a dome as its roof. He also noticed that all the men in the area were entering this grand building, he thought it must have been a gathering for a ritual. He saw the city folk removing their shoes before entering, so he did the same. He was watching them bow then prostrate many times, they then concluded the ritual by looking right then left. He had never seen anything like it, all of them moving in unison as if it were a well-rehearsed ceremony. He went back to the home and waited for ibn Firnas to return from his absence.

He recalled hearing the sound that called people to gather at the large building, but it seemed to have slipped his mind, when he first arrived in the city. He was in deep thought about the white token and the Mermaids. Shortly after, the Stranger appeared from down the hill, sword in hand, wearing a hood that obscured his face. Hannibal looked up and was startled by his unexpected appearance.

Hannibal rushed to unsheathe his sword, as the stranger began to run towards him, with the sword resting on his right shoulder. Hannibal managed to draw his sword, just before the Stranger was in striking distance. He began mirroring his opponent's movements, ready for when the stranger strikes. Both stared the other while walking opposite to each other in a circle. The stranger then rushed forward, striking Hannibal with the first blow starting the duel. Hannibal ferociously blocked the attack then kicked the stranger, but the stranger bashed his calf away, predicting and neutralising the kick. In the moment, he realised that the stranger had grown stronger from the last encounter. The Stranger pounced at Hannibal with a blow to the head, allowing him no time to retaliate. Hannibal quickly raised his sword horizontally to block the attack. This placed him in an awkward position, which the Stranger leveraged by striking Hannibal with his knee, knocking him to the ground. The Stranger then planted his foot on Hannibal's sword hand, rendering his arm useless. The Stranger then stood over Hannibal to deliver the final blow, when suddenly a murder of crows swept in, diving directly at the Stranger, headfirst, overwhelming him. Hannibal quickly stood up and swung his sword at the Stranger's neck ending the duel. Like the previous time, the Stranger turned into smoke, evaporating into thin air. This prompted the crows to fly away into the wilderness.

'Crows are the most intelligent birds in the animal kingdom,' said Abbas Ibn Firnas.

Hannibal quickly shifted his appearance to that of a person admiring the crows, then proceeded to ask, 'Who are you?'

'I am Abbas Ibn Firnas; I am Cordoba's proud polymath. And you are?'

Hannibal began to take deep breaths, still shaken by the Stranger, but pretended as though nothing had happened. He replied,

'Apologies for my curtness. I am Hannibal, son of Ashmoun. By the way… What is a polymath?'

'It means I am an inventor, mathematician, alchemist, and many other things.'

'So, you are a Sage?'

'I suppose I am.'

'Are you the one who wants to fly?'

'Looks like you have heard the rumours. In that case I can use some help if you are not in a hurry?'

Hannibal smiled, replying, 'Gladly. I have nowhere else to be.'

'Excellent!' exclaimed the Sage. He began walking into his workshop saying, 'There is a device I am working on building, but I need to finish studying birds, and how they fly.'

Hannibal asked him, 'Maybe I can help you in that regard. I have a strange ability, which might not make much sense. Maybe it might be a bad idea, but...'

'Well... What is it?'

'I don't know, I'm not so sure I can explain.'

'Can you show me?' the Sage curiously asked.

Hannibal took in a deep breath, then began climbing to the top of the workshop. He stood nervously above the building, praying he would be able to transform.

The Sage was concerned; he asked Hannibal, 'Are you well? What are you trying to do?'

Hannibal still nervous, he told him, 'You'll see.'

He began to slowly lean forward, arms stretched out to the sides. He began to drop, which allowed him to briefly transform into a crow. Ibn Firnas was scared at first, but then realised that this could help him study birds, if Hannibal would be his test subject. The Sage told him, 'I think we can do something with this. Well done.'

Hannibal followed Ibn Firnas, curious and eager to see him at work. The Sage began to explain his findings thus far to him, about birds. Hannibal then explained that he is unable to transform at will or maintain his transformation. Ibn Firnas advised him to keep practising, until he was able to master the ability. He told him that mastering the ability will allow him to closely study Hannibal as a bird, which would help him finish his work faster. Hannibal was glad to have met a Sentinel who was supportive and encouraging like Ibn Firnas.

Hannibal began trying out the advice of the Sage, to take off the same way birds do. Hannibal would make several attempts but made very little progress. Ibn Firnas then suggested watching birds, which might help him work out how to fly. Hannibal did as he was advised and spent hours watching how birds fly. After a long time of observing them, he noticed that many of them ran before taking off. This reminded him of when he chased the crow, and was able to fly, back in Ying. Hannibal then went to a precipice, outside the city, to try to run off the edge. When he did, he was able to transform and begin flying before he fell off the height. The first couple of times, he was so consumed by maintaining his transformation that he was unable to sustain it. After weeks of trying, he grew very frustrated, so he decided to try a new approach. On that day, he went to the precipice, but this time he began running, and threw himself at the wind. He transformed instantly and began flying above the land. In the midst of his frustration, he began to look at the magnificent landscape, which helped him take his mind off his misery. He was flying for a very long time, but he did realise. When he turned around to head back to the city, it then dawned on him that he was still in his transformation. He was so happy that he began to flap his wings, remaining in place. He was so happy that he began diving and then ascending back up, repeating the cycle. It was the best feeling he had ever experienced in his journey so far. When he descended to the ground, he was able to safely land, transforming back to his human self. When he tried it again, he was able to transform this time, without even running. He was so happy with himself, that he flew back to the city. The key was not over thinking it. He was so elated to have broken the mystery of mastering flight.

Hannibal was now able to prolong his transformation, allowing Ibn Firnas to study him in his crow form, up close in person. Ibn Firnas was very grateful to Hannibal because this meant that his work would be finished much faster. The Sage was so ecstatic, that he announced to the city that he was now able to build the glider, which would allow him to fly. Hannibal spent weeks observing the Sage and his apprentices working on building the glider under Ibn Firnas' direction. The Sage was very immersed in his work because he was happy to have finally been able to make his dream come true. After weeks of taking measurements, weighing materials and careful building the glider, the work was done. The following day Hannibal woke up late. The Sage had left him a note saying, *By the time you would have read this message, I will already have been in the sky.* Hannibal quickly rushed outside, eager to see him test out the glider. He was above the vizier's palace positioning the glider, to prepare for take-off. Hannibal wanted to speak to him but realised that the palace was surrounded by guards. Instead, he had to watch him from the streets, like everyone else in the city, just as he saw him do in the vision. When he took off, he was flying above the city. The crowds cheered for the Sage, but Hannibal was worried as to how he would stop the device. Hannibal chased after him, flying behind the glider. He wanted to warn him, but instead he was cawing. The Sage was not able to hear him. Shortly after, tragedy struck, when the Sage tried to safely land the glider and ended up crashing it into the ground. Ibn Firnas died on impact. In his excitement to fly, he forgot to add a mechanism that would allow it to slow down. Hannibal felt an immense pain of sadness grow inside him. Despite mastering flight, it came at the cost of the Sage dying.

Once he had cleared his head, he decided to re-join Hannibal Barca's campaign. He travelled back in time, to the Punic War and found himself in Turdetani territory. Before departing, he came across a merchant from the city, who was trying to sell him winter clothes. Hannibal did not want to buy anything from him, but the man was very persistent. Eventually Hannibal capitulated and traded his gold coins for the clothing, to buy the merchant's silence. The clothes were a coat of animal fur, held together to a thick layer of wool, using a very strong sticky substance that grows on trees, then bound together. The other article of clothing was a helmet like hat, which was a long cloth. The last being woollen pants and leather hide boots. He quickly made his way back to New Carthage, to continue the journey. At this point in time, the second Punic War had not yet commenced, but Hannibal Barca had ambitions to ignite the conflict.

The Carthaginian general amassed an army of Punic troops, combined with Numidian and Iberian mercenaries. Hannibal found it impressive, for a person to command an army comprising of peoples from different lands, who spoke different tongues. Hannibal Barca officially started the war by attacking Saguntum, a city allied with Rome. Hannibal Barca laid siege to the city, forcing his way in with minimal casualties. Hannibal was surprised by the bold actions of the Carthaginian general, but he remained an observer, abstaining from participating. The march continued to Gaul, where Hannibal Barca was at a crossroad, in terms of decision making. He gathered his council to debate what is the best course of action to invade Rome, with the aim of taking the Republic by surprise. Hannibal was outside the tent, closely watching the meeting. When he realised that no one was able to see him, he went inside the tent. When no one reacted to his presence, this gave him the reassurance to observe the meeting up-close in person.

'We are at a crossroads, from where we stand,' said Hannibal Barca. 'Where do we go from here?'

One member recommended that they attack Rome by way of sea, directly striking at the heart of the Republic. Hannibal Barca countered with the fact that the elder Scipio will be expecting them, since he was last seen on his way to Gaul, in the hope of intercepting the Carthaginian forces at sea. Another member suggested that they march through the Ligurian territory into Italia, but Hannibal Barca once again countered with the fact that the Consular army will be waiting for them upon their arrival. Someone else suggested that they order an amphibious assault from Sicilia. Hannibal reminded them that Rome's ally on the island, Syracuse, will help the Latins fend off the attack. He added that every way they had suggested will draw attention to their approach. After they had exhausted all their options, they asked Hannibal Barca what he had in mind. He proposed a daring manoeuvre so inconceivable, that it would shock the Republic. Hannibal stood up declaring,

'The Latins had defeated our navies at sea, during the first war. Naval invasion is futile, as is any other way involving Sicilia or obvious land routes. There is another way that the Romans will not see coming, because no one has tried it before,' the council were puzzled, looking at one another, wondering what that way might be. The general continued, 'We will have to march through the Alps.'

The council raised obvious concerns, but Barca insisted, reassuring them, 'I understand that no army has attempted the crossing in history, but we will be the first to do so.'

The members protested the suggestion, reminding him by stating concerns such as; the winter cold, disease, famine as well as hostile mountain tribes. Unmoved by their concerns, the general continued, 'Be that as it may. It is the only way that will work because it has never been done before and we will have the element of surprise on our side. It will also have the added benefit of masking our approach.'

One member remarked, 'There is no way for us to even pass through the Alps.'

Hannibal laughed, replying, 'If I can't find a way, I will make one.'

Throughout the entire war council, Hannibal was baffled with Hannibal Barca's brash conduct towards the council. He could not tell if it was arrogance, insanity or confidence, but convince them he did, even if they were sceptical about his vision. Hannibal realised that this must be the path of frost that the Spider Queen had told him about, as one of his labours. By the time the elder Scipio had arrived with his forces at the Carthaginian camp, Hannibal Barca and his mercenaries had vanished into the wind, leaving no trail, like ghosts. Although Hannibal was prepared for the cold, he had underestimated the cold of the Alps. This made him glad to have had that merchant annoy him into buying the winter clothes.

Every day of the march started with heavy winds blowing against them. Hannibal felt as if his skull was about to crack open from the intense cold. He was not able to feel his legs from the knees down. The cold was so terrible that he was barely able to clinch his fists, so he hid his hands inside his coat, under his armpits. Like the rest of the army, Hannibal had never experienced cold this harsh nor has he seen snow in his life, except for the frozen lake from his vision. The night-time was somewhat more forgiving because the winds would die down, bringing about much-needed relief. The tents helped shield the army from the winds. The fires made the night-time a tad bit more bearable, and it gave the army time to gather whatever strength they had left, to summon for the next day's march. The journey became progressively worse when the mountain tribes began harassing the army from the mountain tops and cliffs. However, this also greatly encouraged them to flee the Alps, faster. Throughout the ordeal, Hannibal Barca never lost faith, constantly encouraging the men to press on, no matter how dire the situation appeared to be. Incredibly enough, on the final day, just as the army was about to lose heart, they were able to sight the forests in the distance, down the hill from the mountains. The sight of stable ground gave the troops new hope, which bolstered their morale unequivocally, after having barely survived the cold nightmare. The army had overcome a great trail, but it came at a great cost, for a third of the army had perished in the march, succumbing to the frost. Hannibal nearly lost his life during the march too. The cold was so bitter, that he was an inch away from death, but the final day gave him the much need relief to live on. The thing that kept him inspired to carry on, was the fact that he had accomplished so much thus far. Giving up and remaining behind to die would not allow him to reach the end goal in sight: becoming the Herald.

Hannibal Barca first tried to rally the neighbouring Gallic tribes, living on the border of the Republic. The tribes were hesitant to join the cause, in fear of provoking a belligerent Roman retribution, should the invaders fail. Hannibal Barca was warned about a Roman army sent to confront him right away. He decided to take the fight to them, near the river Ticinus, where the Romans had situated themselves. On the promised day, both sides violently clashed, being locked into a fierce melee. Hours later, Hannibal Barca ordered his reserve cavalry to flank the Romans, routing them instantly. The victory allowed Hannibal Barca to receive logistical support from the Gallic tribes, heading into the future.

Hannibal is at the gates, proclaimed the Senate.

They then decided to send another consular army led by Longus to reinforce the elder Scipio's legions at the river Trebia. Scipio and Longus had disagreements regarding confronting Hannibal, which caused a rift between the two Consuls, leading them to separate their forces into different camps.

The night before the battle, Hannibal Barca had ordered a few contingents of his troops, to hide in the forest near the river. At first light, Hannibal deployed his troops in battle formation, with the cavalry on the flanks. Longus marched out, eager to meet his Carthaginian foe, mirroring his deployed formations on the flat terrain. The Roman general charged at his opponent, clashing with the invaders without hesitation, in an attempt to rout the enemy, hoping to seize the victory out from under the elder Scipio. The fight raged on, and during the course of the battle, the Romans managed to push the Carthaginians, having them on the back foot. The tides seemed to turn favouring the Romans, or so Longus thought, since the Carthaginian centre started to fold under the pressure. It was around this time, when the hidden Carthaginian reserves charged out of the forest, clashing into the enemy's exhausted flanks, annihilating them upon impact. The Roman centre quickly retreated, realising what had happened to their flanks, resulting in Hannibal delivering another stunning defeat against the Republic.

During this time in the campaign, Hannibal Barca came across another dilemma. News had reached him of two different consular armies sent to confront him, at the pass to the Apennine mountains, should he attempt the crossing. The two Roman armies where garrisoned inside two walled settlements, on opposite sides of the mountains. The general realised that attacking a well-fortified town would be counterproductive to his war effort, making his campaign lose momentum. He was also aware that besieging those cities will put him in a precarious position and give the Republic time to mobilise more troops against him. He did not have the siege artillery to breach a walled settlement either, so he would be wasting time. He did not have to waste, since he needed victories to maintain Gallic support. More troubling news also reached Hannibal Barca from Iberia, where the Scipio brothers had been sent to subdue his brother, who was left to safeguard the peninsula. Hannibal Barca decided to press on, hoping that his threatening presence in the Italian peninsula would pressure the Republic to recall the Scipios from Iberia.

Hannibal Barca summoned his council and allies, informing them of his next approach to taking the Romans by surprise once again. He made his intentions clear on crossing the insurmountable Apennine mountains, through a narrow mountain pass, instead of taking the road. The council was not thrilled to undergo another crossing, since the last one nearly wiped out the entire army, but it was hard for them to argue otherwise since his methods have yielded great results thus far. The crossing was a gruelling three days forced march, through a traitorous narrow pass. The march led them into a swamp that made matters worse, as it caused disease outbreaks and infections, plaguing much of the army. Hannibal Barca himself suffered an infection, which made him permanently blind in one eye. Hannibal watched all of this unfold, from the safety of the trees, transformed as a crow.

Once they had crossed the mountains and the swamp undetected, the general enacted a scorched earth policy. He burned many farms and towns, to force out his opponent from the nearby fortified city. His opponent chose to remain within the safety of his walls, awaiting the arrival of his comrade from the other side of the mountains. Hannibal Barca did not know the whereabouts of the other consular army, so he decided to lure out the locally garrisoned army by marching past the city, but the Roman general refused to sally out. After a day's march away from the area, he received news that the local army sallied out to pursue him, so he decided to march around Lake Trasimene. Hannibal Barca knew he did not have time to rest the troops, so he had them march around the hill, overlooking the lake to set up an ambush. Hannibal noted that the general had them go around the hill, so as not to alert the Romans of a looming ambush, by leaving marks, had they climbed the hills.

The following morning, the Roman army had arrived at the lake with haste, catching up to Hannibal Barca. While they were on the road, mist had descended over the lake, clouding the area, and restricting the Roman army's visibility. The legions at the front of the column ran into Hannibal Barca's elite Libyan infantry, blocking the road around the lake. The rest of the column halted their advance when they heard the clash. They were oblivious to the altercation unfolding at the head of the column. The Roman army was in a vulnerable position since they were now stuck in the mist and unaware of their current predicament. When the column was in a cluster, the Carthaginian general signalled for the ambush to commence. The Romans started to panic when they heard the battle cries of their foe, from up the hill drawing closer to their ranks. The Roman general had realised that he had been led into an ambush. He implored his men to hold fast, for as long as possible, to try to break out. The Romans were now in a dire situation, as they were hopelessly and completely surrounded, then overrun by the invaders. Once the mist had lifted, the Romans tried to look for any way out to escape the carnage. Unfortunately for the Romans, the only way out was by swimming across the lake, but many drowned in the attempt. The ones that tried to force their way out were cut down by their foe. It was a massacre; the entire Roman army had perished. Hannibal watched all the brutality unfold from the hill. He was surprised by the display of hatred and spite the barbarians had expressed towards the Romans. The victory at Lake Trasimene, created a ripple effect of panic throughout the Republic, as Rome's fate now seemed uncertain.

The Senate appointed a man named, Fabius Maximus as dictator, to deal with the menacing threat of the barbarians in the peninsula. Hannibal Barca and the dictator engaged in a game of cat-and-mouse for weeks, but the elusive Hannibal Barca always managed to slip away. Fabius' non-confrontational approach frustrated and angered the Senate, ordering him to step down from his post. Although Fabius never engaged Hannibal Barca in battle, he provided the Republic with ample time to muster and train a field army large enough to neutralise the invaders. The two new consuls, Paulus and Varro, were given joint command of the new army by the Senate, to eradicate the Carthaginian presence from the Republic once and for all.

After weeks of manoeuvring and following the Carthaginian general around the south of the peninsula, the Romans finally decided to give battle at a flat ground near Cannae. The day before the battle, Hannibal gathered the council explaining his strategy to them. He illustrated how they will deploy their forces in a reverse crescent-shaped formation. He elaborated by stating that the Romans will charge the centre, where they would have to defend in a fighting retreat. The feigned retreat will draw the bulk of the Roman infantry into a tight square. He then explained that the hidden reserves would supress the enemy from both sides of the centre, forcing them into a cluster. On the day of the battle, Hannibal Barca stood in the centre, before his troops, to address them prior to the engagement.

'The Latins stand before us, ready to send us to our graves. They will turn to our homelands once they have killed every one of us, to the last man. They will not show you any mercy if you are to surrender, which is why we will show them no mercy here today.'

An advisor named Gisko remarked, 'But they are so many.'

Hannibal Barca replied, 'They might be, but that doesn't concern me, for not a single one in their army is named Gisko,' the troops along with Gisko laughed at the joke, but Hannibal continued,

'They are only Romans, afraid of their own shadow. That is why they amass in greater numbers and hesitate to give battle.' Hannibal Barca then walked closer to his vanguard, exclaiming, 'Give me victory and I will give you Italia!'

The speech was a much-needed boost, which raised the army's morale. They were in good spirits, and ready to hold their ground, as they nervously looked on at the Roman juggernaut facing them. The two armies had formed their ranks, both having infantry in the centre and flanks, with the cavalry on the outer flanks. The Romans took the initiative and marched out to meet the invaders, slowly closing the distance. The ground shook as they advanced forward. The sound of the march was terrifying, only adding to the horror of the situation. After some time had passed, the Roman centre finally closed the distance, meeting the first Carthaginian contingent in the centre. It was led by Hannibal Barca himself. The Carthaginian lines started to slowly move back in a fighting retreat, giving the illusion of being pushed back. After a few hours, the Carthaginian lines turned into a crescent-like formation, facing the Roman army. The Carthaginian cavalry were able to rout the Roman cavalry, allowing them to join the Carthaginian infantry. The hidden reserves helped funnel the Romans into a cluster forcing them to be trapped in place. The cavalry had finally caught up to the stretched Carthaginian lines, charging the clustered Roman centre, completing the envelopment. Once the Romans were surrounded on all sides, they watched helplessly, as the barbarians hacked their way through them. Only the troops outside the immediate centre managed to survive the onslaught. The disaster at Cannae had brought Rome to its knees. The Senate had lost two thirds of all political and military leadership in one fell swoop. Hannibal was at a loss for words, unable to describe what he had witnessed. He was on horseback, watching the battle unfold from the nearby river. A masterpiece like no other, the campaign from beginning to end was full of surprises.

Curious to see how the Romans would respond to their defeat at Cannae, he decided to travel to Rome. He knew Rome would answer this travesty, but he did not know how. He took this time to race back to Rome, on horseback before the Roman courier arrived there before him. Along the way, he admired the marvellous scenery of Italia's countryside, hills, valleys and forests. The scenery was breathtaking. He really liked the design of the Roman roads, a unique and beautiful look. He travelled from city to city, until he had finally arrived in Rome, being able to get there by following the pigeon.

The first place he headed for, was the chamber of the Senate. Despite his best efforts, the courier arrived in the city before him, which disappointed Hannibal when he found out. He entered the chamber, eager to watch the Senate's reaction, now that they had a limited number of troops at their disposal. He finally had a chance to observe the heart of bureaucracy and politics at work, in person. This was a spectacle he was looking forward to. There was an uproar in the Senate, a display of mayhem. Voices shouting across the chamber.

'Enough!' shouted a young man, sending a powerful echo throughout the chamber, overpowering the other voices.

The voices in the chamber instantly died down. All the members look to the young man, as he walked to the centre of the chamber.

'Look at you! Barking at each other, like sailors and merchants at the docks. Argue over who will take turns to cower from Hannibal and his army of mercenaries. He is at Cannae deciding what lands to distribute among his followers. Time and time again you have sent incompetent fools, to deal with this brute. First it was Fabius; you then appointed the bickering couple. How can we mock these barbarians in contempt? How can we be superior to these barbarians that have brought us to such a critical point in our Republic's history?'

'And who are *you*, boy?' asked a member of the Senate.

'I am Publius Cornelius Scipio, son of the elder Scipio,' young Scipio turned to the senator. 'I was at Ticinus when our forces were overwhelmed by the invaders. I was at Cannae when Hannibal crushed our legions.' Hannibal was surprised to hear that; he continued listening,

'...I fought his forces on many occasions, and as a result, I am the only one qualified to deal with him, for I know him better than anyone here. While my father and uncle lay waste to the enemy in Iberia, I intend to force the invaders back to the place they call home.'

'And how exactly do you intend to do so?' asked another senator.

'I shall sail to Iberia and rout the enemy there. Then I will invade Carthage and force their senate into surrender. The only army they have left to defend their homeland is here. All our generals were lost in the many fights against Hannibal Barca. I am the only one here who has experience fighting against him. Give me an army I can train, to eliminate the invaders, otherwise you will have to deal with him. We have been fortunate, that he has squandered his opportunity to advance on Rome, by wasting time in the south. Give him time and he will have invited the Greeks from across the Adriatic. That is why we must act now.'

It was hard to argue with the young Scipio, because he made a very good argument, but even then, they wanted to hide behind bureaucracy. The Senate unanimously agreed to give him complete authority to command an army. The young Scipio was only allowed to gather the remaining survivors from Cannae. They were dubbed "the broken men of Cannae". The young Scipio put the broken veterans to work, re-training them to suit his tactics and style of command. Hannibal recognised this approach, as he recalled seeing Alexander and Sun Tzu do the same with their forces. Surprisingly, Hannibal Barca continued to squander his opportunity, to pressure Rome into capitulation. Instead, he remained idle awaiting assistance from the Carthaginian Senate.

Scipio wasted no time in drilling his troops as well as making other preparations. Once he was ready to mobilise, he sailed straight for the Iberian Peninsula. He was able to turn the Iberian tribes that despised Carthage to side with him, by offering them favourable terms with the Republic. Through pragmatic diplomacy, he was personally able to gain the favour of the east Numidian king to side with him. This new alliance would prove useful for when he would invade Carthage. In a considerable span of time, everyone started turning against Hannibal Barca, which forced him to sail back to Carthage, leaving Italia and his allies there. The young Scipio then turned his attention to Africa, to invade Carthage, just as he promised the Senate. Along the way, the west Numidian king Syphax blocked the Roman army in west Numidia. Scipio and his new ally attacked his camp during the night, setting the fortification ablaze. The soldiers that tried to escape the inferno were slain by Scipio's men. Another army was sent to halt Scipio's advance at Bagradas; however, he used Hannibal Barca's envelopment strategy to overwhelm his opponent. There was only one obstacle left standing in his way, Hannibal Barca himself. Scipio was on his way to Carthage, his allies had reported sighting Hannibal Barca at Zama, lying in wait.

Hannibal took the time during the march to approach the young Scipio. Unexpectedly, the general spoke to him before turning around.

'Don't think I didn't notice you lurking around since Iberia.'

Hannibal was not expecting to hear him say that; he asked him, 'How did you know?'

'It is my responsibility to be observant. How do you think I managed to become a general?'

'How did you know that Hannibal Barca would depart Italia if you attacked Carthage?'

'When I announced to the Republic that I will be raising an army with the intention of invading Carthage, word travelled far and wide. I knew Hannibal did not have the means to attempt a siege on Rome. Otherwise, why would he hesitate?'

Hannibal took the opportunity to gain an insight into how Scipio's brilliant mind worked. He asked, 'How do you feel about him?'

'I rather admire him. He displayed great skill and military prowess. Not many throughout history will match his genius, but he did not take advantage of his victories.'

'How exactly do you intend to defeat Hannibal?'

'It's quite simple really, I turned his allies against him. He relied on Iberia, so I took it away from him.'

'What is so special about Iberia?'

'It has precious metal mines. It has an abundance of fertile lands and many rivers. I was able to create a chasm between him and his allies. If I deprive him of the source from which he draws his strength, I am one step closer to taking him down. Diplomacy and political intrigue are far more powerful than any army put together. You do not influence people with brute force, you parley with them.'

'So, what did you offer the Iberians?'

'I offered them peace and friendship with the Republic. The Carthaginians were tyrants, and no one likes a tyrant. The only thing they had over the Iberians was fear. I took that fear away from them, now they see me as a liberator, which I am. The only problem is, Rome will become the new Carthage, after they no longer need them.'

Hannibal remarked, 'A tyrant replaced by another.'

'Exactly.'

'What about the Numidians? How did you win them over?'

'In Iberia, I spared the king's nephew and returned him to his family. If it were any other Roman general, they would have sold the boy into slavery. Like I said, diplomacy is more powerful than brute force. Now I have their cavalry to support me against Barca.'

'You used bargaining to isolate him so that you can limit his potential?'

'That is what you call strategy. His men worship him, everyone thinks him to be invincible. If I can influence those around him, he will be alone and isolated, easier to single out. Without him, Carthage will fall.'

Hannibal liked the young Scipio's genius. He appreciated his open-minded approach, and learned so much from observing him, as well as conversing with him. Days later, they arrived at Zama, where Hannibal Barca and his remaining allies were waiting. The Carthaginian general requested to meet with Scipio, and Scipio obliged. Hannibal used his listening ability to hear the exchange of words, as the two great generals met. Hannibal Barca greeted the young Scipio, initiating conversation,

'Publius Cornelius Scipio. We meet at last. I must confess, your reputation precedes you; I am impressed. A fine master of war you are.'

'I have waited years, to finally meet the legendary Hannibal Barca. They called you, Rome's worst nightmare.'

'What can I say? Romans scare easily.'

'I too must confess, I never thought I would be faced with a man of your stature, but I am afraid we are at cross purposes.'

'I never wanted war, despite what most believe. Both our peoples have suffered enough at the hands of the other. Let us both go home.' Hannibal tried to smooth the situation, dismissing the past.

Scipio was baffled and surprised at Hannibal's naivety; he had to redefine reality for the Punic general,

'We both know that's not true, because we cannot reclaim the status quo. How can there be peace when our worlds collide? Two lions are never seen among the pride. There can only be one hegemon, just like Alexander the Great and the Persian empire.'

Hannibal persisted, desperately hoping to change his mind.

'We must let bygones be bygones. Peace is the best option moving forward.'

Scipio shook his head, firmly insisting, 'I made a promise, and I intend to keep my promise. You failed to endure peace. You must now prepare for war.'

The two generals walked back to their camps, preparing their respective armies for the battle of Zama. Hannibal Barca did not have much to say, other than encouraging the men to fight on. Scipio turned to the broken men of Cannae, addressing them,

'Sons of Rome, you were once dubbed the broken men of Cannae. After today, you will be hailed as heroes of the Republic. This day shall be immortalised throughout history forever. We had our Cannae, and this shall be theirs, only this time, Carthage will be no more. Band together and let us end this once and for all.'

They were eager to avenge their loss at Cannae. Now that they had a purpose driving them forward. The units positioned themselves the way Scipio had trained them, back in Italia. The Carthaginian lines slowly approached the Romans, led by the elephants. Scipio expected Hannibal Barca to charge with the elephants first. This is when the light infantry moved out of the way, revealing the gaps between the units, allowing the elephants to harmlessly pass through the Roman lines. Scipio then ordered his cavalry to charge the enemy's cavalry on the flanks. Both Roman and Carthaginian infantry then charged each other in the centre, fighting in close quarters. Both sides were fighting with great fury, as if it were the end of the world, because they knew the cost of defeat after Zama. The Romans refused to give ground, pushing the superior numbers of the enemy forces back. The Romans remembered Cannae all too well and were looking forward to repaying the favour, as well as restoring their wounded pride.

Hours into the battle, the enemy mercenaries began breaking rank and fleeing, disrupting the Carthaginian formations. Scipio knew that the Roman and allied cavalry had won the encounter and have charged into the rear lines of the enemy. Hannibal saw Hannibal Barca flee from the battle, once he knew the battle was lost. It was sad to see Hannibal Barca flee, after his many great victories in Italia, and how he had motivated the men to press on during the march through the Alps. After a great battle, the Romans had won, leaving their enemy devastated on the field. The tables had turned on Carthage once again.

Scipio was searching for Hannibal Barca after the battle, but he received reports that the general had escaped. A part of him was glad because he had great admiration and respect for him. He knew that such a great strategist deserved better than to be humiliated back at Rome. Scipio returned to Rome to celebrate his triumph. This was the first time Hannibal had seen a military triumph, and how the hero was paraded on a chariot. He found it incredible how the masses cheered the victor. After the celebrations, Scipio's enemies in the Senate banded together to discredit him at every opportunity. Rome began turning against its own hero. Scipio famously called it, *An ungrateful Rome.*

He lived out his days in the countryside, away from the Senate and Rome's traitorous bureaucracy. Hannibal hated to see how things ended for Scipio. He hated having to leave this time period even more so. Nonetheless, Hannibal understood that the journey must go on. He decided to leave Scipio's countryside, but he did so with a heavy heart. He began thinking about the next step. Being in Italia reminded him of his gladiator past. He was very vaguely able to recall brief glimpses of his past life, at the gladiator school. He made the choice to travel to Capua, to finish another labour, by helping a rebel. Strangely enough, where he was, was not far off from Capua. Once he made it there, he time-travelled to when Spartacus was first captured by the Romans.

Once he arrived in the city, he looked for the Ludus Gladiatorius, a gladiator school. Hannibal was looking forward to meeting a familiar person from his past. He had to think of a way to get himself into the Ludus. He attended the gladiator trials, hoping to find a way to slip in. He noticed that there were certain individuals placing bets. There was a wealthy local that was known for lending money, for betting purposes. He recognised that this way was risky but would be worth the trouble. Following this thought, he borrowed money from the wealthy local, with the intention of squandering it, purposely betting on the losing gladiator. In accordance with Roman law, he would be turned over to the Ludus, as a slave, to pay back his debts and earn back his freedom—the plan was a success. Come the ides of March, Hannibal was apprehended by the militia men, for his failure to pay his debts.

It was difficult for Hannibal to hold his composure when the wealthy local mocked him, stating, 'You have no idea what awaits you at the Ludus Gladiatorius of Quintus Lentulus Batiatus. I will enjoy watching you die in the arena, if you even manage to make it that far.'

Little did he know that Hannibal was there for a completely unrelated purpose.

He was placed in the gladiator school of Lentulus Batiatus. When he arrived at the place, Spartacus had not yet been bought by the owner of the school. Hannibal and the new slaves were presented before Batiatus, but he noticed that Batiatus did not recognise him. Batiatus did not offer a warm welcome, instead everyone was subjected to a barrage of insult, as well as humiliating each slave individually. The only words of encouragement he did offer, was for the fact that their sole purpose of existence, was to survive and make the owner wealthy. This exact predicament reminded him of Sparta. He was reliving the very thing he hated the most, being impetus, under the mercy of a stranger. He would have to endure his time there, at least until Spartacus' arrival.

The new recruits underwent daily drills, training and sparring, as well as having to endure constant beatings. They were shown how to use all types of melee weapons. The gladiators would often hack away at a large wooden pole, so that their hands and arms were able to endure the shock of a strike upon impact. They were often only provided a shield and a helmet to protect themselves, leaving the rest of the body exposed to strikes. A gladiator was supposed to look like the conquered enemies of Rome. To the average Roman, a gladiator was a performer, a means of entertainment. Every gladiator was nervous before walking out onto the arena because it was a fight to the death. The crowd sometimes decided the fate of a gladiator, with a thumbs up or thumbs down, lest the defeated gladiator gesture with a plea for mercy. Hannibal benefited from this experience because this was a chance to improve his sword skills. He enjoyed sparring, especially with the veteran gladiators like Crixus. It took him a long while, but eventually he was able to learn how to properly fight with the sword.

There reached a point where Hannibal's patience was beginning to wear thin, when he was often presented before the wealthy local and Batiatus, then was subjected to relentless humiliation. This also took place before a private audience, which only exacerbated the embarrassment of the situation. Despite his blood boiling and fantasising about murdering the parties responsible, he often had to forcefully restrain himself. This caused him to develop an anxiety around the two, which he constantly suffered from. He often released his frustration out on the wooden poles, in secret, thanks to his curse, allowing him the discretion to do so. This was made worse by the fact that he could not do anything to harm them yet, otherwise his plan would falter. He would often shake in their presence, looking withered and defeated. It was not out of fear, but out of humiliation, when his dignity was stripped away from him. He used the fact that he outwardly looked broken, to appear helpless and of no apparent threat to them. This convinced Batiatus to make Hannibal a servant slave, who served in the villa and sometimes paraded as a fool. His intention was to further humiliate Hannibal, when in fact he had actually made his most fatal mistake. As a household slave, Hannibal was made to wear a collar around his neck. It was around this time that Spartacus had arrived at the Ludus. The timing was unfortunate, since Hannibal was taken away from the Ludus, making contact with Spartacus more difficult.

Hannibal would use any opportunity, to approach Spartacus, and make friends with him. He would secretly bring him better food. He would try to smuggle into the cells anything the slaves requested, making him very popular. During this time, Hannibal caught the eye of a particular slave named Yunus, a slave captured in Syria, during the Pontic wars, between Rome and Mithridates. Yunus was a very handsome slave, with a strong build. He approached Hannibal, offering to help him learn how to fight with cunning and skill, seeing that Hannibal was frail and quick. In return, he wanted to get closer to Batiatus' wife, Lucretia. This was not unusual, because she was a beautiful woman, who was bored of her husband. Hannibal told Yunus that he would see what he can do for him.

Lucretia was just as cruel as her husband. She often taunted Hannibal, by toying with him, but eventually she grew tired of her ways, being mostly unresponsive. She became so used to Hannibal, that she would string him along, whenever she had errands. Things slowly began to look brighter for Hannibal, as humiliations became less frequent, but cruelty was maintained. Hannibal was often reward for his loyalty when he discreetly helped thwart many slave mutinies. Lucretia would sometimes ask Hannibal to steal things for her, from the women she was jealous of in the city. She would also ask him to spy on people she despised, to blackmail them with that information later. Recognising his talent and loyalty to her, she began to entrust him with more sensitive matters.

One day, she told him that the handsome slave had caught her eye, and that she wanted him for herself. When Hannibal asked her if it was Yunus, she confirmed his suspicions. She wanted Hannibal to secretly smuggle Yunus into the villa on a particular night when her husband would be away. Yunus was delighted, when Hannibal told him that Lucretia felt the same way about him. Although Hannibal was helping avoid the wrath of Lucretia, he was inviting the wrath of Batiatus upon him, should he find out what was happening, and this made Hannibal very anxious. This took place, whenever the opportunity presented itself for Lucretia, when her husband was away, and when the circumstances were right. This new arrangement created a new layer of excitement for her in her life.

During this time, Spartacus had made his intentions known to Hannibal; he was planning on leading a slave uprising. Hannibal was very relieved when he heard that, especially because Spartacus wanted to enlist Hannibal's assistance, to help them escape and find weapons.

The final time Hannibal met with Spartacus, he was informed that the mutiny would take place during the night because there was a celebration taking place in the villa, with many guests in attendance. Hannibal seized the opportunity to hide a dagger in his clothes, in preparation to exact revenge on the wealthy creditor, who was attending the celebration. When the night was upon the city, Hannibal anxiously waited for a chance to slip away, when the celebration began. He wore a mask and a toga blending in with the other guests. He was able to locate the key to the armour and the key to the cells. He quickly made his way to the dungeon, freeing the slaves, starting with Spartacus. All the slaves quietly made their way to the armoury, to arm themselves with weapons. When the celebrations were in full swing, Hannibal found Lucretia.

He told her that there was an urgent matter, that someone wanted to speak with her outside. He took her from a secret entrance, where Yunus was waiting for them. Hannibal was able to steal one of the guards' uniforms, and gave it to Yunus to wear, along with a gladius. The Domina Lucretia was worried because she had no idea why Hannibal was being secretive.

He told her, 'If you want to live, go with him. Flee to Rome, otherwise stay and die.'

Hearing those words, she slapped him across the face. Hannibal was restrained by Yunus from retaliating against her. This is when the screaming and panic was heard from inside the villa. Hannibal knew that the gladiators had begun the massacre. Hannibal quickly rushed back inside and began to look for the wealthy creditor. He took off the toga and kept his collar, so that he would not be mistaken for a Roman by the slaves. Hannibal searched the villa room by room, until he found his target cowering in fear, in one of the rooms. Hannibal called out to him.

'Remember me?'

The local's eyes were filled with horror, as he stared at Hannibal in disbelief. He asked,

'It was you who did this? Wasn't it?' Hannibal slowly approached him, the wealthy man continued, 'They will skin you alive before they crucify you.'

Hannibal replied, mocking him, 'They can try.'

He then began stabbing the local in his chest and belly. The local was trying to keep Hannibal away from him, but to no avail. Eventually, he fell to the ground, with Hannibal on top. He told him,

'I came back, just for you.'

He stabbed him in the heart, ending his life. He then took whatever money the wealthy man had on him. Hannibal proceeded to cut off the collar around his neck and put his own clothes back on. He went back to the chamber, where he saw the guests being slaughtered mercilessly. He found a group of gladiators brutalising Batiatus, before being trampled and stabbed to death. *A well-deserved fate*, he told himself.

When he found Yunus and the Domina again, he took them to find horses, to escape out of the city. When Yunus asked Hannibal what he would do, Hannibal told him that he was going with them to Rome. When they left the city, they spent the first night covering as far of a distance away from the gladiators. When they came upon militia men who were sent to deal with Spartacus, they told them that they were escorting the Domina to Rome. The Domina was able to calm down and carry on the rest of way with them.

When Hannibal asked Yunus how he was able to see him, Yunus revealed to him that he is an Anomaly. Hannibal did not understand what he meant by it. Yunus explained to him that he is able to see things that happen in the Alternate Realm, and he was able to see Wanderers. This gave Hannibal the opportunity to reveal to him that he was not going to keep them company the whole way, because he was going to fly the rest of the way to Rome. The Domina thought that he had lost his mind, as did Yunus, but Yunus believed him somehow, since Hannibal is a Wanderer. Hannibal asked Yunus how he'd ended up being captured. Yunus told him that he was hired as a mercenary to fight by the Pontic king, but when they lost, the Romans took him captive, then sent to Capua, eventually being bought by Batiatus. Yunus embraced Hannibal, expressing his gratitude,

'Thank you for everything. And if you ever need to find me, I will be in Rome.'

As he turned around to leave, she asked him, 'My husband, Quintus. What happened to him? Did he manage to escape?'

He lied to her, stating, 'I tried to go back for him, but I don't know what happened. They were killing everyone in sight.'

This seemed to help ease her conscience insofar as being with Yunus went.

Hannibal transformed and began to fly away from them. He kept flying until he came upon a grove, where he found a tree to sleep under. In his dream, he saw himself at the Colosseum. The child was there too, sitting at the centre of the arena, patting a lion. He approached her; the only thing on his mind was the other rebel he had to betray, as part of his quest. He initiated the conversation, asking,

'Where might I find the rebel, whose face is partially covered in blue paint? The one that wields a two-handed great sword.'

'The claymore you mean. The man you describe is William Wallace. The famous Scottish rebel.'

'Scottish?' frowned Hannibal, 'Where is that?'

'A place in the British Isles, known as Caledonia.'

'Britannia?' he muttered to himself.

'Yes, Britannia, but Caledonia is north of Britannia.'

Hannibal recalled being told about a monument called the Stonehenge located in Britannia. He realised that the pigeon will lead him to find the Stonehenge. He wanted to ask her more questions, but the conversation was interrupted when a stone landed near Hannibal, thrown from behind him. He turned around to see the Stranger.

Hannibal looked at him stating with a disparaging voice, 'I don't have time for you. You will have to wait.'

This prompted the Stranger to back away, which surprised Hannibal.

The child remarked, 'Even though you are not strong nor powerful, there will come a time where it will show.'

'How can I be?' he asked out of pain, he continued expressing his despair with a burning agony. 'No one fears me; everyone be littles me. A millennium will pass before I can be powerful.'

The child stood up, walking towards him. She gently poked him, causing a green flame to burst out surrounding his body, as if he was on fire. He began jumping and screaming, thinking he was lit ablaze. But right after, he realised that it was not burning him.

He was still panicked, he asked her in alarm, 'What is this sorcery? Why have I been set on fire?'

'It is not magic; it is the gift, your inner energy. This is now your aura. It will not make much sense now, but it will in the future.'

Hannibal abruptly woke up, with his heart pounding profusely; he was scared by what he saw. He began inspecting his skin. He was reassured and was able to breathe a sigh of relief, when he saw that his skin was not burned. Nevertheless, he knew he had to go to the Colosseum. He flew the rest of the way until he found himself flying above Rome. Once he found the monument, he landed on the wall overlooking the arena. He took his time marvelling over the Colosseum. He was in awe over the craftsmanship and capability it took to build such a great structure. The level of detail and beauty were breathtaking. Eventually he was able to get himself to focus on why he was there. He made his way down to the arena. He then looked to the sky, closing his eyes. In his mind, he was calling out for help, thinking about Stonehenge. He was trying to see if this way of teleportation would work, because he had never been to Britannia or Stonehenge. When he opened his eyes, he found himself still at the Colosseum. Disappointed with his attempt, he then proceeded to release the pigeon and fly after it, to the Stonehenge. He enjoyed the scenery of going over the Alps, Gual and the body of water that separated Gaul from Britannia. When he finally reached the monument, he felt too exhausted to carry on feeling a strong urge to sleep, so he lay down on the ground to rest.

In his dream, he saw the Spider Queen. It was a while since he last saw her at Ying. She was admiring the Stonehenge. She initiated conversation,

'Beautiful place, Britannia. Is it not?'

'It is.' Hannibal stood up as he spoke, 'I have a question to ask. How can I find William Wallace?'

'You will find him, by looking for the English king, Edward Longshanks. The Druids will help you.'

'And how do I find them?'

'On your journey, eastbound. There will be a consul's army that will land on the island. Whatever follows these events, will eventually lead you to what you seek.'

The Spider Queen vanished, but the dream persisted. He spotted the Aurora, in the sky. It cautioned him,

'Beware of Liars, Traitors and Oath breakers.' He had no idea what the warning meant, but he found it chilling to hear such an unexpected message.

Hannibal woke up two decades later, as a result of the time travel, courtesy of the Aurora. He then entered one of his hallucinations, where he was able to hear distant voices. The monument had greatly amplified his senses, allowing him to detect the voices over an enormous distance. He heard leaders rallying their tribes, to confront an incoming army from the sea. He understood that a traveller from Gaul had arrived on the island, warning the tribes of an imminent invasion. He quickly released the pigeon, then transformed into a crow, flying after it. Along the way, he looked at the land from above. He found that the island was filled with incredible vegetation everywhere he looked. Open fields and forests covered the land, everywhere he went. He liked to fly close enough to the land, to visually consume its beauty. Eventually, he was able to make it to his destination in one day. When he arrived at the coast, he saw painted warriors on chariots, shadowing the Roman fleet. The fleet was looking for a suitable place to land. When the Roman ships find an appropriate place, the legions immediately established a beachhead to protect their amphibious landing. They began erecting palisade walls around their camp, while digging trenches surrounding the camp.

Hannibal felt a powerful presence, something he had experienced before at the monk's temple, but this one was exceedingly more powerful. It was resonating from the Roman camp. He was curious to investigate this strange energy presence. He wanted to see what it was for himself. He waited for the right moment, for when the whole Roman army would leave the fortification, to investigate. He was biding his time by drawing shapes in the mud. He was also using his listening ability, to keep an ear out for developing situations. He heard a group leaving the camp. When he looked up, he saw that it was a foraging party, sent to the nearby woods. He kept watching them closely but did not expect much to happen. After the party had made it to the woods, the locals began harassing them. The attacks persisted with growing numbers, which prompted reinforcements to come to their aid. The situation kept escalating, which forced the commander and his men out of the camp. Hannibal immediately seized the opportunity, flying into the camp. He quickly began following the aura, in search of its source. Much to his luck, the remaining soldiers and Sentinels were at the ramparts or near the palisades. After a while of carefully sneaking about, he was able to track the aura to the commander's tent. He drew his sword, anticipating guards or a Sentinel to be inside. Upon entering the tent, he found it empty. He walked up to a large chest that was near the main table. He slowly opened the chest, revealing the unexpected. His eyes could not believe what he was looking at; it was the

Hourglass. He felt a chill go up his spine, followed with a rush, which made him tremble. Never in a millennium did he ever expect to find the Hourglass by coincidence.

He reached out to pick up the relic, to prove to himself that it was real. Once the relic was within his grasp, his heart began racing with excitement. He began thinking about the Druids, so the relic teleported him to Mona Island. He froze, unsure of what just transpired. He found himself in an open grove, which housed the Druids. The grove had a giant oak tree surrounded by wooden huts. Not long after his sudden teleportation, he saw the Druids emerge from their huts in the woods. He realised then that his instinct brought about the teleportation, triggered by the thought. There was something about these Druids that made him uncomfortable in their presence. They approached him being led by the Elder Druid. He asked him,

'How did you find this place?'

Another Druid then asked, 'How did you find the Hourglass?'

'Who are you?' asked a visibly confused Hannibal.

'We are the Guardians of the Hourglass. We are the Druids of Britannia. You are an ill omen, Hannibal.'

He was surprised to hear them say that.

The Elder Druid then asked Hannibal, 'Have you come to return the relic?'

'Return it?' Hannibal felt scared, but he summoned the courage to ask them, 'How did you know my name?'

The Elder Druid spoke with contempt, 'That doesn't matter.'

Hannibal momentarily gazed at the ground, thinking to himself, *Guardians?* He then looked at them questioning what was said,

'If you are the Guardians of the relic, then how did you lose it in the first place?'

The Elder Druid promptly responded, 'That does not concern you.'

He questioned their claim again, 'You want me to hand it over, based on your word that you are the original owners of the relic?'

'Let me make this simple for you. Do you intend to return it?' enquired the Elder Druid, in a condescending manner.

Hannibal found this conversation bizarre and nonsensical; he persisted with the questions,

'Why do you need it?'

'Once more, that is not your concern,' responded the Druid, in a cold manner.

Hannibal wanted to see how they would react, so he casually responded, 'Well... since you prefer to not answer my questions, I will hold on to it for an eternity, until you give me an answer.'

Being the proud one that he was, the Druid swiftly responded by saying, 'Why would someone hoping to look for Longshanks, be willing to lurk around for an eternity?'

The Druids surrounding the Elder Druid looked at their leader with disapproval. This indicated to Hannibal that they were either Sages or had the ability to read his thoughts. He assumed that, because there was something unusual about them. Hannibal smiled, as he addressed the proud Druid.

'Let us forget about reasons.' Hannibal wanted to present him with an ultimatum, knowing that they couldn't refuse. 'If you tell me how you know this, I promise to return the relic once I no longer have a use for it.'

One of the Druids immediately intervened, exclaiming, 'He is lying!'

There was a pause, where the Elder Druid entered a state of concentration. It looked like he was in another dimension. Hannibal noticed how he entered this state, the moment he had mentioned an ultimatum. He found their behaviour to be very strange.

The Elder Druid finally replied, 'No, he is telling the truth.'

Hannibal found this most unusual. He curiously asked the Druid, 'How would you know I was telling the truth?'

The Druid stated, 'You have no reason to lie.'

Hannibal was sceptical because he could not figure out how they knew what he was thinking, but he was seriously suspecting them to be mind readers.

He said, 'The reason I am here is to find, Edward the Longshanks.'

The Druid eventually decided to help Hannibal with this single request.

'To find the Longshanks, you will have to follow the Lionheart.'

'Is he another king?'

'Yes, and to find him, you will have to first find the Ayyubid sultan, Saladin, in Jerusalem.'

I remember Jerusalem. Alexander passed by the city during his campaign, Hannibal thought.

'What about the Hourglass? When will you hand it over?' asked the Elder Druid.

'Once I have accomplished my quests, I will hand it over.'

The Druid squinted, asking him, 'Quests? In Britannia?'

Hannibal found this encounter very creepy. He could not tell if this was a trick, or if the Elder Druid really was reading his thoughts. He told him,

'I'm not sure.'

Although Hannibal appreciated the Elder Druid's help, he was not thrilled with his cold and unwelcoming behaviour towards him. He left them without saying anything. He had felt extremely uncomfortable interacting with them; it seemed his instinct was strongly cautioning him against them. At this point in his journey, Hannibal wished to travel the island normally, to better understand the topography of the land. He wanted to live with the tribe that confronted the Romans, curious to learn more about the people.

He began his journey heading east, guided by the pigeon. Britannia's ecosystem and vegetation was incredible. He never would have imagined a place, the Romans named "the edge of the world" to be so beautiful. After a week of being on the road, whilst living off the land, he was able to reach his destination. He arrived at the Iceni territory, the very tribe that had resisted the Roman landing.

Living among the Brittonic Celts was a breath of fresh air. It was peaceful and quiet, when compared with the loud and crowded populations of Rome and Capua. The Celts lived on hill forts and in village-like settlements, sometimes in the open or near woodlands. It was very different to Rome's overcrowded and tightly packed cities. The Celts lived a simple life, by being one with the land. It was a different world, from the sophisticated and polluted environment of Rome. Although life seemed relatively peaceful, warring among the tribes was rampant. This led them to adopt a stagnant mentality living in a feudal state. Life devolved to survival of the fittest. The Druids' refusal to record their people's history meant that their life, deeds and achievements died with them, if oral traditions were forgotten. They relied on storytelling, passed down from one generation to the next. He enjoyed listening to the many tales told to the younger generations.

Hannibal noted that the Celts were a proud and stubborn people. He did, however, enjoy and appreciate the simple life they lived. Their culture and civilisation were rich in their own right. They utilised the road system and had advanced metalwork skills. They were skilled craftsmen and artisans, able to fashion many types of clothes and jewellery. They were excellent sailors, and great merchants, which helped them thrive. Hannibal also recognised that they held strange beliefs, which influenced their stagnation, inhibiting innovation altogether. But compared to the Romans, their way of life was perceived as uncivilised.

The decades passed with no Roman encounters, until Caligula. The mad emperor attempted to conquer the island, to earn prestige. He waged war on the coast, ordering his troops to march against the sea, and collect sea shelves, marking his victory. Later on, Rome was eventually able to exert influence in local affairs. It made an ally, establishing a small presence on the island. When Rome's ally in Britannia was attacked by a neighbouring tribe, Emperor Claudius used the incursion as an excuse to launch an invasion into the island. The Romans wanted to secure their northern border, by annexing the island, for its rich natural deposits of gold and tin. Throughout the passing decades, Hannibal travelled the island, discovering everything there was to know about it. By the time he was back in Iceni territory, a war broke out against King Verica by another neighbouring kingdom, forcing the king into exile. Verica sought out Rome's help, to reclaim his throne. He did not know it then, but what he did, would set in motion a series of events that will change the history of the island forever.

Answering the pleas of his ally in Britannia, Emperor Claudius sent four legions to claim the island as a Roman province, once and for all. During that time, Hannibal had had enough of the island and wanted to travel to Jerusalem, to find Saladin, who would hopefully help him somehow find the Lionheart. When news of another Roman invasion had spread throughout the land, he decided to postpone his plans, eager to watch how the events would unfold, sensing a an imminent clash brewing. It had been a while since he witnessed a war, because he enjoyed watching conflicts.

Prior to Roman intervention in Britannia, the tribes were in a perpetual state of war against one another. The power struggles would cease from time to time, but war would always resume. When the Romans invaded the island the first couple of times, they managed to establish client states. This would allow them to insert themselves into the local politics, should their allies be threatened or attacked by the neighbouring hostile tribes. This would give the Romans a legitimate reason to intervene, under the guise of maintaining the peace, to protect Roman interests on the island.

During the current conflict, the legions and their auxiliaries landed in Britannia, immediately mobilising to end the hostilities. The Romans annexed the southernmost part of the island as a Roman province, which was named, Britannia Superior. A prince named Caratacus had survived the first war against the Romans, since it was his tribe that ignited the conflict. Caratacus went into hiding, travelling between the tribes to rally support for another uprising. Years later, Caratacus led the new uprising to reclaim his kingdom, back from Roman control. Unsurprisingly, the disorganised and undisciplined Celts were crushed by the legions. The king was forced to flee to a northern kingdom, in Britannia Inferior. Unfortunately for him, the queen of the kingdom decided to turn him over, not wanting to risk provoking a clash with the Romans. When Caratacus was sent to Rome, Hannibal assumed that it was the end of the monarch, given Rome's reputation when dealing with rebels.

Following the conclusion of the Caratacus rebellion, Hannibal teleported back to the Iceni territory. It was then that Rome had struck an accord with the Iceni people, since they were bound on an inevitable collision course. The ever-expanding Rome had its sight set on the upper half of the island. Hannibal was able to learn through merchants that Rome had transformed its governing style from a Republic to an Empire. Hannibal noticed how Rome under the republic was reluctant to expand, unless provoked to action. But the new Rome under the empire, was more eager to expand its borders.

The peace between Rome and the Iceni seemed to be smooth, until the Iceni king died of natural causes. Before the king's untimely death, he had mistakenly thought that by including Rome in his will, his kingdom would be safe and secure, enduring peace with Rome. He named Emperor Nero as his successor, along with his daughters. But the tribe would soon learn of their king's grave mistake. Hannibal would pay attention to tribal affairs, which helped him follow events closely. He heard the locals talk about a Roman legion marching into the territory. He felt as though whatever followed, would foreshadow the future to be had on the island. The legion looted the tribe's possessions, and when their Queen Boudica protested the legion's actions, she was flogged, and both her daughters were violated. This had greatly disturbed Hannibal, because the legions had never provoked a native population in that way before. He found this behaviour very unusual, even for the Romans, to do so unprovoked. Hannibal did not want to get involved but seeing how the queen and her daughters were treated, he could not help himself. He felt a strong urge to act. He always hated those who abuse power, which was something he couldn't easily ignore. Rather than remaining an observer, as he has done so far in his journey. He had a soft spot for women, thus choosing to go against his instinct, and deciding to act.

Hannibal killed the legionnaires with swift blows to their necks. He then approached Boudica, offering his hand. She was in shock over the legions' brazen acts, but she responded promptly to Hannibal. She took his hand, getting up from the ground. When the other legionnaires saw him, they rushed to deal with him. He quickly took out his bow, letting loose two arrows that found their mark between the soldiers' eyes, killing them instantly. The remaining legionnaires in the square tried to intervene, but Boudica quickly yelled to Hannibal,

'Hand me your sword!'

Hannibal quickly gave her his falcata sword. She violently cut down the legionnaires, with the help of her people's intervention. The other legions in the area were not aware of the incident, leaving with the spoils and whatever populace they took as slaves. The queen then took one of the dead Roman's capes, to cover her back. She then turned to her people, addressing them,

'We have endured humiliation long enough, under the yoke of the Roman heel, bearing down on us, but no more. Tomorrow, we shall call on our allies to join us in our joint struggle, to rid this island of Roman stain. They have shed the blood of our Briton brethren, quelling the many uprisings, of those who came before us. But together, we shall hurl them back into the sea.'

The entire square erupted, with the furious chants of the townsfolk in support of Boudica. This moment had solidified her position as the leader of the new rebellion since no one wanted to face the wrath of Rome. Hannibal had never seen a queen leading before, not like Boudica, if ever. She was tall, with a piercing look, which was matched with a sharp and charismatic voice. She had red hair, something Hannibal had never come across before. All these qualities naturally drew him to her, as well as her air of authority, something that made her iconic. Hannibal fell in love with her; he loved everything about her.

She began enlisting support from neighbouring tribes, until she had amassed an army sizeable enough to take on any Roman legion on the island. Once her army was ready, they waited until the Roman governor was on the west opposite side of the island. Taking advantage of his absence, she mobilised, with Hannibal by her side.

The rebels first struck the city of Camulodunum. Two thousand legions tried to relieve the city, but they were ambushed by the Iceni and crushed on their way there. The city was sacked and razed to the ground. She had exacted Roman-style revenge on the city; burning and looting the settlement, hanging, murdering and crucifying the entire population. Hannibal did not empathise with the Romans, because he had seen Roman brutality and cruelty firsthand. He started having dark thoughts, as well as violent urges to start murdering civilians. It took him all his strength to resist these tendencies. He felt disturbed by the fact that he felt this way. Although eventually he did participate in the carnage, he only targeted aristocrats and bureaucrats. He was very much opposed to the killing of Roman civilians.

When he asked Boudica if the killing of the ordinary citizens was necessary, she stated,

'Blood must be paid with blood.'

He could not argue with that statement, because the Romans had decimated the cities and towns of Britannia Superior, leaving no one but slaves behind. He understood that the violence was a necessary deed, to send a message to Rome, but even so, he was uncomfortable with it. When the settlement was reduced to rubble, Hannibal heard a voice calling him, as if it were inside his head, which Boudica heard as well. He did not know who it was, or where the voice came from. She shouted to him saying,

'It's the Druids! They need our help!'

'I can teleport to them. You wait here.' She was surprised by what he said.

'No! I'm coming with you!' she firmly insisted.

His affection for her prevented him from refusing. He held out his arm, so she could hold onto it. He then teleported with her to Mona Island. She did not feel ill from the sudden travel. He found this unusual, but it was because she was a Sentinel.

'We meet again, Wanderer. Under unpleasant circumstances, I might add.'

'Really? Because the first time was more pleasant?' Hannibal replied mockingly.

'The governor, Gaius Suetonius Paulinus is a day's march from here. And we cannot fight him off.'

'Why not? You told me you were the Keepers of the Hourglass. Which by the way I find very hard to believe. No wonder you lost it in the first place.'

The Elder was indifferent to Hannibal's attempt to provoke him; he casually responded,

'Our illusions and magic are powerless against a Sentinel. That is why we need you.'

Hannibal found this hard to believe, because what was said sounded dubious and strange. He asked,

'Why would I help you?'

'You get to keep the relic. As a show of our appreciation,' said the Elder Druid.

'Don't be coy with me,' Hannibal replied harshly.

'He will do it,' interrupted Boudica, as she firmly held his hand.

Hannibal felt her hand, without looking. He had a floating sensation in his stomach and chest. He thought that she might be falling for him because he certainly was falling for her.

'Fine. I will do it for her,' he begrudgingly agreed. 'What do you need?'

The Druids briefly glanced at Boudica, noting what she was up to, they then looked to Hannibal, as the Elder explained,

'So far, he has been informed of the rebellion's latest endeavour. And as a result, he is turning back east, to confront the coalition. All you must do now is defeat him.'

'Just like that?' wondered Hannibal.

'Yes, we have to go now,' Boudica interrupted once again, as she grabbed onto Hannibal's hand, forcing him away. 'Take us back,' she softly commanded him.

Hannibal teleported to Camulodunum, and as soon as they were back, she embraced him.

'Thank you for doing this,' she said.

Hannibal smiled, following her back to the settlement.

The second city to face the wrath of Boudica was Londinium. It was a bustling hub of trade and local bureaucracy, and it was one of the key Roman cities in Britannia. Suetonius managed to reach the city, only with his cavalry, leaving his legions a couple of days' march behind, in a forced march. He decided to leave the city to its fate, since he was vastly outnumbered, not wanting to risk the loss of his cavalry. The city suffered the same fate as Camulodunum, with the total destruction of the city and the complete annihilation of its inhabitants. Hannibal did not participate in the carnage this time, feeling very hesitant. He knew that this was wrong, despite his hatred for the Romans.

Suetonius retreated along the main road north, to a nearby hill that overlooked the main road, positioned between two forests that were covering his flanks. He waited for the rebels to meet him there, instead of confronting them in the open, severely limiting their numerical advantage. Boudica marched her army on the main road, in pursuit of Suetonius. Along the way, Hannibal rode next to her chariot.

'Do you have a plan to confront Suetonius?' asked Hannibal, with an eager tone to his voice.

Boudica glanced at him before looking straight ahead,

'We will charge them, head on. We Britons fear no one,' she remarked with an expressionless face.

'What if the battle does not go according to plan?' he asked with a slight smirk, expecting her to ponder over the possibility.

She turned to him befuddled, asking, 'Why would that happen? Have you not seen our numbers?'

Hannibal always being the cautious schemer, suggested something while briefly looking away.

'What if there is another way to resolve the battle? Minimising the risk of failure.' He looked back at her as he said that.

'How so? What strategy do you have in mind?'

'I am no strategist. But why not allow the battle to unfold? No matter the outcome. Should you be defeated, you simply reverse time.'

She let out an abrupt laugh, remarking, 'The Hourglass.'

When she smiled with approval at his suggestion, followed by nodding, his heart warmed to the fact that she agreed with him.

When they reached the hill, where the Romans had positioned themselves, she instructed her army to place the wagons behind them. Next, they formed rows, that looked like a human wave of men that were ready to ascend the hill. She rode out to the centre on her chariot, inspiring the troops with a moving speech.

'When I told you that I intended to wipe this island from Roman stain, I meant every word. This army marks the beginning of the Roman heel, for the rest of the body moving that heel, stands in Rome, dictating how we live our lives. Once they have been crushed, we will move on to cleanse the rest of our beloved island from their presence. Any memory of them will be one of their great defeat, and how we fought back to claim our rights, with fire and blood, because it is the only language they understand. I will not stand back and give orders, I will be with you, in the thick of the fight. Because I want history to remember me as part of the fray. Let us put an end to their miserable existence once and for all.'

The horns sounded the start of the battle, with all the chariot riders approaching the Roman positions. The riders began hurling projectiles and insults. The legions were under cover, in a testudo formation, which had the front row of legionnaires holding their shields facing the enemy, with all the other legions behind them, holding their shields up, covering their heads. The formation gave the legions a fish-scale look, and was intended to cover them, as a turtle does, when it hides inside its shell. The projectiles continued, but had no effect on the Roman position or morale. Realising this, Boudica ordered the entire army to charge up the hill. This showcased Celtic bravery, but it was outmatched by Roman tactical genius in terrain warfare. The Britons struggled to climb the hill, which caused them to break formation, when they were forced to funnel through the choke points up the hill. The Romans seized the opportunity to charge at the rebels down the hill when the rebels were in disarray. Hannibal realised what the Romans had done. They forced their enemy to fight an uphill battle, reducing their impact and numbers advantage. This was the first mistake that Boudica had made, which was allowing the enemy to choose the battle grounds, especial one that is favourable to them. Hannibal understood this, because he witnessed how Sun Tzu outwitted his Chu opponent during his military campaign, always choosing the battle ground. The Britons folded under the Roman charge, falling back, with many dying. With no cohesion, they were being cut down by the legions.

Boudica was shocked to see her inexperience causing the destruction of her army, during her first battle against Rome. She rode out of the fray, to encourage the troops to fight on and push back the Romans. But her words fell on deaf ears, in the midst of the pandemonium. The shock of witnessing her failure left her mortified. Hannibal came to her with the Hourglass in hand. He presented her with the relic, which she took from him. When he did so, he had forgotten that once he hands over the relic, he can no longer take it back if he intends to use it. He also unknowingly had marked her, which meant that she cannot harm him, but neither party knew nor realised that. She closed her eyes, concentrating on reversing the battle by hours before its commencement. Unsurprisingly, she managed to do it with ease, since she was a Sentinel. Hannibal had unintentionally committed his first act of changing history, by manipulating events to deviate from their natural historic course. By doing so, he had transformed Boudica from a Sentinel to a Rogue. Boudica opened her eyes to see her army intact, and the Romans back above the hill, as if the battle never took place. She breathed a huge sigh of relief, smiling as she burst into laughter. She looked over at him, stating,

'Simply reverse time!' She smiled, telling him, 'You shall have a place in my kingdom.'

Hannibal liked that, even though he did not quite understand what that meant. He suggested that she ought to have her troops move to the flanks, surrounding the Romans, the next time the Romans pressed forward; a manoeuvre he remembered Hannibal Barca perform against the Romans, many times throughout his campaign.

When the battle commenced for the second time, the troops were oblivious as to what had happened. When the Romans charged them down the hill, Boudica rode around with her chariot instructing the rear guard to slowly move around, so that they would not alert the Romans of their movements. As the battle progressed, the Romans were slowly overwhelmed, being fully surrounded, unaware of their situation. The day ended with a spectacular Celtic victory, resulting in the Roman army being completely wiped out, just as Boudica had claimed in her speech. She was hailed as the one and only queen of the Iceni. She rode out with her chariot to the centre once more, addressing the troops.

'Today we made history, as the first Celtic confederation to defeat an entire Roman army in a single day. Tomorrow we shall be their overlords.'

Boudica realised that the Hourglass can change everything. She relished the notion of being the master of time. Something far too powerful for her to relinquish. The relic was the gateway for an unbreakable future. She knew she would have absolute obedience. After the masses had believed that she managed to achieve such a great victory on her own. Word of her great deeds spread like wildfire throughout Britannia. There was a slow ripple effect, which saw the tribes either slowly join, or be forced into joining her new kingdom. Her actions had great sway over the tribes because she was the first to ever defeat a Roman army, with resounding success. Not long after her prospects, she began thinking about the future, and how to defend the island from future Roman invasions.

Hannibal recommended that she allow her people to learn and adopt Roman craft, skills, tactics, technology and style of governance, instead of extinguishing their influence entirely. She was reluctant at first, but then she recognised that this would give her an advantage over her rivals. She tasked Hannibal with overseeing trade with the Romans. Hannibal was more than glad to be of service. Under his supervision, he was able to win over skilled craftsman, and freed Gladiators. He ensured that Roman philosophy and education made its way to the island. She realised how talented Hannibal was with diplomacy and governance. So, she appointed him as the main ambassador, to dealing with the Romans. He was able to maintain good relations with Rome, preserving a long-lasting peace. On occasion, he would sometimes visit Gaul, where he would consult Roman bureaucrats and experts regarding certain matters he was tasked with. Luckily for her, Rome was too embroiled in conflict with the Persians in the east and the Germanic tribes from behind the Danube and the Rhine Rivers. This allowed her kingdom to quickly flourish, under Hannibal's stewardship. Using her charismatic charm, she was able to persuade her people to slowly adopt Roman methods of agriculture, administration and technology. Hannibal was able to strike an accord with Roman mercenaries. They helped train her people in the Roman tactics and art of war. This was made possible because Hannibal was well liked by the mercenaries.

Throughout his short time with Boudica, he never really felt comfortable enough to open up to her. Eventually, Boudica and the Druids had to discuss a future without Hannibal. He was always far too trusting, to eavesdrop on Boudica. But when he saw that he was being increasingly alienated, he felt unwanted. Whenever he tried to reach out or get close to Boudica, there was always an excuse to keep him away. Later, he found that he was being given tasks beneath his skills, which felt demeaning. He felt that it was by design, which led him to suspect that something was a foot. One day he decided to visit the Stonehenge. He wanted to learn what was happening. He wanted to find out why her attitude had changed towards him. During one night, he made his way there, when he felt that he was no longer being watched. He used his listening ability to pinpoint Boudica's voice, or the Druids'. Much to his surprise, he was listening in on a secret meeting that was planned without his knowledge. The Druids were voicing their concerns.

'We don't know why you allowed a foreigner to be involved in our way of life.'

'He has helped us grow to where we are now. He helped the Iceni secure their rightful position among the tribes. Why do you disapprove?'

'That is not the point. We don't know who he is, nor where he came from. We felt that he was an ill omen, from the day we met him. It was hard to discover the reason, but it seems that he wants to become the Herald.'

'That is impossible; no one has managed to even come close.'

'When he came here with the relic, it was a sign. We believe he might be the one to awaken the Herald.'

'What are you saying?'

'He is the ill omen that will bring about the about the end of the world.'

'And what does this mean for him?'

'It means he must be dealt with. Before it's too late.'

'How?'

'Bring him to us, and we will take care of the rest. That way he will not suspect a thing.'

'It's a shame because he has done wonders.'

The Elder Druid concluded by stating, 'It is the only way.'

Having learned what was discussed shattered Hannibal; he felt utterly betrayed, after having spent years helping Boudica transform her kingdom. He felt heartbroken, after having given her knowledge of strategy and governance. Worst of all was that he had given her the Hourglass, as a show of his admiration and affection for her. He felt lost and abandoned; his whole world came crashing down. He could not believe this would be his thanks, after what he had done for her and her people. He decided to depart immediately and leave Boudica and the Druids behind to continue his journey. In his heart, he knew he had made a mistake, when he did not listen to his instinct, by interfering with her fate, back at the settlement when the legionaries came sacking.

From the Stonehenge, he decided to teleport to a giant aqueduct in Gaul, which he had seen when he travelled there. Once he was above the aqueduct, he was observing the majestic view, overlooking the land. He knew that they could not reach him in Rome, should they ever decide to pursue him. This would be a new start for him.

Hannibal spent his time practising his archery skills, with some Roman troops and mercenaries. Eventually he became an excellent marksman. He practiced sparring with the sword on wooden poles and with mercenaries, to maintain his pacing and footwork, as well as training to enhance his reaction, timing and reflexes. Improving himself helped him recover and forget about Boudica and the Druids. He enjoyed flying over cities, which helped him understand the different regions and locations.

Throughout the decades he witnessed civil wars and peace treaties, periods of prosperity, triumphs, defeats, progress, innovation, disasters, famines and plagues. He decided to move on, during the third century, which had brought about a crisis to Rome's very existence. He briefly followed the events of the third century. He saw how Emperor Aurelian masterfully dealt with the usurpers. Hannibal was very impressed with Aurelian's pragmatic nature; he dealt sensibly with every situation he faced.

Hannibal was even more impressed with how decisively and quickly Aurelian was able to crush the secessions threatening the empire. In a very short span of time, Aurelian neutralised his enemies. He was also able to restore order, reviving Rome from the brink of imminent collapse. His deeds saw him being hailed as *'Restitutor Orbis'*, meaning 'restorer of the world'. But sadly, as a result of being murdered by his senior officers, Aurelian would not live long enough to see the fruits of his labour. His justice scared the corrupt generals, leading to his demise, in a time of morale decline.

Hannibal time travelled to the second half of the fourth century. Curious to see what awaits the aging empire, and calamity is what he found. The powers that be wanted to punish Rome, for succumbing to decadence. He knew this all too well, based on the teachings of Greek observations and philosophy.

Around this time, the great Hunnic migration began, from the steppes of Asia, into Pannonia. This caused a mass exodus of the Germanic tribes into Roman territory. During these events, the Roman empire had split into two halves: east and west. He recognised the name of the horde because Alexander had foretold of a Hunnic king to come. His heart was beating to the mere mention of the name, 'the Huns'. This was the signal he had been waiting for, to move on. He then released the pigeon, to guide him to Pannonia.

During that period, a conflict broke out between the Huns and the Western Roman Empire. The Huns raided territory in both eastern and western Roman empires, wreaking havoc and destruction, which forced both empires to pay tribute in gold and slaves to avoid the wrath of the Huns. To end the hostilities, Rome sent a nobleman's son, as a ward, to live among the Huns. The boy was one Flavius Aetius. This was a show of goodwill, and in recognition of their new alliance. The boy grew up in the court of King Ruga, the current king of the Huns. Aetius had formed good relationships with the Hunnic elite, chief among them a young Hunnic prince named Attila.

Hannibal lurked around, being used to evading the watchful eyes of Sentinels and Seekers. But this time he had to be a lot more careful, because he found the Huns to be very vigilant. He lived among the Huns, witnessing the atrocities they committed outside their territories. He understood why the Germanic tribes migrated into Roman territories, either by means of invasion or diplomacy. The Huns massacred entire populations with utter impunity, indiscriminately murdering everyone in their wake. For the better half of the century, the Western Roman Empire managed to pay off the Huns, as mercenaries, to eliminate their opponents in Gaul. This was at a time when Rome was on the edge of total collapse, marking the beginning of the end. This explained why the Romans abandoned Britannia and all other provinces. The Western Roman Empire was reduced to a state of never-ending civil wars. This allowed ambitious Roman generals and Germanic warlords to exploit Rome's weakness. The Rome that Hannibal now saw was no different from the Republic. Rome was always a city of liars, schemers, traitors and opportunists. He remembered the words of Scipio Africanus as he properly called it, 'An ungrateful Rome.' The days of the western empire were numbered, now that the tables had turned. The barbarians were now at the gates, reminiscent of Hannibal Barca's accomplishments.

The Vandals migrated from Germania to Gaul, looting and pillaging every Roman settlement in their way. They managed to eventually settle in North Africa, with Carthage as their new capital. The Visigoths migrated out of Germania as a Roman ally at first. But after a series of false promises and persecutions, the Visigoths, under King Fritigern, rebelled against the empire. The Visigoths had to endure humiliation before the rebellion, so terrible that most were forced to sell their children into slavery, in exchange for dog meat. Finally, at the battle of Adrianople, the Visigoths decimated the army of the Byzantine empire, the new name of the eastern empire. The Visigoths earned their freedom and independence at Adrianople. They settled in west Gaul, then later occupying most of Hispania. This was a reoccurring theme with many Germanic tribes, like the Suebi, the Franks and the Burgundians. Witnessing the horrors of this particular century was a jarring and harrowing experience for Hannibal. He recalled the words of the Spider Queen, of how there would come a time when he would begin to question humanity. But this was only the beginning because he had not yet fully embraced this notion. It was hard to reject this notion, when he saw the levels of malice man was capable of, as people devolved to levels of cruelty unbeknownst to the pure human consciousness. This period was rightfully called 'the Dark Ages', as humanity plunged deeper into darkness.

Following the death of King Ruga, Hannibal saw the ascension of Bleda and Attila, as co-rulers over the Huns. Bleda was proclaimed king, leaving Attila to rule as a prince. The kingdom was split between them into east and west. Years later, Bleda mysteriously perished, in a supposed hunting accident, making Attila the new king of the Huns. Attila went a step further, claiming to have found the sword of Mars, who was the Roman God of war. Although the Romans had converted to Christianity, they still held on to their old polytheistic beliefs, because it was part of their identity. This claim had the Romans trembling, especially when Attila would gain victory after victory against them. This led them to believe that his sword really was the sword of Mars. During this time, Flavius Aetius had become a general, gaining prominence in the western empire, with growing ambitions. The current western emperor, Valentinian, was threatened by the general's influence since he was a weak ruler and a pretender to the Roman throne. Sensing the danger, Flavius Aetius used his contacts at the Hunnic court to solidify his position back in Rome, by becoming the official emissary between the two powers. The emperor's mother, who was the true ruler of the western Roman empire, accused Aetius of treason, when he marched on Rome. But with his diplomatic endeavours and status, he was able to clear the charges against him, with the Huns at his back. Hannibal saw how Aetius was able to use his

Hunnic allies to manoeuvre around the traitorous political scene in Rome.

Aetius asserted his dominance, by clashing with the Visigothic King Theodoric and was able to soundly defeat him. He annexed a sizeable portion of his lands and in the end, he was able to force the king to capitulate to end hostilities. When the Vandals, under king Gaiseric, first moved from Southern Hispania into north Africa, Aetius recognised them as the true rulers of the province, allowing them to live there, in exchange for tribute to pay his troops and maintain a steady supply of grain into the empire.

Later, the Vandals and the Visigoths had an alliance through marriage, which placed Aetius in a precarious position. This concerned him, because most of Gaul was under his direct control, and was considered his personal possession. Outside interference would upset the balance he had created. The Vandals then invaded Sicilia and stopped paying tribute, as well as cutting off the grain shipments, exacerbating the already volatile situation. In response, Aetius once again, being the political fox that he was, made Gaiseric an offer of alliance, by proposing a marriage between Gaiseric's son and Emperor Valentinian's daughter. This created a rift between the Visigoths and the Vandals, breaking up their alliance. The offer was too tempting for Gaiseric to refuse, since it would give him a direct claim to the Roman throne. The ploy secured Aetius's position in Rome once again, making him the most powerful man in the western empire.

Following this incident, he aided the Visigoths against their enemies, south of the Pyrenees mountains, averting another clash with the barbarians. All these events were slowly weakening his grip on Gaul. Surrounded by enemies everywhere, he knew that another incident would prove to be his undoing.

The emperor's ambitious sister, Honoria, tried to have her brother assassinated, but the plot was uncovered. She was forced to marry a senator whom she despised, who also kept an eye on her. Around the same time, the death of the Frankish king resulted in his two sons calling on Attila and Aetius, respectively, to help them secure their throne. Simultaneously, Honoria secretly sent Attila a letter with a ring, pleading with him for her freedom. Naturally, Attila interpreted this as a marriage proposal, asking for half of the western empire as a dowry, knowing that Valentinian would refuse. When the news arrived at the Roman court, the empire unequivocally refused, which Attila saw as a pretext for war. This gave him the legitimate excuse to march to his Frankish ally's aid. This put Aetius in an awkward position since the emperor called on him to face the Huns. This was the inevitable that he was trying to avoid, but he felt compelled because he was unable to refuse. This time, there were no tricks for the general to employ, only a waking nightmare he had to live through. Flavius Aetius managed to win over the Franks, the Visigoths, the Burgundians, the Saxons and the Alans, forming a Germanic coalition against Attila. Aetius chased Attila for weeks, until the Hunnic king decided to give battle, in an open field, at the Catalaunian plains. Attila chose this location because it was more suited for his horde.

The battle commenced with the Huns and their allies, facing the Romano-Germanic coalition. The Huns drew first blood, by charging the allied centre, with their cavalry in a wedge formation. The charge was strong enough to break up the centre, which caused the Alans to rout. The Huns then split up, in opposite directions attacking both Roman flanks. The Hunnic horse archers were easily repulsed by the Roman foot archers. This was followed by the Hunnic allies' shock cavalry, attacking the Romans and their Gothic ally on the flanks. King Theodoric died rallying his troops, while leading the defence against the Huns, on the right flank. Both sides were now locked in a brutal melee, with neither side having an advantage over the other. Aetius took this opportunity and managed to rally back the routed Alans. While that was taking place, a hidden Gothic cavalry contingent, behind the Roman right flank, emerged to join the fighting. They charged the Huns from the rear when Aetius gave the signal. They were able to break the stalemate, forcing the Huns into a mass retreat. For an arbitrary reason, Aetius instructed his forces and his allies to cease any pursue of the enemy. Hannibal found this strange, as did the Germanic tribes, because the Huns were a devastating force in Europe. He suspected that Attila and the general, had a mutual understanding, a form of agreement, since they needed each other, to fend off their respective political opponents and rivals in the region.

The threat of Attila looming over the empire bought the unpopular general some time in Gaul and Rome. Aetius was allowed to exist, since he was the only deterrent to Attila and the Huns. Attila was not the type to rest, especially after such a humiliating defeat. This undermined his position among his allies, and as a regional hegemon. The Hunnic king crossed the Rhine, the following year, raiding and razing any settlement in his way. The Pope requested to meet with him. Around the same time, a plague broke out in Italia. Using the news of the plague and gold, the Pope was able to persuade the savage king to return to Pannonia. Hoping to avoid the plague, Attila went back to his kingdom; Hannibal decided to follow Attila back to Pannonia.

The king had decided to marry a Germanic noblewoman, to strengthen his alliance with a Germanic tribe. Hannibal saw this as an opportunity to strike. When Attila was none the wiser since the king would be too busy celebrating. Hannibal also had noted over the years, that the king was an avid degenerate drinker. So, he snuck into his tent, as a crow. He then dropped a sharp black stone he had picked up from the River Rhine into his wine jug. He laced the stone with poison, to contaminate the wine. He then hid behind the shrine of Tengri. When the king and his new wife came into the tent, Attila began drinking from his jug. He gulped larges sips, until the stone had swiftly slipped into his throat. The stone was very sharp, tearing at his throat, causing him to choke. He tried to cough, to spit it out, but instead, he choked on his own blood, leading to his death. The tent turned into a white void, making

Hannibal transform back to his human form. Attila was still coughing, not paying any attention to his surroundings, his eyes red and covered in tears.

'I did not know if I would ever find you. But it is funny how the world leads you, to those whom you seek,' remarked Hannibal, with amusement, while maintaining a neutral expression.

'When they find you, you shall be impaled for days, before you beg for death,' the king angrily responded, struggling to speak, while coughing.

Hannibal laughed before answering, 'How typical of you. To think that I will be apprehended, not realising who I am.' He then knelt over the king, who was still coughing. 'You died, choking on your own blood as a result of haemorrhaging, due to your excessive ways of indulging. That is what the truth will be, and it will be remembered this way.'

It was hard for the king to accept this painful reality.

'Why was I targeted?'

Hannibal sighed before responding, 'You are the savage king, whom I was tasked with killing. Some things you cannot escape.' He stood up afterwards, pacing around in the void.

'The final one you seek, is a warrior king, called the Lionheart.' With those parting words, Attila had expired. His eyes were fixed looking up.

Hannibal's stomach was clenched, when he heard, 'the Lionheart,' realising that the Druids had pointed him towards his final act of regicide. The death of Attila, concluded the hallucination, bringing him back to reality.

He quickly took Attila's sword and recurve bow, whilst Attila's newly widowed wife, began screaming in horror over the dead savage king. He then hurried back to Rome, curious to learn about the general's fate, now that the threat of Attila was over, before word reached the emperor.

When he arrived in Rome, he continued on his way to Ravenna, the new capital of the empire. He travelled forward in time, to see what happens to Aetius. As anticipated, the general was summoned to the emperor's villa, under the pretence of discussing state matters. Emperor Valentinian ordered his guards to kill Aetius on the spot. The general's personal guards, then killed the emperor in retaliation. Having witnessed this act of betrayal, he time-travelled back to Gaul to warn Aetius. He quickly rode by him, trying to warn the general, but his guards immediately intervened. They were able to block Hannibal, defending Aetius, fearing that he was an assassin. Hannibal realised in hindsight that he should not have worn his cloak. Hannibal conceded that the matter was out of his control. He decided to leave for Rome, to visit the Colosseum.

Before leaving, he snuck into a local garrison, where he took chainmail armour, a helmet with some chest-plate armour. When he arrived in the Eternal City, he realised that the atmosphere of this once great city had become dark and gloomy. The people would often go to watch gladiator games, to distract themselves from the imminent collapse they faced. The city that was once graced by Augustus, Scipio, Claudius, Marcus Aurelius and

Aurelian, was now a prized possession, waiting to be claimed by anyone.

During the night, he went to the monument to teleport to Jerusalem, but instead he experienced a deep state of hallucination. A great dense mist had descended upon the monument, followed by the Spider Queen emerging from the fog.

'I hope you haven't forgotten about me?' she remarked, with an uneasy sinister tone to her voice.

'I was too engrossed in my quests.'

'If I remember correctly, your quests were not the only task you were engrossed in. But I cannot fault you, for you are only human.'

He felt judged, since she did not approach him, maintaining her distance. Being reminded of Boudica once again. This brought up a deep regret, which was painful to supress.

'Deviating from your task, will result in you making mistakes and being reckless. Like what you did with the general, a great risk that could have been the end of you. But since you are likely to continue being like the rest of them, I can prescribe a solution. When the time comes, a son of Rome, whom you will find immortalised in the mosaic, will help you.'

'I don't understand why you are doing this.' She smiled as he said that in frustration, but did not reply. He continued, 'What makes me so valuable? And how will this son of Rome help me?'

'Let me worry about the underlying reasons. But more importantly, when you present him with the token, he shall find you, when the time is right.' She then abruptly walked past him, only stopping for a moment, suggesting, 'A word of advice. Approach him at a time when is vulnerable and unaware.' She then vanished into the fog.

When the hallucination ended, he saw the Stranger entering the arena, the same way he'd seen him do in the dream, many centuries ago. He panicked, trying to reach for the knot, in an attempt to make a hasty escape. As he looked for the knot, he heard the Stranger's footsteps speeding up. When he looked up again, to see the Stranger, he was now a few steps away from him, with his sword raised. Hannibal reached for his Falcata sword right away, quickly parrying off the first attacks. Blow after blow, he was barely able to keep up with the Stranger's relentless strikes. After a short while, fighting for his life, the Stranger raised his sword. He struck with a mighty blow, shattering Hannibal's sword on impact. Hannibal quickly transformed, trying to fly away to the top of the monument. The Stranger took out a spear, throwing it at him, wounding his right wing. This forced him out of the transformation, tossing and tumbling on the ground. His shoulder was badly wounded, but the rush he felt helped him numb the pain. He pretended to be incapacitated, dragging himself away, trying to lean against the wall. The Stranger quickly caught up to him. Hannibal waited for him to get close enough, releasing Flavius to distract the Stranger. Flavius was able to knock him down, before being bludgeoned by the Stranger. Hannibal quickly drew Attila's sword, and with all the strength he had left, he struck him, aiming for his head. The Stranger's sword was forcefully thrown from his hand, due to the power of the weapon. Hannibal spared no time, quickly dealing a fatal blow to the Stranger, launching him away to the other side of the arena. The Stranger perished upon impact. His heart was pounding from the unexpected encounter. Even more surprising, was the power Attila's sword possessed, which was unreal. He quickly tended to his wound, wrapping it with any cloth he had with him, in the shrinking sack. Once he caught his breath, he teleported to Delphi, to visit the Oracle, since he was only able to expect her during the night.

Upon his arrival, he quickly went inside the temple, heading directly into the Oracle's chamber. He fell many times to the floor, trying to make his way to the chamber. Once he was able to enter the chamber, he experienced a light state of hallucination, allowing for the Oracle to appear.

'Greetings Hannibal. What does the Wanderer seek?' she said with her calming voice.

Hannibal was still visibly shaken by the incident at the Colosseum.

He asked in a low and tired voice, 'What does the mosaic look like?'

She revealed the mosaic to him. He saw an emperor in the centre, flanked by soldiers, clergymen and bureaucrats.

'I presume the one in the centre is an emperor,' he curiously remarked, while intensely staring in concentration on the mosaic.

'Yes, the one in the centre is Emperor Justinian.'

'I don't suppose a member of the clergy would happen to be a son of Rome?' he rhetorically asked, with a sarcastic tone.

'Everyone in the mosaic is a son of the empire.'

'Wait!' he exclaimed when he had an epiphany. 'Was Justinian a Roman emperor in the East?'

'That is correct. He was a Byzantine emperor.'

He knew that if he asked the right question, he would be able to find what he is looking for.

'What was Justinian remembered for?'

'Many great deeds. Chief among them, commissioning the construction of the Hagia Sofia and reclaiming the city of Rome from the Goths.'

He realised that the son of Rome the Spider Queen had referred to, might possibly be a general. Because if Justinian was to reclaim Rome, he would have sent an army to do so, rather than an emissary.

'Who was the general that reclaimed Rome, in Justinian's name?'

'Flavius Belisarius,' she told him.

When he looked at the mosaic, it was apparent to him that the closest members to the emperor must have been of utmost importance. He made this assessment based on the fact that the members on the right were soldiers wielding shields and spears. He had a strong feeling that the iconic man to the emperor's immediate right was most probably Belisarius. Because whoever created the mosaic had put great detail in his image, placing emphasis on his character. He was not entirely certain, but his instinct was strongly hinting to Belisarius being the son of Rome.

Hannibal began to feel weak and sickly. He knew it wasn't from the visit or the teleportation because he had never felt this aching pain before. It seemed to have stemmed from his muscles and bowels. He quickly fell to his knees, then collapsed to the ground, on his side. He then felt the pain slowly growing in his stomach.

He desperately said to the Oracle, 'I need a healer. I need someone who can help me.'

'The one who can help you is a man called Ibn Sina.'

'Where might I find him?'

'He will be in Baghdad. Which is the new city that replaced Ctesiphon.' Right as she said so, he fell unconscious.

In his dream, the child appeared in a dark void, like the one in the graveyard. He still felt the same agony, but he was unable to stand because of it; he was on his hands and knees. It was then that he saw a large, hooded figure standing behind her, holding a scythe. The terrifying scene made him recoil and momentarily forget his pain.

'Who is that?' he cried out in horror.

'He is the Grim Reaper,' she calmly replied, as she always does, with her childish voice.

'The what?' he shouted. 'What is he doing here?'

'You are dying, Hannibal.' Those words hit him like a tree branch ramming into his chest. His whole world was shaken, by her shocking revelation to him. She continued, 'He only appears to claim a person's soul. But he can't reach you now.'

'Why is that?'

'Because you are dying, not yet dead. Wake up.'

He immediately awoke, both rush and fear coursing through his veins, drowning out the pain, momentarily. When he awoke, he was in the period of Ibn Sina. He knew where the city might be located, because he knew the region well, when he followed Alexander, during his campaign. He first teleported to Jerusalem, forgetting that he was supposed to teleport to Baghdad. He then teleported to the Abbasid capital. He found himself in the Caliph's palace, surrounded by the Caliph's court. Hannibal did not know how to get to Ray, and he could feel his state deteriorating. He acknowledged that he was not going to make it. So in a last ditch effort, he called out the name of Ibn Sina, right as the world around him began to slowly fade away. Hannibal fell unconscious, surrendering to his fate.

He found himself again in the dark void. This time there was no pain, only silence. He thought this marked the end of his journey. He believed he was already dead, having succumbed to the poison. He had lost all hope, plunging him deeper into a state of despair.

Is this the end for me? he asked himself

It felt like he was being punished. He felt that he played a dangerous game, gambling away his chances and having lost, due to his recklessness. The more he thought about it, the less things made sense. The doubt had consumed him so much that his despair left him in deep spiritual agony. He broke down in tears, crying away the pain, of everything that had come to pass. The worst part of his predicament was the fear of the unknown, of being in a strange and uncertain place. Believing that all hope was lost, he closed his eyes, surrendering to whatever happens next. He felt that if he was to be thrown in Hades. The least he could do was spend his final moments resting. Shortly after, he heard the Aurora speak out,

'Arise, Hannibal. Your hour has come again.'

Hearing this made his heart thud. This gave him renewed hope, and a great appreciation to strictly follow and complete his quests. Because he was happy to have a second chance, at redeeming himself, to prove that he is worthy. This was the ray of hope, that he so desperately needed. He opened his eyes, waking up in reality this time. He slowly raised his head, to see where he was. He saw a man, wearing a turban and a long white cloth that looked similar to a toga. His back was turned towards him, and he seemed to be busy creating a concoction. Hannibal concluded that it must have been the healer he was looking for. After having fully acknowledged that he was no longer in imminent danger, he put his head down, breathing a sigh of relief. He was exhaling heavily, after having survived that terrible ordeal.

'Oh, thank God you're alive. I was beginning to think that the solution I poured down your throat did not work,' said the Sage, relieved at the success of his antidote. 'Unfortunately for you, the solution I gave you, will make you barren. Meaning you can no longer produce offspring.'

'Thank you, kind healer,' replied Hannibal, with a sickly voice.

'People call me, Ibn Sina,' he enthusiastically answered. The Sage then showed Hannibal the concoction.

'I would like to recommend a solution to your problem if this happens again.' He approached Hannibal, with a bottle in hand. 'This is a poison that you must consume in very small doses. I strongly recommend that you ingest a single drop every day, to help your body and organs become familiar with any poison you may come across. That way you will become immune to being poisoned.'

'Wouldn't that kill me?'

He reassured Hannibal, explaining, 'On the contrary, it will help your body become familiar with poisons.'

'Clever,' he remarked, with his eyes firmly shut, suffering from his burning wound.

Ibn Sina then gave him the concoction, which he tucked away into the shrinking sack. The Sage told Hannibal to rest for the next week, so that he could monitor his symptoms, to ensure that his body was recovering normally, without any mishaps.

Hannibal spent most of the week sleeping. His body was not adjusting well to the wound, and it was slow to heal. He was often sweating, which only added to his growing discomfort. The experience was excruciating and dreadful, especially since he was helpless. His mental and physical state were in decline, getting worse by the day. This is when he had a vision. He saw himself back at the ice lake. The child appeared to his side, humming to herself, while playing with a strange object that looked like a small bear.

'Why am I here?' he asked her.

'This is where it all ends,' she replied, then continued humming.

'About that deathly figure, whom I saw behind you. Who is he?'

'The Grim Reaper. He can be frightening.'

'I'm assuming he reaps souls. What happens when he does that?' There was a pause before she replied. He also did not realise that he asked about the Grimm Reaper before. Seeing her playing with that toy made him forget about his pain for a moment. It brought a smile to his face, as he reminisced over long-lost memories. The humming sounded very pleasant, which he liked.

She explained to him, 'Once the Reaper claims your soul, you cannot be recalled back from the dead. You join the realm of the dead, to rest.'

In the distance, at the edge of the lake, he saw a raiding party singing a sea shanty. He noticed that her humming, was part of the same melody of what they were chanting. He was unable to hear them, because his pain made it hard to concentrate or focus on the distant voices. He closed his eyes, and tried to think about something, to distract him from the pain. But all he was able to hear was the humming of the little girl. When he opened his eyes, he found himself alone on the ice lake.

'At the lowest point in the land lies the Dead Sea, where the might of two powers clashed,' spoke the Aurora, which did not make much sense to him.

'The one you will follow through the sands, is Ibn al Waleed. The Rashiduns will guide you,' spoke the child, with her voice echoing through the valley, but he was unable to see her.

Before he could ask for clarification, he was awakened by one of Ibn Sina's students. Hannibal was told that he was shaking in his sleep and sweating. They gave him a strong herb to inhale, to help him relax. The aroma of the herb had put him at ease, almost instantly. He felt so relaxed, that he could feel his body floating in mid-air. Once his vital signs had stabilised, he was left alone to recover. The following week, he was being assisted to walk and balance himself again. After many attempts, Ibn Sina had concluded that although the poison did not kill him, it had damaged his nerves in his right arm, which caused him to shake. The poison had other effects on him, such as making him lose his balance and making him dizzy. Ibn Sina gave him a concoction that caused him to experience a kind of surge, a rush. This substance helped him cope temporarily, but he was warned to use it only when absolutely necessary. He was warned that once the effects wear off, he would experience fatigue, to varying degrees, depending on how much he had exerted himself. Ibn Sina also explained to him that, since he was a Wanderer, wounds take longer to heal. Hannibal figured that it must have been part of the curse, which only added to his suffering.

Once Hannibal was healthy enough to walk on his own, he was allowed to leave the Sage's residence. He did as he was instructed, by applying a single drop of poison with anything he drank, once every day. He tried to use Attila's sword, but he was not strong enough to wield it.

He liked the weapon, because it had a uniquely incredible power, when used. He tried to fire arrows with his bow, but his aim had faltered. He often released Flavius, to ride around to his destinations or to keep him company. Flavius became his support while walking. He found that Flavius somehow helped him cope, and seemed to exert positive influence, but he could not understand how. The experience reminded him of his time in Crete. He kept exercising his right arm, to help him with his nerves. He tried to transform into a crow, to see how well he could fly. He found that the transformation made the pain and shaking stop. It felt different, and he was at first unaware of this fact. He appreciated the that his bird form heals much faster than his human form.

Next, he wanted to see discover the sites that Baghdad had to offer. He heard that Baghdad rivalled Cordoba in its magnitude. When he began to hour the city, he was stunned by Baghdad's beauty and vibrant culture. The city did indeed rival Cordoba in its beauty. He wanted to stay, but he knew he had no time to admire the city's magnificence. Growing impatient with his quests, he wanted to complete his labours. He then time travelled to the period of the Rashiduns. He did so by time travelling until he found himself among the populace who spoke the Persian tongue. He was in awe of the Persian capital Ctesiphon, when he saw the grandeur of its monuments. He released the pigeon to guide him to Ibn al Waleed and followed it in flight. Not long after leaving the capital, he found it hovering over the Rashidun army. He quickly recalled the pigeon, to travel with Khalid's army. He rode with them until they reached the city of Walaja. He was anxious to integrate himself into the Rashidun army, under the command of Khalid Ibn al Waleed. He was worried that he would be seen as an enemy or a threat, so he decided to keep his distance for the time being.

When the Persians finally arrived at Walaja, they positioned themselves against a hill, mirroring Khalid's position, who was also facing them, with his back against the adjacent hill. Hannibal watched the battle unfold in his bird form, atop the hill behind the Persians. The Persian general was waiting for another Sassanid reinforcing army, which was mere days away from Walaja. Khalid understood the severity of his situation. It felt like watching Hannibal Barca's campaign in Italia, only this time in the desert. Khalid could not risk allowing the two armies to merge and had to take the initiative. The Sassanid general's orders were to wait for reinforcements. Understanding this dilemma, Hannibal was anxious to see what the Rashidun army did next. The day had passed without any fighting taking place. During the night, he was curious to observe the morale in both camps. He wanted to know, what each camp thought of the other.

He first listened in on the Sassanid camp. He heard the Persians boasting and bragging, about their greater numbers. They were so confident, that they believed their numbers will bring them victory. They were eager to be the ones to defeat the unstoppable Rashidun general. They considered the Arabs inferior to them, belittling and mocking them. It was the exact mistake that the Roman Republic had made when they initally faced Hannibal

Barca. He then flew over to the Rashidun's camp and saw a different scene entirely. They were encouraging and inspiring one another. They constantly reminded each other about how God would bring them victory if they remained steadfast. There were groups praying, others reading and reciting their scripture. The rest were standing guard, tracking the enemy's movements, outside their camp. When dawn was upon them, the Sassanids were getting into formation. The Rashiduns on the other hand, were finishing their morning prayer. He had never seen an army praying before a battle, in their enemy's presence, the way they did.

Khalid made his way to the vanguard, ordering all the lines to charge the enemy at once. Hannibal was amazed, by the great level of determination the men had in their mission. The unwavering faith they had in their leader, was incredible. Once the Rashidun army clashed with the Persian lines, they placed the Sassanids in a deadlock. He watched them for hours, as they were slowly being pushed back. The Persian counterattack seemed to be working because the Rashiduns were pushed all the way back to their hill. Hannibal was perplexed by Khalid's bizarre decision. He was anticipating the Rashidun army to be overwhelmed at any given moment. He kept observing the slow progress of the battle unfolding. He felt that there was something afoot, since the Rashidun army was still holding on, instead of routing. He could not tell if the Persians were committed or being hesitant. Khalid's forces were finally pinned against the hill. Once all the Persian troops were fully committed. Hannibal closely followed the battle, from the Rashidun's hill. Khalid gave out a secret signal to a flag bearer atop the hill. Hannibal began looking around but saw nothing. He continued to look right and left, anticipating something to happen. Moments later, Khalid's legendary cavaliers emerged from their hiding position, behind the enemy hill. When he saw this, he recalled Hannibal Barca using the same tactics against the Republic, many times. He now realised that Khalid was simply luring the Persians, as part of a carefully orchestrated plan. The hubris Persians took the bait, abandoning their defensive position. It didn't take long for the cavalry to charge the Sassanid forces from the rear, taking them completely by surprise. This caused the Sassanid army to mass rout, being caught in a pincer. The Rashidun cavalry and foot soldiers began to hunt down their fleeing foe. The entirety of the Sassanid army was obliterated. Amidst the frenzy and panic, the remaining survivors fled into the desolate desert. Days later, their corpses were discovered by Khalid's army, when he was marching to meet the second army. They had perished succumbing to dehydration, having lost their way in the desert.

Next, Khalid met the second Sassanid army at an open field, near the town of Ulleis. The Persian general had positioned his forces between the Euphrates and an offshoot river. This strategic position was intended to prevent Khalid from using his cavalry. The Persians wanted to avoid what happened to their troops at Walaja. This time Khalid knew that there were no tricks or deceptions to be had. Only brute force, to break the

Persians for good. Upon arriving at the battlefield, he found the main Persian army still feasting. He wanted to press his advantage, despite his men being weary of their journey. He ordered them to assume their positions, to strike once they were ready. Once the Persians realised that Khalid was serious about fighting. They quickly scrambled their forces, to repulse the Rashiduns. The two armies were now facing each other. This was the part of the battle, where men would volunteer to duel. They would challenge anyone from the enemy lines. An Arabian chieftain, who had lost his two sons at Walaja, personally challenged Khalid to a duel. Khalid gladly obliged, seizing the opportunity to eliminate a key member of the enemy leadership. The two men immediately began exchanging blows. The duel didn't last long, as the more skilled Khalid was able to kill the chief with a decisive strike. Khalid capitalised on the chief's death, signalling for his army to charge the enemy lines.

The two armies then clashed in a bloody melee. Neither side was able to gain ground, staunchly holding on, steadfast. Khalid had reminded his men that if they won this battle all their efforts in the past few months would pay off for the rest of the campaign. For hours, the Rashidun forces tenaciously fought on. They proved far more resilient than their Persian foe. They were able to break the Arabian-Persian vanguard. This caused a rapid cascading effect of mass retreat, quickly turning into panic. Another brutal battle was won; Khalid's gamble had paid off. Khalid ordered his cavaliers to hunt down the remaining survivors. He recognised that allowing the survivors from past battles to escape proved problematic. He decided to take drastic action, in an extreme show of force. He wanted to send a message to the Persian emperor, one that would be sure to deter further aggressions or reinforcements. He gave the order to execute the remaining survivors. He threw their bodies in the river, to make an example out of them, to prove a point. He who stood in his way, shall face the same fate as the men of Ulleis. As a result, the Persians offered very little resistance after Ulleis. His word rang true, just as he had promised his troops at Ulleis. The remainder of their campaign was a smooth sailing endeavour, thereafter.

Hannibal could not comprehend the events he had witnessed. He was struggling to understand how Khalid was able to storm through an empire without having to flee or being pursued once. He always kept the Persians guessing; it was the exact opposite of what Hannibal Barca had done in Italia. Most importantly, he was very impressed with Khalid's genius, his ability to read events and react to unpredictable circumstances was incredible. Shortly after capturing all key cities in the south, Khalid received orders from Arabia. He was to quickly march to Syria, to assist and reinforce the other forces sent there. Warning of a great Byzantine army that had amassed, threatening to destroy their presence in the Levant. Khalid understood the severity of this news, and knew he had to act quickly.

Khalid held a war council, seeking his generals' and close friends' advice. He wanted to know which route to take that would get them to Syria the fastest. Most of them made suggestions but those, if taken up, meant that it would take weeks to reach Syria. Being pressed for time, Khalid rejected those ideas. One man told Khalid about a path that is rarely traversed by travellers, through the desolate desert, separating Mesopotamia and Syria. He told him that it was the fastest way to Syria, but he had warned him that there would be no water for five days. They would have to race to find the small oasis at the end of the five days, if they hoped to make it to Syria alive. Khalid made the difficult decision of ordering a fast march through the desolate desert. Hannibal realised that this was the path of scorching sand. The heat was already unbearable. He had no idea if he would be able to make the march. Khalid forced the camels to drink, until the beasts' bellies were full. He then ordered everyone to stockpile as much water as possible. He instructed the foot soldiers to stay behind. He only wished to travel with his cavaliers. Everyone said their farewells before separating. The ones who stayed behind, prayed for their comrades' safe travel. The Rashidun cavalry began the march, without looking back.

The first two days passed with relative ease for Hannibal, but the heat of the desert was unbearably strong. The night was unexpectedly cold and harsh, reminding him of the march through the Alps. The third day started to take its toll on everyone, especially Hannibal. His wound began to hurt, causing him to shake. The heat was so terrible that he would hallucinate and see a mirage, many times throughout the day. Every day at noon, Khalid would order his men to slay some camels, so that the other beasts can drink the water stored in their bellies. Because they needed them alive to fight the Romans. What amazed Hannibal was that they would pray joint prayers, twice a day throughout the march. They were constantly encouraging each other, to help keep their morale lifted. The fourth day was a test of everyone's endurance. Hannibal had to rely on Flavius to help him through the march. Being used to barely drinking any water at all, Hannibal gave Flavius most of the water to drink. But after a while, he began feeling parched. Hannibal was barely hanging on to life. The final day, everyone had run out of water. The heat only adding to the already dire situation, likely expediting everyone's demise, should they not find the oasis. Hannibal felt as though his soul was ready to depart at any second, with the heat burning his skin and organs. A few men had to be placed on the backs of horses and camels as they no longer had the strength to march. Most of the army struggled through the day, in aid of their comrades, to ease their pain. Alas, the man that was leading the expedition, started running towards a small hill. There he called over a few men at the front of the column to help him dig. They all began frantically digging around an old tree stump. Despite having no luck in finding the oasis, they did not dare stop searching. They kept relentlessly digging because their lives depended on finding the water. Their perseverance was reward when they saw water flowing from the sand, promptly thanking God for the discovery. They quickly rushed water jugs to their parched brethren. Hannibal felt like his head was ready to burst at any moment, from the scorching sun.

Being deprived of water, under such severe heat, made him lose consciousness. Flavius made it to the oasis, with Hannibal still on his back. The horse threw Hannibal next to the water, which forcing him to wake up. He still felt very weak and unable to drag himself to the small oasis. With whatever strength he had left, he grabbed the substance that Ibn Sina gave him, pouring it down his throat. Moments later, he felt a great jolt of energy, which made him jump like a demon. He dipped his face in the oasis, drinking his fill. Flavius had done the same, by his side. This gamble by Al Waleed risked every man's life, based on the memory of one soldier who had travelled the desert in his youth. Once Hannibal was hydrated, he lay back down on the hot sand, facing the sky. His heart was still racing from the concoction. He could not understand how he was able to survive the journey. It felt worse than marching through the Alps.

The substance left him so fatigued that he was unable to walk on foot. He had to resort to riding on horseback for the remainder of his journey. The army quickly mobilised after they replenished their wares from the small oasis. The following day, they managed to reach Byzantine territory in the Levant. Hannibal wanted to break away from Khalid's army, having overcome another great trial. He shrank Flavius, once the horse devoured its fill of grass. He began flying around, with the aim of finding a fortification. Whilst hovering over the land, he was able to immediately spot a local fort; landing on top of it. Using his instinct, he was able to hear the Roman commander conversing with the local bishop. The holy man was warning the garrison, having heard of Khalid's accomplishments in Mesopotamia. He was asking them,

'Is the standard of his army a black one? Is the commander of this army a tall, strong built, broad-shouldered man? Does he have a large beard, with a few pock marks on his face?' When their answer to all questions were yes, he cautioned them, 'Then beware of fighting this army.'

Hannibal was baffled by Khalid's reputation, being perceived as death itself. The garrison did as they were advised by the priest, leaving Khalid be, without confrontation. At this point in his journey, despite his curiosity to follow Khalid, he was growing impatient with his labours. He wanted to press on, desperate to conclude his quests, because he still had a long road ahead of him. Having already accomplished so much, instilled in him a sense of pride in his efforts, and motivated him to carry on. He spent the night above the fortress, thinking about what the Aurora said in his last vision. He knew that he had to follow the events of the battle that transpired, between Persia and Rome. He rested until nightfall, then carried on with his journey, despite not feeling well. He released the pigeon and began flying after it. Hours later, he was able to reach an isolated sea, the locals named the Dead Sea. Upon landing, he was able to hear the Mermaids singing. When he looked into the water, he saw nothing.

He called out, 'Hello! I cannot see you. What is this?'

The First Mermaid responded, 'Hello Hannibal. Our presence is felt in any body of water.'

Hannibal thought he was suffering a sonic mirage. He began clearing his ears. He paused for a moment, to try to assess whether he had gone mad.

'Are you really here?' he asked, feeling bewildered by the absurd situation.

'If you submerge yourself into the water, we can bring you to us,' the First Mermaid casually stated.

'But I have somewhere else to be first,' he told her.

She instructed him, 'Come back when you are ready.'

Hannibal was curious to witness the battle between Persia and Rome. He recalled hearing the Rashidun troops mention a battle that took place a few decades ago, between the two powers. This mention had been made during one of their recitations of their scripture.

He kept time travelling until he found himself at the confrontation that took place near the Dead Sea. After their defeat, the Roman forces retreated to Antioch. He witnessed the second and decisive Roman defeat at Antioch, which broke the empire. He followed the Roman army back to Constantinople. The Sassanids were able to annex every Byzantine territory on their way to Constantinople. This to the world, looked like the end of the Roman empire. The Byzantines were deciding what to do next, anticipating a blockade.

Once Hannibal arrived at the Byzantine capital, he came across the Hagia Sofia, which had been mentioned by the Oracle. Upon entering the temple, he found the mosaic of Justinian. He felt butterflies in his stomach, seeing it in person, because It was so surreal. It looked as though the characters in the depiction were frozen and trapped in time. He then kept time travelling, until he reached the time when Belisarius was an infant. He approached the young general-to-be in his residence when his father had visitors. He chose to visit Belisarius as a child, because he was not yet a Sentinel. He recalled how young Leonidas did not recognise him as a Wanderer. Hannibal wore the Centurion's outfit, which he stole from the garrison back in Gaul. Despite the attire being outdated, he looked like a Roman soldier. He unwittingly had implemented the Spider's Queen's advice, of approaching Belisarius in a time when he would be vulnerable. He approached young Belisarius, presenting him with the white rose.

As he gave him the white rose, he told him, 'Find me when the time is right.'

Once Belisarius took it, he slowly began to vanish and Hannibal was taken back to the previous time period that he'd come from. This allowed him to follow the events, right after the siege of Constantinople. While the Persians and Bulgars had surrounded the city, by land. The Byzantines still had the sea, from which they could sally out from. During the siege, the current emperor had died, prompting the army to elect a general called Heraclius as their new emperor. Hannibal was intrigued to see how this new emperor would save the eastern empire. Heraclius instructed the army that he would be leaving the city, to embark on a secret mission. He claimed that this mission will likely take him a year to accomplish. He instructed them to hold the city in his absence. He also told them that should he never return, they are to presume him dead or captured. Should he not return afte a year, they were to elect a new emperor in his stead. He made his preparations with haste, secretly leaving the city under the cover of darkness. He managed to sneak out with his elite cataphracts. He ferried his army to a port in northern Anatolia. He then quickly made his way to a holy Zoroastrian temple in Armenia. He razed it to the ground, to create a diversion. This prompted the Persian emperor to recall the army laying siege to Constantinople so that it could defend the empire. This forced them to mobilise immediately to defend their capital, Ctesiphon. Heraclius wasted no time by marching on Ctesiphon, to force the Persians into submission. His mission was a success. Once he was able secure favourable terms, he then quickly raced back to Tarsus where he was able to intercept the Persian army returning from Constantinople, in a surprise attack. He soundly defeated their forces, taking many prisoners, which he used to renegotiate for the return of all annexed territories, during the decades-long war. Hannibal was at a loss for words, after having witnessed Heraclius' great feat, in such a short time.

After reliving the conflict, he wanted to meet Saladin, since he was already in the Levant. He first teleported to Jerusalem, then kept time travelling and listening to the locals, until he heard mention of Saladin. He saw the city being reinforced, preparing for a siege. Saladin was anticipating the Anglo-Frankish alliance to lay siege to the holy city. Hannibal began roaming the walls, in his bird form, observing the fortification efforts. The tools, technology and weapons looked different. Growing impatient, he began looking for Saladin. He did not have to search for too long, because he found the Sentinel on one of the ramparts, overlooking the fortification efforts. He landed on the same wall, maintaining a safe distance. He did not know how to approach him, hearing a violent reaction. He decided to walk up to him, but ready to time travel should there be trouble. Once he approached the Sultan, he fidgeted, anxiously thinking of something to say. Saladin unexpectedly began speaking with him, while overseeing the workers.

'What are you doing here, Wanderer?'

Hannibal already surprised by what he heard, asked him, 'How did you know I was here?'

Saladin replied softly, 'I saw you when you transformed back to your human self.' He then turned to him. 'But what brings you here?'

'I was told that you can help me find the Lionheart.'

'In that case, you needn't go anywhere, for he is on his way here, along with his coalition.'

Hannibal could not contain himself, having just learned that the Lionheart was on his way.

'What can you tell me about him?' he curiously asked Saladin.

The Sentinel started walking, Hannibal following close behind as they conversed,

'From what I've heard about him, he is a man far away from home. Conflict follows him everywhere he goes, or as I understand, he goes looking for it. Naturally, a warrior king is drawn to fighting. Although we are enemies, I must admit, he is quite the warrior, brave and daring.'

Hannibal spontaneously commented, 'He sounds like a true war monger.'

Saladin raised his hand to Hannibal's chest, prompting him to stop. He cautioned Hannibal, saying, 'I would like you to remember that whatever you seek to accomplish, always remember that actions have consequences. If you ever intend to spill blood, know that blood never sleeps.'

Hannibal nodded in agreement. Saladin then bid Hannibal farewell, saying, 'Peace be with you.'

The Sultan then left to prepare for the upcoming siege of the city.

Hannibal had to assess the situation. He had to determine which best way to stalk the Lionheart, without raising suspicion. He wanted his final act of regicide to keep attention away from him. This felt like following Alexander around all over again, only this time, it would be during the medieval period.

When the Lionheart arrived outside the city walls, Hannibal flew around and above the camp, to carry out his reconnaissance. He saw many Seekers and Sentinels. This meant that he had to keep his distance. He kept looking for the Lionheart and was able to finally spot him after a while. He discovered that getting anywhere near the Lionheart, even if he kept his distance, would not only prove dangerous, but impossible because he was always closely guarded. The Lionheart was also renowned for his swordsmanship and martial prowess, so he could not challenge him head on. This limited his options to the bow and arrow. The other problem was that the monarch's men were vigilant. While eavesdropping on the camp, he learned from soldiers that the king was on high alert for a group called the Assassins. The locals referred to them as, the Hashashin. The following days, word had reached Richard, from England that his brother and King Philip of France were annexing his lands. This compelled the king to return and deal with the situation right away, forcing him to leave the holy land at once.

The unexpected developments made matters worse for Hannibal, because the king was now on the move. It meant that Hannibal could not be on their trail, otherwise he would be discovered, and his efforts very much compromised. He decided instead to spend a year in the Ayyubid territory, to train for the kill. He approached Saladin, enlisting his help to be inducted into the Mamluk training in Egypt. Saladin wrote him a letter, so that the garrison commander would accept him upon arrival. He trained for a whole year to become a cavalry archer. He was also given a composite bow, which was much more powerful than his Hunnic recurve bow. The training helped him regain much of his strength, to use the bow. He still did not have the strength to wield a sword. He spent every day, practising for the kill. He practised performing the execution, considering every possible scenario. Once he completed his training, he was given a Kurdish sword, as a reward for his accomplishment. He liked his new curved sword, and how beautiful it looked.

After the year had passed, he flew towards the Dead Sea. He was anxious about meeting the Mermaids because they did not inspire trust nor confidence. On his way there, he enjoyed looking at the sea castles and fortified cities. The architecture reminded him of the buildings and fortifications, he saw in Cordoba. He was able to arrive at the isolated sea by sunset. Upon his arrival, he heard the Mermaids singing, just like before. When he approached the water, they instructed him to submerge himself. He hated the fact that he had to rely on them, for the long-distance journey. Once he was fully submerged, he made sure to close his eyes. He remained in the water, not feeling any movement or shift in the water. Moments later, he thought he was still in the Levant. When he began losing his breath, he quickly swam to the surface, breathing heavily for air. He opened his eyes and saw that he had been teleported to the secret lake. He then dragged himself out of the water. He was still gasping for air. The First Mermaid requested that he bring back with him, the crown of Edward Longshanks, as a price for his passage to the secret lake. She also warned him that should he refuse or fail to bring it on time, the hex that was placed on him would summon him back at the lake, allowing them to claim him. He would spend eternity drowning. She also informed him that he had a year to carry out the task before the hex is triggered. He acknowledged that a year was barely enough time to find Wallace, the Lionheart and Longshanks.

He started by flying south, with the aim of finding a harbour. News from merchants and sailors would help him locate the Lionheart. It took him days to reach the south. When he made it to a harbour, it took him a short while, until he discovered that he was in Kent. There, he managed to learn that England had territorial disputes in northern and western France. A week later, he learned that the Lionheart was being held captive, and was being transferred to the Holy Roman Empire. Realising that time was already slipping away, he teleported to the giant aqueduct in Frankia. He was glad to be back at the monument because it held many fond memories.

Before setting out to follow the Lionheart, he wanted to familiarise himself with the English holdings in France because the land had changed so much since the days of Gaul. He started by flying to Western France, following the pigeon there. The scenery was beautiful and breathtaking, especially since he had a bird's eye view of the scenery. He found this experience very cathartic. It was a good distraction from all the wars, deaths and chaos.

When he reached the province of Aquitaine, he landed on the nearest castle top that was within sight. European castles had a unique design, which looked appealing to the eye. They looked completely different from the ones he had seen in the east. He felt compelled to discover more castles in the region. This was his newfound temporary fascination, which served an educational purpose but also distracted him for weeks. He toured the English domain, visiting castle after castle. This knowledge also had the added benefit of helping him understand the new region.

His final tour of the forts led him to a small-town castle at Chalus. He liked small towns, because they were little quiet havens, tucked away from view. Unlike the cities, which were loud, chaotic and overcrowded with people. Whilst admiring the town, taking in the serene environment, from the castle top. He began to experience hallucinations, allowing for the Spider Queen to appear before him.

'Greetings, Hannibal. What troubles your ever fragile mind?' she mockingly asked him, initiating conversation.

Hannibal kept gazing at the scenery, ignoring her disparaging remarks. His experience had taught him, to ignore naysayers like her. This was primarily because he was tired of her mind games. She acknowledged that she exerted power over him, through ambiguity with the need for guidance.

'I must congratulate you on a job well done. What you did was ingenious, the way you managed to get young Belisarius to accept the token. More impressive was your ability to solve that riddle.' It became apparent to him that she was using this treatment, to keeping him at arm's length.

'If you say so. Either way, your advice has brought me this far,' he replied, as he kept staring at the open countryside.

'Quite the little wise man you have become. But I can't yet place it. Is that humour?'

'If I had a sense of humour, I would not be so obscure from the rest of the world. But I suppose it is best kept this way.'

'Oh Hannibal. You are far too valuable to be given away to the world. But I have a feeling, that this is exactly what the future holds for you,' giving Hannibal a chilling foreshadowing. But he did not know what it meant.

'Valuable or not. I would rather be rid of this useless journey, and my worthless life with it.'

'On the contrary. You are the Herald awakened. Without you, the Herald would remain a fairy tale.'

He turned to her, and said, 'The last time you spoke about the Herald, you mentioned powers. Is there more to the Herald, or is it only powers?'

She gave him an unusually exuberant response, as she enthusiastically explained, 'The Herald is a marvellously wonderful thing. He can match his opponent's size. His powers are ever-growing, until the host can no longer bear or contain the Herald's powers – but that is based on the frequency of use. The Herald significantly improves the host's physical strength. He allows the host to hold their breath under water, for a whole year. The Herald can endure extreme pain, as well as the harshest elements of weather. His resilience is legendary, making him very difficult to kill. And the Herald greatly enhances the senses of the host.'

'When you describe the Herald in such a manner, he truly sounds legendary,' he remarked, trying to picture what that would look like on him.

'That is why becoming the Herald is a near impossible feat.'

'This all sounds wonderful. But why me? Why not someone else, who is more deserving of such a great stature?' he genuinely asked her, trying to coax out a partial truth.

'You are unlike any other human that exists on this earth. Very few possess your level of intellect, in your own way. Your mind improves with time, while most lose their mind with time. You are able to see the greater picture, in the grand scheme of things. Can you imagine what you can do as the Herald? The power to smite those who have wronged you. You can even reshape the world the way you see fit. Any man would kill for the chance to possess such power, even for a moment. The reason why you truly stand out from the rest, is for the fact that you are a paradox. You are able to exercise both good and bad, without compromising yourself. That is the rarest of qualities found in a man.'

'I would agree more with self-loathing, but a person at odds with himself also sounds accurate, if that's what you meant by paradox,' he added.

'You shouldn't be so cynical, Hannibal. No men who came before you have made it this far. And those who have, failed, because they did not heed advice nor caution. It is quite the accomplishment; you should be proud. You are halfway there. Why turn away now?' she reminded him, with a pandering voice, masking her twisted rationale with sincerity.

Hannibal nodded agreeing with her rationale. This allowed him to repurpose his self-hatred, to channel it towards something that could help him make sense of his endeavours. Hearing what she had to say made him realise that there was a partial truth to what she told him. His motivation to being brought back to life, was to exact revenge against the Praetor, but he lost focus. He recalled how good it felt to kill Batiatus and the money lender. He thought, *Despite her intent, I might as well make the best*

of becoming the Herald, to change the way things are,
since becoming the Herald is likely to be inevitable.

Ironically enough, the existence of the black token had completely slipped his mind. He had been too occupied with fending off the Stranger, rushing from one quest to another, and being overrun with emotions, which were being used to misdirect and manipulate him. It was becoming harder to make sense of everything, making it easier to accept her paradigm. So, he decided to turn it into his mission. He found it bizarre, how after a short conversation with her, he now had something to live for, not realising it will not be what he expects.

'Perhaps you might be right. I will never know until I get there,' he responded, with a miserable expression on his face.

'That's the spirit!' she exclaimed. 'We shall meet again, after a long absence.' She was happy with having broken Hannibal down to accepting her way.

When she disappeared, Hannibal was reverted back to reality. He saw crows gathering around him, cawing at him. He understood that he was in danger but did not know how. He looked in every direction and saw nothing. When their cawing intensified, he looked down. He was shocked to see the Stranger, making his way into the castle. He time travelled into the future, in hopes of escaping the Stranger. He looked back at the fields, and saw the town being surrounded by a small army, led by none other than Richard the Lionheart himself. He could not believe his luck. He began assessing the situation to pick the opportune moment to strike. While he was formulating a plan to assassinate the monarch, the crows surrounding him suddenly dispersed. Hannibal quickly turned around and saw the Stranger standing behind him. He was alarmed by his presence, thinking he had gotten rid of him. The Stranger had a dagger in his hand, he then quickly advanced stabbing Hannibal in the belly. Unfortunately for the Stranger, Hannibal was wearing chain armour under his clothes. In the spur of the moment, Hannibal threw himself off the castle ramparts to get away from the Stranger. He quickly transformed to a crow and made a smooth landing. The Stranger then raised his crossbow, but Hannibal was too quick in proactively responding to the situation. He released Flavius, mounted him and immediately rode towards Richard's position. The Stranger was unable to fire at Hannibal, so he jumped down from the castle. Hannibal knew that the stranger would be in hot pursuit. He had to act swiftly, otherwise the opportunity to kill the monarch would be forever lost. He retrieved his composite bow, taking the risk of riding straight for Richard, in plain view of his men. He had only a moment to strike him before they realised what was happening, but he needed to get as close to Richard as possible. He turned around to see if the Stranger was behind him. He saw him closing the distance on horseback as well. He was aware that he had no other option but to fully commit. Rush began coursing through his veins; he made sure to ride erratically, so that none of the stranger's arrows would find its mark. While evading his pursuer, he saw his narrow window of opportunity arise, when the king was preoccupied with shouting orders, during a skirmish between the townsfolk and the king's mercenaries. He drew closer until he was within range to let loose his arrow accurately. He drew the bow, holding and waiting for the right moment to release his grip. While concentrating, he felt an arrow bounce off his helmet, that was intended to distract him, but he remained focused, ignoring the commotion. When he saw his moment, he released the arrow while holding his breath. Moments later, the arrow found its mark, deep into the king's shoulder. Hannibal's patience and efforts were rewarded. The surgeons tried to quickly remove the arrow, but their efforts only resulted in the king's demise. The king's death made the Stranger vanish, bringing both the king and Hannibal into the white void.

Unlike the other regicides, both Richard and Hannibal found themselves inside the Hagia Sofia. There was a beautiful woman standing before a choir and chanting in Latin. Richard smiled in joy, stating, 'There she is. The fair maiden of Brittany, Eleanor.'

Hannibal sat down a short distance away from the monarch. They listened to her chant, with the choir behind her, humming and repeating phrases,

'*Orbis factor rex aeterne, eleison. Kyrie... eleison.*'

Richard was repeating her words, to himself, aloud, 'Creator of the universe, eternal king, have mercy. Lord... have mercy.'

'Soft and gentle words. They crumble any man, wearing him down to tears. This is quite marvellous!' Hannibal said, showing how he felt listening to Eleanor.

They continued to listen to her intently, being reduced to tears, in silence.

'What becomes of us?' Hannibal asked the king, wondering what lies beyond death.

'I shall find out soon enough, then you shall follow and see for yourself,' replied the monarch.

When Eleanor finished chanting the Latin song, they were taken back to the white void.

'Where do I go from here?' asked Hannibal, having no clue what to do next.

'Follow the king, to help you find the king. From father to son, you shall find the rebel.'

'What about the swordsman?'

'You will find him in the Sengoku Jidai time period.'

This brought an end to the interaction, taking Hannibal out of the void and back into reality. The Stranger was nowhere to be seen. Hannibal had managed to escape his clutches once again.

Following the death of Richard, his brother John was proclaimed king as his successor. Hannibal understood that the coronation was what the Lionheart was hinting at, when he said he should 'follow the king'. John's reign as king was rife with civil war, as his followers went to war against the neighbouring kingdoms. After his death, his son, King Henry, ascended to the throne. Unlike his father, King Henry was able to restore order and settle disputes among his nobles. When his son, Edward, came of age, he was married to a Spanish princess from the kingdom of Castile. Hannibal paid very close attention to the young prince, following him closely, to better understand him.

He was given the name Longshanks because he towered over men. He was prone to anger and had sudden outbursts, while remaining pragmatic and calm at other times, making him unpredictable. He inspired no loyalty in his actions, even going as far as to oppose his own father, on the political scene. His tendency to shift alliances when it suited him put him at odds with many nobles. Eventually, when his father died, he was crowned king of England. Despite his strange behaviour, his achievements had made him both feared and respected. When the matter of the Scottish rebellion arose, the monarch was all too eager to put an end to the problem, using his nefarious methods. Hannibal took an interest in the matter, when he heard the name William Wallace. Hannibal went in search of him and was able to locate him. Given the nature of the dire situation, he had to act with caution. He had ten months to betray Wallace and acquire Edward's crown. This was a dangerous gambit, but one he would have to take.

In the early stages of the rebellion, Longshanks left the matter to his subordinates in Scotland to deal with it. Unfortunately for him, his policies and taxations were the spark that ignited the rebellion. This was superseded by his soldiers' mistreatment of the Scottish people. Hannibal watched the events unfold, which would help him better understand all the parties involved. This knowledge would help him insert himself onto the scene, to get closer to Wallace. After closely following the events, he quickly realised that Wallace was an opportunist, much like every other Scottish noble. The only difference was that he was more popular than the other nobles. The English king's men were not able to quell the rebellion, culminating in a surge of support for Wallace's cause. This further alienated the Scottish nobles, who were trying to appease Longshanks. Realising the emerging rift, Hannibal looked to approach a prominent Scottish nobleman, John Comyn. The nobleman wished to gain favour with the English. Hannibal knew that he could exploit this to his advantage, since John Comyn was closely involved in Scottish affairs.

During one dark and quiet night, Hannibal waited for the nobleman in his private quarters. He understood that failure at this stage of his journey would prove fatal. He was praying he had made the right choice by choosing to meet John Comyn in his home. He knew that John would be the most vulnerable in the place he least expects to find company. When the nobleman arrived there, Hannibal barricaded the door, once he made sure that John Comyn was not carrying a weapon on his person. The nobleman recoiled when he had realised what happened, shouting,

'Guards!'

Hannibal had chosen that particular night, because most of the guards were drunk, after they had celebrated their commander's wedding.

'I come in peace,' he reassured the nobleman.

'How did you get in here?' Comyn shouted once again.

Hannibal raised his hands, to show that he was unarmed.

'I am here to talk to you in private.'

'Concerning what exactly?' asked John Comyn, in a shaky voice.

'About Wallace.'

'I'm listening,' he replied, while remaining on the opposite side of the chamber.

'I understand that you wish to hand him over to the English. I can help you.'

'Who are you and why the offer of hand?' enquired the nobleman, suspecting Hannibal to be a spy.

'Wallace killed my father who was garrisoned in one of the towns.' He paused, hoping the bluff would work. 'I came to you because I heard rumours that you wanted to hand him over to the English.'

'How are you going to help?'

Hannibal had his face concealed, making it harder for Comyn to see him.

'You needn't risk sending any of your men. I will find Wallace's whereabouts. And when I do, you will find a message tied to an arrow, here in your private quarters.'

'How do I know you are not working for Wallace?'

'If I was working for him, we would not be having this conversation. Instead, they would have found you with a slashed throat.'

John Comyn thought about it for a moment, realising it to be true. He told him,

'Very well. I will be waiting for your arrow.'

Hannibal left from the window, then started flying away, once he was out of sight. His search for Wallace resumed, after having left him for days. It took days to locate him again, which he did by following his rebels. He saw that the Sentinel was under constant guard, which made approaching him impossible. He decided to try and approach the rebel, under circumstances where it will be hard to refuse him. Fortunately for Hannibal, he did not have to wait long. The events were building up to the battle of Stirling Bridge.

One day, he saw a rider approach one of Wallace's men, outside their camp. He used his ability to listen to the conversation.

'Where is Sir William?'

'State your business.'

'I bring word about the English. They are heading north.'

'Come with me at once.'

Once they were inside, he heard them talking over each other. Wallace was informed by the herald of the English troops' movements. He called out to everyone in attendance.

'Quiet all! The English are converging on Stirling Bridge! We have to beat them there, before they ford the river! Gather the men. We move tonight!'

Hannibal wanted to send a message to warn Comyn. He knew that John Comyn's scouts would reach him fast as soon as the rebel's movements became common knowledge. He wrote a message, on a small parchment, that read:

'Wallace awaits the English at Stirling bridge.'

He was pacing around thinking of a way to send the message. To his luck, there was a small murder of crows, just outside the camp. He gave it to one of the crows, after he had enlisted its help. He then made sure to keep a close eye on Wallace, not wanting to miss the battle.

On that night, Hannibal had a vision. He saw himself being rowed along in a narrow boat. The scene was familiar because he recalled seeing the boats, in the cloud. He tried to talk to the natives rowing the canoe, but they did not seem to hear him. He started looking into the blue water, which reminded him of the Mermaids. He began thinking of Edward's crown. His thoughts were interrupted by a voice ordering the canoes to stop rowing. He looked up to see their king pointing to something in the distance. Hannibal looked over and saw an eagle with a snake in its beak, standing on a floating log. The native king spoke in his tongue, proclaiming,

'This is the sign we were looking for. We will build the city here.'

The king then turned to Hannibal, calling on him to wake up. Hannibal abruptly woke up, to the voices of the troops, as they were heading out of the camp. He followed the rebels at a safe distance, on their way to the Stirling bridge. Days later, Hannibal watched the battle take place.

On the day, the English were boasting with a show of force, trying to intimidate the rebels. The rebels from across the river, were mocking and hurling insults at the English. As he watched the emotional display of the pre-war ritual, he could not help but wonder if he had made the right choices.

Finally, the English blew the horns, ordering the men to assemble. Once the soldiers formed their lines, they began charging the rebels, who were holding the bridge.

Amid the battle, Hannibal was watching the fray from the rebel's side of the river. The battle intensified, where both sides were at an impasse. Then suddenly, the bridge buckled under the weight of the cluster. This forced the English to cross the river, but yielded little success, making their troops vulnerable to the rebels'. Hannibal was watching Wallace very closely. He noticed a man lurking around him, for far too long. He turned his attention towards that individual, ready to act with his bow. At one point, the man sneakily approached Wallace. He drew his concealed blade, ready to strike the unsuspecting rebel. Hannibal quickly drew his bow, and waited until the rebel was close enough, then let loose his arrow. The arrow struck the would-be assassin in the head and neutralising him. Wallace was alarmed to see the dead assassin. He looked into the distance and saw Hannibal lowering his bow. He acknowledged that Hannibal had helped save his life. Hannibal saluted Wallace, and then approached him when he was signalled to do so. At this point in the battle, the English had to retreat, after suffering too many casualties.

Hannibal was given silver by Wallace, as a show of thanks and gratitude. He then followed the events after Stirling bridge, keeping close to Wallace. He found it odd how Wallace did not recognise him as a Wanderer. Eventually, the rebels' efforts led to the Battle of Falkirk. This time, the English had equipped their archers, with the new longbow, a very powerful and effective weapon at long range. The battle commenced, with both sides engaging each other. The English kept firing volley after volley into the Scottish ranks. The longbows were able to keep the Scottish knights at bay, rendering them redundant. This took its toll on the Scottish rebels, causing the Scottish cavalry to rout under the constant barrage of arrows, exposing the Scottish flanks and rear. The English were able to surround the rebels with their reserves. Hannibal quickly swept in to save Wallace once again. He had another horse, to allow Wallace to flee unscathed. Despite the English knights' best efforts to capture Wallace, Hannibal managed to help him escape. The notion of having the ever-elusive Wallace on the loose greatly irritated the English monarch. But crushing Wallace at Falkirk restored his reputation among his nobles.

After weeks of hiding and being on the run, Wallace approached Hannibal, with a request.

'You were the one that saved me from the assassin at Stirling. And then you again saved me from capture at Falkirk. I know you already went above and beyond, to save me. Might I trouble you for your help one more time?'

Hannibal nodded his assent, replying, 'For you my lord, anything you desire.'

'I have received word from one of my heralds that John Comyn wants to help, I need you to parley with him, and arrange a meeting; I wish to hear what he has to say.'

'Are you certain, Sir William?'

'You proved yourself capable, but I can't risk any of my men, because Comyn will recognise them, but he won't recognise you.'

Hannibal could not believe his luck. Everything was now falling into place. But he felt the terrible burden of having to betray Wallace. Worst of all was that Wallace suspected nothing. Hannibal knew that he was being used by Wallace, because should he, Hannibal, be captured by John Comyn, Wallace would have risked a stranger who can be replaced. However, in reality, Hannibal had Wallace right where he needed him. He felt happy to have accomplished his quest, but he had the terrible price of betrayal on his conscience to pay for.

Pretending to be reluctant, he told Wallace, 'Give me a week to prepare; I don't trust John Comyn.'

'Take your time, but not too long, we need to act quickly.' Hannibal agreed then took his leave.

Before Wallace had a chance to act or escape, Hannibal travelled that same night to John Comyn's villa. He wrote a letter that read, 'The rumours are true,' hinting that Wallace was in or around Glasgow. He then tied the scroll to an arrow, despatching it into the nobleman's chamber. The weight of accomplishment that had initially brought him relief was now replaced with the burden of betraying a rebel with a cause. He felt that by betraying Wallace, he had also betrayed all of Scotland. The magnitude of his actions filled him with guilt and great sorrow. He felt that what he did, left a hollow void in his soul. He was torn by it, but it was a necessity to ensure his survival. He acknowledged that no act of redemption, no matter how grand, could ever absolve him of this crime.

The plan worked, because John Comyn was very charming and disarming, which lulled Wallace right into an English trap. Hannibal could not bear to witness the rebel's downfall, but he had to stay long enough to see it happen, ensuring the deed was done. He next had to quickly acquire Longshank's crown before his time ran out.

With only a week left to finish his quest, Hannibal time travelled through the years, keeping an ear out for military movements or anything that would indicate drastic action. He was successfully able to quickly learn about a new Scottish uprising, led by Robert the Bruce, the new king of Scotland. Edward was still alive at that time; however, his health was failing him. The stubborn monarch persisted on marching north with his army, to quell the new Scottish rebellion. Along the way, near the Scottish border, Edward's health deteriorated irreparably; he was suffering from dysentery. Hannibal was closely following the monarch and decided to risk his chances to seize the opportunity, seeing that he was pressed for time.

One night, he quietly entered the king's tent, when the king was fast asleep. He took his crown, slowly placing it in the shrinking sack. When he turned around to leave, he saw the Stranger approaching him, spear in hand. The Stranger made to thrust the spear into his chest. Hannibal reacted instantly, dodging the attack. The two then struggled for control of the spear. After a short while, Hannibal was eventually pinned to one of the tent's poles, with the sharp end of the spear, against his chest. The Stranger seemed surprised, because every other encounter, he was able to catch Hannibal off guard. Hannibal swiftly reached for the nearest weapon he was able to pick up, which was a metal staff. He swung the staff at the Stranger's head. The Stranger saw it coming and was able to stop it, grabbing the weapon mid-strike. Hannibal then quickly kicked him right between the legs, dropping the him to the ground. This gave him enough time to create a safe distance away from the Stranger. While he was reaching for the knot in the sack, he ran into the king's servants, all of whom immediately ran to call for help, upon seeing him. This awoke the king, who saw what was happening. Hannibal quickly turned around, right as he began time travelling. Simultaneously, the stranger had hurled the spear at him, aimed at his head. Just in the nick of time, he managed to escape the attack. Had there been a flicker of hesitation from Hannibal, the spear would have penetrated his skull. During the panic, he accidently travelled back in centuries, because he was only thinking about getting away. His mind was thinking to travel a long duration away from the incident, to create a safe length of time between him and the Stranger.

When he looked around him, he saw small villages and towns. The buildings looked different to anything he had seen before. The rush of a near-death encounter left him mentally frozen. He released Flavius and rode towards the villages. As he drew nearer, he saw that they had been raided and looted. He travelled on until he came across a farm. He entered the barn, to see if there was any straw for Flavius to eat. Upon entering the place, he was struck on the head, with some kind of heavy object. The blow knocked him down, but luckily for him, he had his centurion's helmet on, which absorbed the strike. He called out in panic,

'No! How did you find me so soon?'

But a woman's voice responded, 'Wait! You're not a Norseman. I thought you were one of them.'

He was dazed and discombobulated from the blow, but he replied in frustration, 'Of course I'm not a Northman!'

'You're wearing Roman armour. What are you doing here?' asked the voice, with great concern.

Once he regained clarity, he saw the woman behind the voice.

He replied, 'It doesn't matter. I have to journey north before the week is over.' He struggled to get up from the ground.

'North? Why would you want to go north?' she said, as she helped him up.

'I have business to attend to,' he told her, as he leaned against the wooden wall.

He tried to recollect his thoughts for a moment. She asked him, 'How did get away from the Marauders?'

'Marauders? I didn't see any raiders on my way here.'

'You are in luck then.'

He interrupted her, with his hand still on his head.

'Is there a city called York anywhere near here?'

'Yes, it is not far from here,' she responded, but then asked him, 'What's at York?'

He ignored her question saying instead, 'Excellent, I will ride there at first light.'

'You must have fought them, to have this many cuts all over you,' she commented, looking at his wounds and torn cloak.

He looked at his clothes and realised that they were destroyed. He saw the holes and cuts, most likely caused by the many struggles and encounters he had lived through.

'Thank you for your help. I will be on my way,' he told her, as he pulled Flavius away.

'Stay the night at least,' she pleaded, adding, 'You cannot travel with such wounds.'

Hannibal did not want to stay, but with great reluctance, he agreed, nodding, still dazed by the blow. Later that night she tended to his wounds. He noticed that she had a strong build, maybe as a result of having lived and worked on the farm. She had vibrant yellow hair, which added to her beautiful features. She had a kind face, emphasised by her piercing blue eyes.

While she was dabbing his wounds with a wet cloth, she asked, 'Where did you find this horse?'

'I found him in Athens.'

'He is beautiful!'

Flavius neighed in response.

'He offers his thanks,' smiled Hannibal.

After an hour of resting from the blow to the head in the soft candlelight of the barn, they conversed well into the night.

'How did you see me?' he asked her, while watching the candle burn.

'I heard a strange noise outside the barn, so I looked from one of the holes, but I was only able to see your feet approaching.'

'You must be an anomaly,' he thought aloud.

'What's an anomaly?' She looked at him with curiousity.

'It means you are able to see someone like me, a Wanderer.'

'Are you a traveller?'

'I am a traveller lost in time,'

She kept pressing him with questions.

'Where do you come from?'

He looked at her, then back at the candle, replying, 'I hail from Carthage. The old empire.'

'Are you mocking me?'

'It's complicated.'

He felt scared talking to her, because the last time he spoke to a woman, he was played for a fool. He was anxious and it was showing.

She realised he was nervous, so she reassured him, 'I believe you, but Carthage was conquered by Rome, many years ago. How would you still be alive, from back then?'

'It's a long story.'

'I'd like to hear it.'

'I am happy to tell you it, but I need to rest for now.'

They slept apart from each other, on opposite sides of the barn. Hannibal was so drained by the day's events, that he fell asleep right away. When he woke the follow morning, he found the woman talking to Flavius. Flavius seemed to enjoy her company because he was very responsive. Hannibal liked the fact that she was so bright and full of hope. She was very exuberant in her interactions with Flavius. He closed his eyes and recollected the moment he saw the spear, as it slowly made its way to his forehead. He began moving his head, muttering under his breath. While he was reliving the struggle, he felt a hand touch his shoulder. He abruptly opened his eyes, breathing heavily, recoiling away. When he was fully conscious, he realised it was the woman. He apologised and told her how he thought she was someone else.

'Who else were you expecting?' she squinted at him, looking confused.

He quickly replied, 'It doesn't matter.'

She was concerned for him, asking him, 'Are you well?'

'Always,' he told her, whilst breathing heavily.

'You were asleep for days.'

When she told him that, he looked panicked. He told her that he had to leave. Despite her concern, he headed towards Flavius, who did not respond to him, refusing to cooperate.

'We have to go boy. We can't take her with us. She will be safe here.'

'I'm still here!' she snapped irritably.

He breathed a sigh of frustration, he then said, 'I can't take you with me to where I am headed.'

She rushed to him, grabbing his arm and pleading.

'I have nowhere else to go. If I stay here, I will die. We have no livestock or plants. The Norsemen took everything. Please, don't leave me here.'

Hearing those words shook him, as they reminded him of his parents disappearing before his eyes. He reassured her, relenting,

'Very well, you can come, but you have to do exactly as I say.'

She quickly embraced him, as a show of appreciation.

'Thank you, thank you, thank you!' she interrupted.

Hannibal then told Flavius to take her to York. She was puzzled by what she heard, thinking that he had gone completely mad. Flavius responded well, neighing in approval, which only added to her confusion. As he was rushing out of the barn, she called out to him.

'Wait! How will I know how to get there?'

'Flavius will take you there.'

'How?'

'You just climb onto Flavius's back, and he will do the rest.'

'How will you get there without a horse?'

'Don't worry about it; I will meet you there.'

While she was mounting Flavius, he slapped the horse on the rear, which triggered him to gallop away. He waited until sundown to release the pigeon. He followed it to York, reaching the city in the dead of night. The woman was able to reach York within a single day, through the night, and managed to reach the city walls at dawn. Hannibal was glad to see Flavius, but was worried about having to bring her along, since she was a responsibility that he was not prepared for. But he saw that Flavius seemed happy with her, and she too enjoyed his company. When she awoke, she found Hannibal feeding Flavius.

'How did you get here?' she asked him again.

'I will explain everything to you later. For now, we must be on our way since you have become part of this journey.'

He presented her with loaves of bread and apples he bought with the silver Wallace gave him. After they satisfied their hunger, Hannibal presented his hand to help her down to the ground.

He asked her, 'Do you trust me?' He had a strangely optimistic smile on his face.

'Why?' she asked, looking sceptical.

Hannibal shrunk her, along with Flavius. The experience felt magical because she found herself dwarfed yet she was horrified because she thought she was being abducted. Hannibal teleported to the secret lake, where he too was terrified to meet the Mermaids. He approached the lake and stood at the edge of the water. He anxiously waited, with his heart hammering. Once they emerged onto the surface, they spoke.

'Greetings Hannibal.' Once again, he heard those enchanting voices, but he was petrified, fearing they will discover the woman.

'Do you have what we asked for?'

He handed them the crown, without responding.

'Why so tense, Hannibal? Is something the matter?'

He anxiously responded, 'I don't know what lies ahead.'

The Mermaids sensing that he was telling the truth, so they submerged themselves, making way for the First Mermaid.

'Quite the clever man you are, unlike anyone we have ever dealt with,' she told him, as she emerged from the lake's surface, her voice ever so mesmerising.

'I have nothing to give you, as a price for safe passage.'

While all this was taking place, the woman was carefully listening to the conversation.

'Oh, but you do.'

Hannibal felt his heart beating in his stomach, thinking that he was about to be exposed.

'You have an interesting relic that we would like to have.' Hannibal held his nerve, despite the tension he felt.

'What might that be?' he quickly asked, being incredibly nervous.

'You have...' said the First Mermaid as her smile grew, making him even more nervous, with the fear growing in his stomach, 'the sword of Attila the Hun, which is really the sword of Mars. Quite a powerful weapon.'

He was relieved to hear that because he was willing to forgo the sword instead of failing the woman in his trust, despite having just met her. He handed Attila's sword to the First Mermaid, which she gave to another Mermaid, who then dived into the lake with it. The First Mermaid then offered her hand, which Hannibal was hesitant to take. She reassured him that he had nothing to fear, since he had carried out his end of the bargain. After a pause, he reached out and took her hand. He had no other option but to go along with her.

She then told him, 'I have never been fond of any human before, but you are someone special. I just wanted you to know that.'

He did not know how to feel about what she had just told him. Before he could formulate any reply, she slowly pulled him under the lake, and he closed his eyes. He decided it was easier for him to surrender to his fate. When he opened his eyes after a short while, just like his experience in the Dead Sea, he saw himself in open water, with no Mermaids around him. When he swam to the surface, he was discovered by the native populace, who were fishing in the lake. They helped him onto their narrow boats and greeted him in their native tongue; he greeted them back, they then rowed to the city. This was the same scene he recalled seeing in his vision. He was in a canoe, being rowed to the city, by the natives. After a short while, he looked in the distance and saw the city above water. It was miraculous, seeing a city floating above the lake; he could not believe his eyes. He turned to one of them asking,

'Is this really Tenochtitlan?'

The native smiled in response.

Once they reached the city, Hannibal was at a loss for words. His mind was unable to comprehend what he was looking at. The locals were staring at him as he was escorted to the king. Once they reached the centre of the city, Hannibal was still visibly in awe of what he saw around him. The king spoke to him,

'Welcome stranger. I am King Acamapichtli. Ruler of the Aztec people. I was informed by our priests of your arrival.'

'Thank you for your kindness, and for welcoming me into your home,' answered Hannibal.

'Tenochtitlan will always be home to those who are our friends and allies.'

'I apologise for my appearance; I am weary from a long travel, and I need to rest.'

'Of course, the guards will see to it that you are looked after. Join us at the temple when the night sky is upon us. By then, you would have had all the time you need to rest.'

Hannibal thanked the king, and was then escorted into a secluded home that was built for him. Once he was alone, he released the woman, who looked scared and was shouting at him, for shrinking her without warning. Hannibal apologised stating that he had no time to explain. He left her to calm down, after having gone through a frightening experience himself. He began wondering if there was a purpose to him being at Tenochtitlan. Unable to find answers, he thought about how he might find the spirit world. He recalled that he would find it in the Dakota territory. But he had no idea how to get there. The woman was able to calm herself, after much time to rest. She approached Hannibal, who seemed troubled, gazing at the wall, in deep thought.

'I never asked you for your name,' she politely said.

Hannibal turned to her and replied, 'My name is Hannibal. What's your name?'

'I am Rowena.'

'Clever name, White-haired,' he commented, smiling.

'How were you able to speak to the natives?'

'Like I said, it's complicated, but as I said before, I will explain everything once we make it to the Dakota territory.'

'Dakota territory? Where are we?'

'I have no idea. Trust me, I will explain everything to you once we make it to the Dakota territory.'

She silently nodded in agreement, seeing that he had been honest with her thus far. For the remainder of the day, he slept on the ground, vacating the bed for her. She, on the other hand, spent the day watching the natives going about their daily lives. She was amazed by what she saw. She never thought she would ever leave her village, to see such an incredible and serene part of the world. In his sleep, he had a vision, where he was back at the ice lake. This time he was alone. He was vaguely able to hear the rhythm of the sea shanty; the marauders were singing. When he stepped forward to get closer to them, the vision abruptly ended. He then transitioned into a normal dream. He found himself in the black void, typically what he would see when he was revisiting or reliving his thoughts. He was trying to imagine what the spirit world looked like. But he was unable to, being deafened by the silence of the void. After enduring the much-needed silence, he awoke to Rowena singing a song.

'My mother told me, someday I will buy
Galley with good oars, sail to distant shores.
Stand up on the prow, noble barque I steer.
Steady course to the haven, too many foemen.'

As he sat up, he said, 'That's a nice song. Where did you hear it?'

She turned around.

'Welcome back, stranger,' she humorously commented, smiling at him.

'It's good to be back, but where did you hear that song?'

She sat down.

'A traveller from our village read a poem from Egil's saga. He also sang the words in the same way you heard me say them.' She ate from the fruits on the table, looking at him inquisitively, 'The last time we spoke, you mentioned that you were a Wanderer, or traveller, I don't quite remember which one. What did you mean by that?'

Even though he had promised to explain later, he noted that she was very persistent. He looked at her, taking in a deep breath, and tried to explain himself,

'When I was a child, I volunteered with my father for the Carthaginian army. The second Punic war was on the verge of breaking out. I deserted the army after my father died. I came across a relic, which preserved my youth. I had lived a previous life, in service of Rome. Later, I happened upon a governor, who took the relic from me, then had me killed, for whatever reason. When I died, I was offered the chance to have my life back, ever since I had touched the relic. You see… only a person who has interacted with a relic, can become a Wanderer, after death. But that is if you wish to return, and every Wanderer does so by choice.'

'I have heard many stories, at our village gatherings. But none were quite as far-fetched as what you have told me.' The moment felt sombre for her, recalling the raiders, killing and looting in her village.

'But I have travelled many places, far and wide. I have seen many worlds, but none like this one. These people are different from anywhere else I have ever come across. They are peaceful and welcoming. Not like the hostile world I have witnessed, which I hope is far from here.'

'You are a man full of mystery and intrigue. I would like to hear more about your adventures. I also want you to know that, for someone who seems dull and gloomy, you are a very interesting person.'

He could not tell if she meant what she said, but she seemed genuine. This had reminded him of his time with Boudica, and how she used her charm to acquire the Hourglass from him. He really liked Rowena, but was afraid to relive that experience, should she turn out to be another Boudica. He appreciated her endearing and warm demeanour. He sensed that from her, every time she spoke to him. She was also very pretty. He liked the fact that she had a strong build, unlike most women he had seen around the world. Despite being honest and formidable, she was also very feminine and gentle, which only added to her qualities. When he looked at her, he realised she was holding something in her hand, that was around her neck. She kept it in her hand as she gazed outside, through the doorway.

'If you don't mind me asking, what is that thing around your neck?'

'It is a wooden cross,' she hesitantly responded, with her mood reflecting her defensive response.

'Are you a Christian, or was it a gift?'

'I am. Why do you ask?' she responded in a truculent tone.

Hannibal smiled in response, which she found reassuring, yet strange, given the intensity of the moment.

'If you liked a poem from Egil's saga, then you will love Eleanor's chanting.'

'Eleanor? Who is Eleanor?' she curiously asked, having never heard the name before.

'I heard her sing at the Hagia Sofia.'

'You have been to the Hagia Sofia? In Constantinople?' She looked surprised.

'You know about the Hagia Sofia?' he foolishly asked her, being oblivious to her time period.

'Everyone knows about the Hagia Sofia. The greatest structure in Europe.'

For some arbitrary reason, this prompted him to ask about the song, from Egil's saga.

'Was Egil a Saxon?' he asked her.

'He was a Norseman. Why do you ask?'

Her response gave him a feeling of butterflies in his stomach, sending chills up his spine. The look on his face indicated he was having an epiphany.

'The marauders are Norsemen!' he thought aloud. 'The child. She brought me to the ice lake, in Norway. Because that's where the black rose will be. I will find it in Egil's time period. That is what they were singing. I recognise their humming now.' He knew he must have looked like a madman, saying nonsensical things out loud. Her expression was of deep concern for him.

'Is everything all right?' she asked him, looking worried.

'No,' he quickly replied. 'As soon as I venture into the spirit world, I must find the swordsman, and then the Praetor. Afterwards I can look for the token,' he rambled on.

He was interrupted by the voices calling him from outside his abode. Rowena hid in the small room. When he opened the door, he was met by two eagle warriors, holding torches, as it was getting dark. They instructed him to come with them, he nodded and followed them. After walking through the city, being escorted by the warriors, they reached the pyramid temple. He was stunned by what he saw. The structure looked magnificent and grand in stature. The locals were standing at either side of the great steps, leading to the top of the beautiful looking pyramid. As he ascended the pyramid, his eyes were fixed, staring at the local's decorative clothing. They had strange and colourful patterns of paint on their faces. He was astonished to see their attire. This was reciprocated by them looking at his chain mail and armour. The irony was that neither party had seen the other before, which only added to the amusement of the moment. He watched as they quietly gossiped among themselves, while they looked at him. When he reached the top of the pyramid, he saw the elders and priests flanking the king. They were all gathered around a small pyre. He felt elated, when he was on top of the pyramid, looking down at the city at night. It looked amazing, being lit by many torches and small pyres. One of the priests presented him with a wooden bowl that contained a mud-like substance, mixed with water. He took the bowl and drank the contents. He began to experience a state of hallucination he had never felt before.

The king instructed him, 'Look into the fire.'

Hannibal did as he was told. He saw the fire being extinguished, taking reality with it, leaving only the smoke rising in the air. He heard Rowena calling from behind him. He quickly turned around. When he did, he found himself looking at her, but they were inside a treasure chamber. The place was filled with mountains of gold coins, artefacts and trinkets. The chamber had many elevated stone heads, high up on the walls, near the ceiling. After looking around the chamber, he turned to Rowena, and saw that she was afraid.

'Take the Medallion,' the king instructed softly in his authoritative voice.

Hannibal looked behind Rowena, and was able to see the Medallion, placed between the hands of an ancient statue. He gently told Rowena, 'Come with me.'

They rushed to the Medallion. Before he was able to grab it, the place began violently shaking, as though an earthquake were taking place. The mouths of the elevated stone heads began pouring down sand into the chamber, slowly filling up the space. She took the Medallion then followed Hannibal out, running towards the entrance arch, which led out of the chamber. Before they reached the archway, the Stranger appeared into view, obstructing their way out. When they first saw him, they stopped running. Hannibal told Rowena to stand back, and to escape the chamber, while he kept the Stranger occupied. Hannibal pounced on the Stranger, not giving him anytime to unsheathe his Roman Gladius. He had him up against the wall. She ran past the archway, but the Stranger was able to escape Hannibal's clutches Hannibal quickly reached for a golden rod near him but the Stranger reacted by skewering Hannibal in the stomach. The blade went right through, penetrating his back. The Stranger turned around to chase Rowena, but Hannibal furiously tackled him and held him tight in place. The stranger tried to break Hannibal's grip, but it proved too tight for him. The chamber then collapsed, burying them alive. The king instructed Hannibal once more.

'Open your eyes.'

Hannibal had his eyes firmly shut, but slowly began opening his eyes. He was tense, breathing heavily. He quickly placed both his hands around his back, expecting to feel blood gushing out or a sword wound. He felt nothing, which was odd, because he had felt the pain of the sword piercing his flesh. He looked scared and bewildered, after this terrifying experience. When he looked at the king, he saw the Medallion in the king's hand.

'The treasure that you saw really does exist. I wanted to see for myself, what type of a person you are before I gave it to you. You proved to be an invaluable and loyal friend. Your altruistic qualities dictated your actions. You chose to save a stranger, over yourself, allowing her to take the Medallion, amidst the disaster. You didn't even think twice about it. I can attest that most men would fold, leaving their friends to their fate, but not you. He who seeks power, yet is unwilling to wield it, deserves this relic. I present you, with the Golden Medallion of the Aztecs. You have earned it.'

'Why do I deserve it?' he cynically asked.

'It was a test, and you prevailed.' The king smiled, suggesting, 'I think your friend might agree with me.'

Hannibal turned around, seeing a teary-eyed Rowena, gleefully smiling at him. She rushed to embrace him. He was happy to embrace her back, but he was still disorientated. He then turned to the king, who approached him.

'I would like to bestow upon you this relic. Use it well.' The king then took a mask from one of the priests, explaining to Hannibal, 'We had a traveller, from the Inca people journey to our lands. He presented me with this mask. It is a relic that I would also like you to have. I have no use for it.'

Hannibal took the mask from the king. The king explained that it would help hide him from his enemies. When Hannibal asked about the Medallion, he was told it glows when he is in danger or when he is close to what he wants. When Hannibal took the Medallion and placed it around his neck, he heard a strong wind howling by, but felt nothing. The king explained,

'What you heard was the spirit of the elder calling you.' He then looked to the sky, calling out with a loud voice, 'Black Hills of Dakota, accept the brave Wanderer. For he is a true friend of the native folk.'

Moments later he found himself at the Black Hills, the voice of the king echoing the words, 'Farewell, Hannibal! I hope we meet again!'

He began looking around him, until he found Rowena. She looked surprised at what had happened to them. He sighed in relief, after he saw that she was well, and had not been affected by the teleportation, which was odd.

He asked her, 'Do you feel ill?'

'No. But what was that?'

'That was teleportation,' he looked at her, wondering. 'What compelled you to follow me up the pyramid?'

'Can a woman not be curious?' Once again, her truculent spirit shone through.

She felt as though he was scolding her, despite smiling and having a calm tone to his voice, as always. She looked at him, and asked, 'Have you never taken risks before?'

He conceded to her, stating, 'One too many.'

'Look!' she exclaimed, pointing into the distance.

He saw a group of riders, following their chieftain, who was wearing a large headdress, with many feathers. Their horses were marked with funny looking symbols. They had red and white dye, on their faces. It reminded him of the Britannic Celts, who painted themselves with blue dye. He released Flavius, so that Rowena can ride on his back. The approaching riders looked intimidating, but he felt reassured when they were not rushing him. Once they were within talking distance from each other, the chief spoke to Hannibal.

'Hau, Dakota.'

Hannibal responded to the greeting of the chief in kind. 'And greetings to you friend. We come in peace.'

The chief introduced himself, with an assertive, yet disarming voice, 'My people have bestowed upon me the name Tall Oak.'

'I am Hannibal, and this is my travel companion, Rowena.'

'You must be the brave Wanderer. And she shall be known as, White Woman.'

Rowena smiled, hinting that she liked her new name. Hannibal smiled in agreement with the chief. He liked the way the Dakota name each other.

'I am here, seeking the spirit world. How can I find it?'

'One thing at a time, brave Wanderer. First, you must surrender your weapons, for you are on the sacred Black Hills. Weapons are forbidden on sacred grounds.'

Hannibal complied, handing over his sword and bows. When they were offered horses, Rowena chose to stick with Flavius, as she took a liking to him. Hannibal was given a red horse called, Running Spirit. The horse seemed strange because it did not behave like a normal horse. The natives kept making clicking noises and other sounds with their mouths, which made the horse obey Hannibal. Rowena rode by Hannibal's side, admiring the majestic surroundings of the Dakota territory.

When they all reached the camp, the chief exclaimed, 'Welcome to the new world!'

He then turned to them.

'We will vacate a teepee for you both, during your stay with us.' Both Hannibal and Rowena looked to each other, exchanging smiles.

The teepees looked identical to what he saw in the cloud, at the amphitheatre. The feeling was unreal, because it marked a great milestone, in his journey. This was a reminder of how far he had come. Even now, he was still in disbelief.

The chief showed them to their teepee tents, then left them to rest for the night. Hannibal felt embarrassed to be in a tent with her. He made up an excuse about wanting to see the plain for himself, during the night. She was able to recognise his excuse, pretending to be oblivious. He spent the night roaming the plain, prowling through the forest. Before the night was over, he spent the final hour above the black hills, overlooking the land. He found it beautiful, quiet and peaceful. As the sun began to rise, he transformed into a crow, to see the land from above. It looked stunning because he had never seen a plain like the plains of Dakota. When he returned to the tent, he found Rowena rearranging their living quarters.

'Good morning. It looks like you were very busy.'

She looked up at him, while on her knees. She stopped her work to ask him, 'Where were you last night?'

'I was roaming the plain. I couldn't sleep.'

'Is something troubling you?'

He vaguely responded, 'Yes, many things.'

She then asked him an unexpected question, 'Back at the pyramid top, in the fire. Why did you choose to save me from that hooded man?'

He casually responded, 'Your life is worth more than mine.'

She smiled wondering aloud, 'Why would you say that?'

'It's true. You have something to live for, I don't.'

She asked, 'Who was the hooded man? Is he someone you know?'

He felt uneasy, but he explained, 'He is called the Stranger. And he is constantly haunting me, throughout my journey,' he then accidentally let slip, 'Part of the curse I guess.'

She looked puzzled, inquiring, 'What curse?'

He quickly snapped out of his gaze, realising his mistake. He then responded, 'Nothing! I must go!'

He left the tent in a hurry. He headed to a different side of the camp. While looking around, he heard someone call him.

'Greetings, brave Wanderer!' and saw it was Tall Oak.

'Greetings, Tall Oak,' he nervously responded.

'There is someone I want you to meet,' the chief enthusiastically suggested.

'Yes, of course,' Hannibal promptly responded, seeming on edge.

Hannibal quickly fetched Running Spirit, then followed the chief. While riding through the camp, he saw the natives look at him as though he was from a different planet. The chief eventually led Hannibal to an odd corner of the camp. It was a lonely and unique-looking teepee, surrounded by totem poles, skulls, and a giant eagle-shaped wooden carving.

Hannibal felt uneasy; he asked Tall Oak,

'Why are we here?'

Tall Oak responded. 'I want you to meet the Future One. She is a blind elder woman, who communicates with the spirit of the Elder.' Hannibal was speechless. Tall Oak continued, 'Proceed into the tent,' leading him inside.

Hannibal took several deep breaths, then cleared his throat whilst entering. The moment he stepped inside, he found her chanting several native chants. She stopped when she felt Hannibal's presence.

'You must be the one they call Brave Wanderer,' spoke the future one in her old, soft voice.

Hannibal's fear intensified, but he tried to remain calm. He responded, 'I must be.'

'I understand that you seek the spirit realm.'

'I do.'

She smiled at him, 'A beautiful coincidence, because we never thought someone like you would ever tread these lands.'

Hannibal interrupted. 'Might I ask why you are called the Future One?'

'I can see things in the future. A gift which cost me my sight.'

'A curse or a gift?' asked Hannibal.

'You must see everything that happens as a gift because things happen for a reason. That is why you are here, for a reason,' she explained to him.

Hannibal nodded and began wondering.

'What happens now?'

She signalled for her servants to close the tent so she could begin the ritual. As the preparations were being made to fill the tent with smoke, she explained to Hannibal,

'Before you become smoke like, your body must be conditioned, to help you enter the spirit realm. Once the ritual smoke fills the air, you must inhale it. You will hear sounds, and see strange things, but you must remain focused on my voice.'

The servants started a fire which began giving off white smoke. It didn't take long for the smoke to engulf the tent. The Future One began chanting and humming. Hannibal began coughing from the smoke. The servants began blowing smoke, after smoking the ritual pipe. Once Hannibal inhaled the ritual smoke, he began to experience intense hallucinations. He felt as though he was in a different place, as was intended. This different place made it feel like he was floating in the air. He began to see all his victims, circling around him, while asking him questions. He tried to concentrate on the Future One's humming, but it was difficult. He briefly saw himself at the ice lake, but the ice cracked open, making him fall in the water. He then saw the Mermaids circling around him, with tridents pointed at him. When they swam towards him, he closed his eyes. He began to hear a man calling out, saying, 'This is violence.' When he opened his eyes, he saw a battle taking place, in a land he had never seen before. He recognised the colourful armour because it looked like the swordsman's armour. The same armour he had seen in the cloud, at Epidaurus.

He asked, 'Where is this?'

'In Japan,' spoke the Future One.

'In what time period did this battle take place?'

'Sengoku Jidai.'

He urged her asking, 'Why am I seeing all of this?'

'You are being shown the past and the future, Hannibal. I cannot control what you see.'

A strong sandstorm swept in, obscuring his vision. When he looked down, he found himself standing on a sand dune. He realised he was in a desert terrain. He heard the winter wind howling in the air. The sound was unique, different to the sound produced by a sandstorm. This prompted him to ask,

'What is that? I heard this sound back at the Aztec city.'

'That is the spirit of the Elder calling you to him.'

He called out asking, 'Is this what the spirit realm looks like?'

'Yes. It is a place filled with fog, smoke, blizzards, storms and sandstorms. That is why it is very hard to navigate.'

At this point, Hannibal had reached the end of the hallucination and he was drained from the experience. He collapsed to the ground, falling unconscious.

He had a dream where he saw his younger self in his family home. He was asleep on his mother's lap. She was singing a lullaby.

'Strangers come, and strangers go. The skies will rise; the winds will blow. Your star will shine, your deeds will glow. You will traverse so many roads. Go on my son; the world is yours.'

This was the night before he was conscripted into the army. He did not recall this memory consciously, because he'd never known about it. The joy of witnessing this moment, brought a tear to his eye. He said to himself, *If only she knew that her words have rung true.* He called out to her. 'Mother!' but this caused the dream to abruptly end.

He was awakened by Rowena, who told him, 'You were calling out to someone in your sleep. What happened to you, Hannibal?'

He took a moment to catch his breath, before replying, 'I saw my mother, on the night before I was conscripted.'

'Are you well?' She was very concerned for him; she kept pressing him. 'Hannibal talk to me. What is happening to you? Ever since we were in Alba, you've been in a state of hurry.'

Hannibal wanted to explain things to her. He began by explaining the quests he had to complete but left out any mention of William Wallace. He was reluctant to explain the regicide aspects of the labours, but he did so with great hesitation. He explained to her that undergoing these labours would allow him to become the Herald. She thought he was a messenger; she asked for clarification.

'Are you a scout? Is that why you were at the village?'

Hannibal let out a brief laugh, he then clarified what he meant.

'The Herald is not a messenger. The Herald is a powerful entity.'

She did not quite understand what the Herald was, much to his relief. She asked him about the voices she'd heard when she was in the shrunken sack.

He cleared his throat, before he told her, 'They were Mermaids. I was speaking to the First Mermaid. We had an accord, whereby I would bring them the crown of Longshanks, as a price for bringing me to the island.'

'Where from?'

He gazed into the distance, telling her, 'It doesn't matter. I have been continually rushing around, from one place to another.' Then he accidentally let slip the following, 'I suppose that within itself is part of the curse.'

She then pressed him on that statement once again like before, gently insisting, 'You mentioned that the other day. What did you mean by it?'

Realising he was cornered this time, he tried to feign being busy again. But she firmly pushed him against the tent, insisting that she deserved to know, as his travel companion. He finally relented.

'Returning from the dead comes with consequences. I refer to them as a curse. I can no longer recall memories from my past life. I am also lost in time, meaning I cannot see my family, only in my dreams. Being back from the dead also changes a person, but I am not sure how it changed me. The worst part of it all is that I am immortal, cursed with eternal youth or life. That is how I was able to time travel, and how I was able to visit the different corners of the world. But having said that, should I be attacked or harmed by certain individuals, I will die. The silver lining is that I will be sent to Hades—'

She interrupted him asking, 'Do you mean Hell?'

'Whatever Hell is sure sounds like Hades.' Hannibal seemed indifferent.

'What about the Stranger? How does he fit into all of this?'

'The Stranger is part of the curse. He hunts me down, everywhere I go. He came very close to having me killed on several occasions.'

It was all starting to make sense to her, but it still seemed far-fetched. She could not understand all of it, and said, 'How is all of this possible? I believe you, but it seems so supernatural and unreal.'

He reminded her, remarking, 'Some things are beyond the scope of reality, not meant to be understood. Even though I went through everything I have described to you, I myself still am in disbelief. The mind is incapable of explaining the inconceivable.'

She remembered the teleportation and the hallucinations in the fire, stating once again, 'Having experienced some of these things myself, I tend to agree.' She then wondered aloud, 'Is this where the journey ends?'

He lied to her as he said, 'There is more, but I don't know what.'

'You must have so many stories; I would like to hear them some day.'

'All in good time.' He changed the subject, asking her, 'How have you been spending your time?'

She smiled, telling him, 'It took me all day to rearrange the tent. Afterwards, I fell asleep.'

He promised to help her find something to do, rather than waiting around for him. Hannibal then left the tent looking for Tall Oak. He found him at his teepee, speaking to prominent members of the tribe. He was able to enlist Tall Oak's help, to allow Rowena to help the chief's wife in everyday matters. Rowena was pleased with this new arrangement; having something to do, meant she was now able to spend her days productively. The chief told Hannibal to approach him once he was ready to venture into the spirit realm.

Hannibal often spent time helping Rowena learn the native tongue. He also spent plenty of time teaching the natives how to create composite bows, which were far more powerful than their hunting bows. He also trained them how to use the bow effectively. He showed their artisans how to make the leather gloves, which helped a marksman release arrows safely. Tall Oak was so impressed with Hannibal's marksmanship, often taking him hunting. He also appointed Hannibal to teach his eldest son, Tecumsah, how to use the composite bow. Hannibal also taught them how to wrestle, which quickly became a form of entertainment and showmanship among the tribe. Hannibal would spend a lot of time with Tecumsah. He taught him how to think like a strategist, and how to analyse events. Hannibal would share with him wisdom from around the world, but he never swayed him away from his own beliefs. As a result of Hannibal's mentoring, the boy became more aware and was shaped to be a clever man, more so than any man from his tribe.

Rowena was also making her mark on the native women. Hannibal saw her influence among the natives when she added her own decorations as part of their clothing. She also shared the way her people prepared food with them. At first, this was negatively received, but that changed over time for the better. He was so proud of her, especially when he saw her innate leadership skills and how influential she was. It was a testament to her strong and truculent character. It didn't take long for Rowena to hound Hannibal into teaching her the martial skills he knew. He did his usual of trying to come up with excuses, but she was relentless. It ended the same way with him conceding to her. She knew how to use her charm to get what she wanted, and it always worked on him.

He would often take her to a nearby territory, near the Dakota lands. It was at a lake, in a forest, secluded and away from other people. There he taught her how to use a sword as well as a bow and spear. He also taught her how to wrestle. He was impressed by how fast a learner she was. Although she was physically stronger than him, he was a very elusive target, making him a difficult opponent to best. With every duel, she would pioneer new ways to bridge the gap. Eventually she was able to find ways to out duel and best him at everything. He would often tell her stories from his many adventures, after every lesson. Rowena always looked forward to the stories because Hannibal was a very talented storyteller. She always credited him with being a great teacher as well. Because he had the natural ability to explain anything — no matter how complex.

Hannibal became somewhat attached to Rowena. She had an irresistible charm about her, that drew him to her. He made efforts to get closer to her, but his awkward attempts ruined his advances. He was trying to be someone he was not, which she detected and was repelled by. Despite his best efforts to get close to her, his deeds did not have the desired effect of bringing her closer to him. His awkward nature around women made him undesirable. Despite being very clever, he was not socially intelligent. She often hinted at him that she liked him back, when she would tell him to smile more often. She wanted him to open up, rather than hiding behind his outer stoicism. Unfortunately for him, he was not well versed in matters of the heart. Tall Oak often reminded him that he was a very clever man because he had the ability to solve problems. He told Hannibal that he was smarter than anyone he had ever met before. The irony was that even though he was reminded of being clever, repelling Rowena made him feel very foolish.

It wasn't long before Hannibal noticed how Tecumsah would always approach Rowena. It was apparent to him that Tecumsah had taken an interest in her. Soon that very quickly turned into Rowena taking a liking to Tecumsah in return. Hannibal was amazed by Tecumsah's ability to get close to Rowena, even though he could not see how Tecumsah was charming. Even though it greatly irritated him to lose her, he was happy for them. She never noticed his presence when he would watch them. This was something he had mastered over his many years of experience, remaining undetected.

The chieftain's eldest son was the total opposite to Hannibal. He was charming, handsome, dashing and always commanded an assertive presence. However, he did not possess Hannibal's levels of intellect in deviousness and strategy. Rowena liked the fact that he was confident and persistent, yet pragmatic. Hannibal realised that his quality of being understanding was mistaken for being a pushover. He was happy for her and Tecumsah, but the idea of someone else being able to succeed in love where he had failed burned a hole in his heart. This time, it was his own making that drove Rowena away, and he accepted that the fault lay with himself. His silence and quiet demeanour were also mistaken for not being confident.

This led Hannibal to ask himself, *Is this part of the curse too? Or is it just me?*

This was the tipping point that helped him make his decision to move on. This was another quality that Rowena did not like about Hannibal; he easily gave up on love. But she was oblivious to the true level of pain that he had endured for centuries. Hannibal was not a broken man because he was weak, but he recognised that the world was quick to judge him. Hannibal became more withdrawn from the tribe. This became evident, when his presence was not felt as strongly any more. The once roaming Brave Wanderer became scarce. When Rowena told Hannibal that she was to be wed to Tecumsah. Hannibal hid his agony behind a strangely genuine smile. He really was happy for them both. However, this was all the more reason for him to move as far away from the new world as possible. When she asked him about what follows next in his journey, he excused himself saying he was being summoned by Tall Oak. She blocked his way, concerned for him, asking if he would stay—he told her that he didn't know. He gave her the knot of Gordium as a wedding gift, stating,

'This has been my companion from the very beginning. We have been to all corners of the world together. I pray it serves you well. I am not sure what lies ahead for me in the future, but I would like you to have it. Give you a chance to see the world for yourself if you choose to do so.'

She was saddened to hear him say that; she was worried about him, voicing her concern,

'Is this a farewell?' she asked him, with a sombre tone to her voice.

'I'm not sure, but Tall Oak has summoned me for a private affair. I cannot keep him waiting.' He sounded defeated, but she did not want to press him.

She did not expect him to give her something so precious. She could not help but embrace him, because she did not forget how much he had helped her. Tecumsah then approached them. He was able to sense Hannibal's sorrow, but he was not able to place the reason behind the sorrow. When he learned from Rowena that Hannibal was leaving, he too embraced him. Tecumsah greatly appreciated Hannibal, and everything he had taught him. Hannibal had been a profound influence on him, being a great mentor.

He was always able to confide in Hannibal. Hannibal reassured them both that he would visit if he could. They jokingly threatened him if he didn't, which made him smile. That night, Hannibal approached Tall Oak, informing him, 'I believe it is time, old friend.'

This was five years since he was asked to 'come when he was ready.'

Tall Oak smiled in response, repeating, 'It is time, my friend, the spirit of the Elder awaits you.'

The chief took him to the Future One, where he would resume his journey. Hannibal was anxious to venture into the unknown. When they reached her tent, he turned to the chief for the final time stating,

'I suppose this is farewell.'

Hannibal looked back at the camp, thinking about Rowena. He said to Tall Oak, 'I don't know if I am ever coming back.'

Tall Oak smiled reassuring him. 'There will always be a place for you here, for you are a true friend.' He stretched out his arm, offering his hand to Hannibal.

Hannibal shook his hand, telling him, 'I hope we meet again.'

Hannibal parted ways with the chief and headed into the tent. He had an uneasy feeling in his stomach; it was an incredible pressure.

The future one said, 'Greetings, Hannibal. This is a rare opportunity for the Dakota.'

'What is?' asked Hannibal, with a shaky voice.

'For centuries, we never thought it would ever be possible... for the world to send a Wanderer to the new world. You see Hannibal, only a deceased person can enter the spirit realm and survive it. But there are exceptions.'

'Why is it a triumph for the Dakota?' asked Hannibal, hoping for an explanation.

'Because many chiefs have tried to retrieve an ancient relic, which graced the Elder's head. The Elder's headdress. It is a relic that would allow you to navigate the spirit realm. The other relic that can also help you do so is the one around your neck, the medallion. The difference is the medallion helps you find what you seek in the real world as well, but it does not show you the way, not even in the spirit realm, unlike the headdress.'

'How do I know what to do once I am in the spirit realm?'

'Fear not brave one, my voice will be your travel companion.'

Hannibal was presented with a ritual pipe, which was another relic. He was told it was one of the gateways into the spirit realm. The ritual began like the last time, with the servants filling the tent with smoke. The future one began chanting, as Hannibal smoked the ritual pipe. He began coughing because he had never tried it, despite seeing the ritual many times. He felt the world around him change, but he couldn't see it. Shortly after, he felt the sand dunes beneath his feet, as the smoke cleared. When he stepped out of the smoke, he was met with a sandstorm. In the midst of the storm, he could not hear anything, not even the storm itself, but he could feel it on his skin. He was able to think, in the calm solace. The silence was broken by a howl. The howling was far away, but the echoes were heard by Hannibal.

He thought, *What is that?*

The future one's voice answered him,

'That is the spirit of the Elder calling you.' Hannibal heard her breathe a loud sigh of relief. 'Follow the voice,' she softly instructed him.

When Hannibal looked in the direction of the voice, he could see a beacon of light, marking the origin of the voice. When he looked down at his chest, he saw the medallion glowing. It was not very clear, nor easy to spot the light in the distance, because the sandstorm was obscuring the light. Hannibal began walking through the storm but had no idea if he was heading in the right direction. Occasionally, the howling would help him discern the direction. He spent days following the howling in search of the light. In the end, he was able to reach the end of the storm and saw an oasis. When he rushed to the water, he was able to make out a skeleton, with the headdress above the skull. The future one's voice spoke to him,

'That is where the Elder died. He was parched. He thought that the water in the spirit realm would sustain him. He was not aware that the living cannot survive in the spirit realm, but he overstayed his welcome.'

'A terrible fate for anyone to suffer.'

Hannibal retrieved the headdress. He did not wear it, because it didn't feel right. While inspecting the relic, the future one spoke to him again.

'Place it on your head.'

Hannibal obeyed her instructions. When he did, the storm lifted, and he was able to see the desert.

'All I see is the desert. What do I do now?' he called out in distress.

'Close your eyes and think of something. Think of somewhere you have to be.'

He began thinking about the battle he saw in the smoke. He began to hear the clash of swords and horses neighing, with arrows whistling by, across the field. He heard raging voices calling out, in the midst of battle. When he opened his eyes, he saw the battle. Warriors with colourful armour, some wearing masks. He began looking for the swordsman, amid the fray. It didn't take long to find him, duelling any man he faced. Hannibal was fascinated by his prowess. It was like watching someone trying to slice water or smoke. He was elusive, fast and struck true with his blade. He would often hurl insults at the men, prompting them to furiously charge him. He was using their rage to his advantage, cutting them down one after the other. During that moment, while gazing upon the battlefield, Hannibal began thinking about bows. He was too engrossed in his thought to realise what was happening around him. When he turned around, he saw guards chasing a hooded figure, with a longbow on his back. He followed the men into a cabin in the woods. When he entered, he found the bow and the green cloak on a table. He picked up the longbow, which was, in fact, a relic. He also took the cloak, placing it in his sack. When he went outside, he saw the Stranger staring at him, hiding behind a crowd. He raised the longbow and loaded the arrow. He released it when he found an opportunity. The arrow passed through the settlers harmlessly, hitting the Stranger in the chest. Hannibal was shocked by what he saw.

The voice informed him, 'The bow belonged to the hood, another relic — this one you get to keep, since Rowena received your arms that were confiscated from you at the Black Hills.'

'What happens now?'

'Come to me.'

Hannibal found himself inside the tent, but he was still in the spirit realm. The tent was still filled with smoke.

He asked her, 'Why am I back here?'

'I needed your help to retrieve the headdress.'

'I need weapons; a bow will not suffice.'

The future one began laughing. She told him, 'The elder would like to bestow upon you more gifts, to compensate you for your loss. The first will help you become smoke-like. The other will be to guide you to find a very powerful relic, Wukong's staff.'

Hannibal liked the sound of that. When he handed her the headdress, he felt a strong breeze.

He asked her, 'What just happened?'

'As a show of gratitude, the elder has turned your own body into the shrinking sack. You can now summon and shrink objects. You are now smoke-like as well, ready to become the Herald.'

When Hannibal firmly held the longbow, he began squeezing it, which made it shrink into his body.

'This doesn't feel right, but it is convenient,' he told her, stating his approval.

'With time, everything will feel right. Be free, brave one; the Elder appreciates what you have done, for the Dakota.' Those were her parting words to him.

Hannibal now felt lost because he had enjoyed life with the Dakota. He was free to roam again, which was unsettling, since he had gotten used to having company. He began to think about how to train to become a better swordsman. The thought of the Stranger besting him in every duel greatly frustrated him. This prompted the spirit realm to bring him back to the desert. He remained distracted by his thoughts, until a voice called him,

'Welcome stranger. What is your name?'

When Hannibal looked up, he saw a rider. It was the spirit of a legendary Arabian knight.

'My name... is Hannibal,' he answered him, feeling bewildered.

'Welcome to Arabia, Hanni-Bal. I am Antara Ibn Shaddad,' proudly spoke the spirit, with a flamboyant flare to his voice.

'Why does your name sound familiar?' Hannibal asked curiously, not being able to recall the name.

'My legend has been immortalised among the many tribes in Arabia. I was renowned for my bravery, chivalry, strength and poetry.'

Hannibal noticed the similarity between how spirits and the Oracle interacted with him. The only difference was that the spirit of a certain person was animated by their character. It also dawned on him that this was the first time he had spoken to a spirit, helping him complete another labour.

Antara took Hannibal under his wing, teaching him proper swordsmanship. Hannibal would spend a year living a nomadic life with Antara, in the deserts of Arabia, out of the spirit realm. Hannibal was taught to be fearless in a duel, no matter who the opponent was. However, despite having practised so much, Hannibal was never able to come close to besting Antara. He was too fast and too strong. Hannibal was always overpowered by the Arabian knight. Antara often stressed the importance of being decisive when wielding a sword. He reminded Hannibal, stating,

'You must never hesitate. Fight every duel as though your life depends on it. Always punish your opponent, taking advantage of their mistakes. Read their movements and try to anticipate their next strike.'

This sounded logical to Hannibal, but it was easier said than done. Hannibal would only spend a year with Antara. He saw him travel among the tribes, winning countless duels. He challenged others to poetry. He was celebrated and hailed everywhere he went. Hannibal was in awe of his charisma, confidence and magnitude among the tribes. Hannibal found that people saw him as a paragon of bravery and strength. This only solidified his legend.

After the year was over, Antara bid Hannibal farewell, telling him,

'Ready or not, life must go on. Your journey awaits you, Hanni-Bal. It was a pleasure hosting you.'

Hannibal said his farewells, which made Antara disappear, taking Hannibal back to the spirit realm. In that moment, he acknowledged that the spirit realm, was like using a relic. He could find spirits with his thoughts. He reflected upon the need to practice his coordination, pacing, endurance, parrying and dodging. He wondered if there was a cleverer way to defeat an opponent, by being sneaky. This prompted the spirit realm to take him to a temple of sorts. Where he was presented before the head of a ninja clan, a ninjatsu master, to teach him how to become a ninja.

'Welcome, Wanderer,' the enigmatic man greeting him.

'What is this place?' asked Hannibal, as he glanced around.

'This is where you will learn to hide from your enemies, follow them, spy on them, and when the time is right, strike them.' Hannibal did not say anything in response, because he was interested in what the master had to say.

'Ninjatsu is about striking at your opponent, when they least expect it. I don't know how much you may know about cunning, but once you have completed your training, you will be like a shadow in the night. Do you think you are ready? Do you have what it takes, to become a ninja?'

A smile formed on Hannibal's face, as he realised that this was an opportunity to making himself even more elusive. Hannibal gladly replied to the master, 'I am willing and ready to learn the way, master.'

'Very well then, Wanderer.'

Hannibal was first put to the test, by being stripped of all his weapons and armour. He was tasked with stealing letters of correspondence from a wealthy merchant, who was heavily guarded by mercenaries. This task was especially difficult, because his physical appearance gave him away as a foreigner. His first approach was to adorn himself to look like a local, by stealing the clothes of a peasant.

He followed his target around for weeks, watching them closely, but from a distance. He noticed that servants and peasants alike were barely recognised and that no one really acknowledged their presence. Having studied their routine, he waited until the merchant's caravan would stop to set up camp. He seized his opportunity to integrate himself and help them set up the caravan camp. He was aware that getting close to the merchant's belongings would take time, so he would have to be patient. Incredibly enough, he was able to infiltrate the camp, without being noticed. He was able to remain obscure by accepting tedious and menial tasks to perform. But to his luck, the menial tasks sometimes involved serving the merchant and his inner circle. Even though it was unusual for foreigners to be part of Japanese society, the merchant and his fellows never took any notice in him. Hannibal maintained his routine, by behaving in a subservient manner, which made him invisible to everyone. The opportunities to serve the merchant allowed him to study the inside of the merchant's tent. At night, he would eavesdrop on the inner circle's conversations, without using his ability. After weeks of enduring the painful cycle of being a peasant, he was never able to find a chink in the merchant's security, and therefore could not sneak into his tent.

One day, when everyone in the camp was unusually busy, using his duties as cover, he waited for the merchant to leave his tent. He then went over to the baggage wagons to set fire to them. This quickly attracted the attention of everyone, including the guards, as their belongings were among the wagons' baggage. Hannibal then quickly snuck into the tent, once he made sure that it was empty. Since he had been in the tent many times, he knew exactly where to look. It wasn't hard to find the letters, and so he quickly made his way out before being spotted. When he left the tent, he was surprised to see the master before him. The master began clapping, as he congratulated him,

'Very impressive. You are quite the little spy. Aren't you? Even more impressive when I heard that you were patient for weeks.'

Hannibal wasn't able to hide his surprise; he promptly found himself back at the temple.

The master explained, 'Yes, that is right, you were being watched the whole time. You did all that was necessary, lying in wait, remaining undetected and creating an opportunity when none were made available. The preliminary phase is over.'

Next, Hannibal was trained to use his instinct to be able to feel the presence of others. This was a difficult exercise, but with practice, he was able to harness his senses to detect other's presence. He was then trained in the many different methods to quietly subdue an opponent without causing an incident or struggle. This aspect of the training was surprisingly easy for Hannibal. He was also taught how to scale and overcome obstacles. It was basically the kind of acrobatics monkeys performed, to move around the wild and to navigate their environment. This took Hannibal plenty of time to get used to performing such manoeuvres. This kind of training took a lot of courage to be able to perfect, but after many trials, he was able to master it. This would serve the purpose of infiltrating into places or escaping dead-end situations. He was trained to make his own sedative agents, which was difficult. He learned how to move in smoke, and how to set traps. He was trained to detect someone's presence, when observing his environment, especially if someone was hidden. He had been taught to use his situational awareness to tell if something seemed out of place. Finally, he was trained to fight like a ninja, and how to improvise, to survive encounters with opponents, no matter the situation. He was drilled by being placed in certain situations and was tasked with escaping or fighting his way out. He managed to succeed every time, which greatly impressed the master. His final test in the training was to be able to fight multiple opponents. This was the hardest test and Hannibal would spend a year before he finally succeeded in surviving multiple opponents. This is when he was brought before the master, where he was surrounded by the ninjas of the temple, in the main hall.

'Well done, Wanderer. You have come a long way in training. There is one final task you must do, to prove yourself worthy of being called a ninja.'

Hannibal never felt so proud and was glad accept such a honour. He replied,

'I am ready, master.'

'Good,' said the master, sounding pleased. 'Your final task is to infiltrate a monk's temple and steal a bronze staff in the meditation chamber.'

This sounded very familiar to Hannibal, he asked the master, 'Before I do, there is someone I must find, and I need your help to find them.'

'I see.' He fell silent, contemplating Hannibal's request, then said, 'Since you have exceeded expectations, I will allow you this one request. Who is it that you seek?'

'I don't know his name, but I have seen him fight in a great battle that took place in the Sengoku Jidai period. He is a very skilled swordsman.'

The master let out a brief laughter before expressing his approval, stating,

'You are very ambitious and daring, because the man in question is Miyamoto Musashi. In this case, he can be your first obstacle, before the final task.'

Hannibal was given back all his belongings and was guided to the battle of Sekigahara. Hannibal left the spirit realm back into the real world. It felt relieving to be able to breathe fresh air, to feel the calm breeze against his skin and see sunlight once again. He released Running Spirit, and began guiding the horse, by using the clicking noises that the Dakota taught him, to control and lead the horse. He took out the longbow since he did not possess a sword. He watched the battle unfold. It was unlike any battle he had ever seen take place. The fighting on both sides was intense, fervent and filled with passion. Each side was fighting for their lord. Many Samurais died, protecting their masters. Hannibal kept moving around the battlefield, remaining outside the fighting, looking for the swordsman. After looking around for hours, he was able to finally spot a man insulting others, before every duel. When he saw who it was, he immediately recognised him from his armour, and the fact that he wielded two swords. He kept his eye on him the entire battle. He waited until the fighting was over, then rode up to him. Before the swordsman had a chance to turn around, Hannibal fired an arrow, hitting Miyamoto's thigh. Hannibal quickly fired another arrow that penetrated his neck. He felt sick to his stomach to have to resort to such dishonourable means.

With great displeasure, Hannibal told the immobilised Miyamoto,

'I am very sorry.' he then despatched Miyamoto with a final arrow to the head.

Miyamoto's eyes never left Hannibal's face, as he collapsed to the ground.

Hannibal used the ritual pipe, after lighting it, to make his way back into the spirit realm. Upon entry, he found himself still on his horse, in the hall, before the master.

'Masterfully done, Wanderer. Masterfully done. It is rare to see an outsider carry out a task with such ruthless efficiency. I am impressed, but now to your final task. The staff you are to steal you will get to keep, as a final reward.'

Hannibal was given Miyamoto's sword, as a reward for his actions. Afterwards, he was guided to the temple he once visited, back in the middle kingdom. Before leaving the spirit realm, he was surprised to see the little girl waiting for him.

He asked her, 'The last time I asked about the inner energy, I saw a green flame around me. How do I summon my energy?'

She replied, reassured him, 'The gift will come to you when you need it.'

When she touched him, a green flame aura surrounded him. He was scared, even though he had seen it before.

'What does it do?'

'It will help you match the strength of your foe.' She then abruptly faded away.

He left the spirit realm for the temple. He was still surprised, to revisit the Shaolin temple he visited centuries ago. He walked around, expecting to find the monks, but the place was empty. Sensing the energy of the staff, he walked to the chamber. He found a shrine room, which was also empty. He carefully made his way inside, walking to a wall, covered in flowers and decorations. Upon closer inspection of the wall, he was able to find the bronze staff, cleverly hidden in plain sight. He then carefully took it off the wall, after having to untie the knots holding it in place. He began to admire the symbols and curves engraved on it. His new discovery was cut short by a familiar voice taunting him,

'All this time, and the Wanderer has the audacity to come to this scared place, and steal?'

Hannibal did not turn around; he was too busy admiring the staff.

The monk continued, 'Instead, you came back, infiltrating and thieving. I knew you were not worthy to tread such sacred grounds.'

Hannibal responded mockingly, 'For an old man, who lives in isolation, I can tell you that you know nothing about me.' He turned around. 'And it pleases me to tell you that you are wrong, old man.' Hannibal smirked at him.

The monk calmly stated, 'I may not know what lies beyond these mountains, yet many travel a great distance, seeking my wisdom.' He then asked Hannibal, 'How do you think this will end?' He then added, 'There is no way out for you.'

'Is that a threat, old man? I don't think you will like my answer,' Hannibal casually warned him.

'You are not leaving here with the relic. We have the chi on our side. The staff will not help,' the monk proudly stated.

Hannibal could no longer tolerate the monk's condescendence.

Hannibal issued a final warning, speaking sharply.

'I don't think you quite understand the situation, you old cretin! Even if there were a thousand of you with chi, you will not stand in my way. But again, I do not expect a fool like you to understand.'

'You shall be punished for your insolence,' shouted the monk.

Hannibal smiled, knowing what came next. He looked up and saw them all intensely frowning at him. They were confident, being surrounded by their chi auras. Hannibal unleashed his green aura, surprising all of them.

'It always has to come to this. And I keep asking myself. why? If this is the game you wish to play, then you have only yourself to blame.' Hannibal began slowly walking forward, waiting for them to rush him. He concluded his remarks, stating, 'I do not enjoy violence, even when it is necessary, even now I still loath it. But dealing with you will be a pleasure.' He hinted at him, 'You first old man.'

The monk snapped at him, 'So be it!'

They rushed Hannibal, hoping to overwhelm him. He quickly responded, by bashing the first one in the chest, violently catapulting him into the others behind him. They were shocked by how fast he was. He quickly began dashing around them. They foolishly did not expect him to know how to use the power of the staff. With every strike, he sent each man flying into an object. He purposely left the monk for last. Once he made short work of them, he turned his attention to him. The monk, angered by Hannibal, furiously charged him. Hannibal feigned a strike to the head, forcing the monk to dodge it. He quickly struck out his knee, with the other end of the staff. This forced the monk to the ground. Hannibal quickly crushed his arms, rendering him impotent. Before he was able to say a word, Hannibal quickly mounted his chest, placing both his hands around his neck.

Hannibal told him, 'You thought your numbers would help you. Unsurprisingly, a group led by a simpleton like you, will never accomplish anything.' Hannibal continued, 'I could ill afford advice from an old fool. Look at you now.'

Hannibal then increased the pressure on the monk's neck, pressing down hard into the ground. After struggling for some time, but to no avail, the monk expired before his eyes.

Hannibal remarked to the dead monk, 'What a waste.'

When he made his way back into the spirit realm, he was rewarded by the master. He was given a large handful of black dust and a small pinch of blue dust, enough to be used once. Hannibal carried on traversing through the spirit realm. After many days of travelling through the realm, to help put his mind at ease, he wanted to visit a place where things didn't remind him of the past. He was looking for something to cheer him up and lift his spirit.

He was taken to a boxing gym. When he looked around, he saw pictures of people wearing immaculate and colourful clothes. He saw column-shaped bags suspended by chains. He saw a ring, with ropes attached to four corners. He saw many devices he had never seen before. Everything he saw did not make sense to his ancient mind. The silence of the chamber was broken by a crowd of people dressed in strange-looking clothes. They were following a black man; whose picture he had seen earlier on the wall. He saw them pointing devices at him, asking him questions.

'Cassius, how will you beat Sonny Liston?'

Cassius confidently responded, declaring, 'I'm gonna float like a butterfly and sting like a bee.'

Hannibal had never heard such a flamboyant voice speak with such vigour and conviction. He especially liked the boxer's smile. Hannibal took an instant liking to Cassius. He kept close, watching and listening to the crowd asking him a barrage of questions. Each time he would respond with a witty remark.

When his opponent's name was mentioned, Cassius asked the journalist, 'Ain't he ugly?'

The man next to Cassius could not contain his laughter. Cassius continued. 'He's too ugly to be a world champion. A champion should be pretty like me.'

Hannibal closely watched the events that followed. Hannibal watched as Cassius would antagonise Sonny Liston at every encounter. He noticed how Sonny would respond to the provocations and insults aimed at him, trying to attack Cassius. Hannibal remembered the swordsman using the same ploy, to provoke an emotional response, rather than allowing them to use their wit. There were several exhibition events where each fighter was showcasing their training to the public. Hannibal was very intrigued by the boxing that he saw. When he tried on some gloves to mimic what he saw, he kept failing. His arms would flail, unlike how Cassius was boxing. Having failed at working out how to box, he gave it up out of frustration. The events culminated in the final showdown, where the two opponents faced each other in a ring. It looked identical to the one he had seen in the gym. He recognised that the arena was shaped to look like a colosseum. When the bell was sounded, it marked the start of the fight. He saw Cassius dancing around his bigger opponent, just as he had promised. For every punch Cassius received, he would quickly respond in kind but made sure to land several more in the process. Round after round, Cassius would dismantle Liston, wearing down his confidence. Halfway through the fight, Sonny Liston would concede the contest in Cassius Clay's favour.

He watched Cassius celebrating in disbelief. Cassius leaned over to the ropes, shouting into the crowd repeatedly,

'I told you! I told you! I told you!' pointing at the judges, who sat by the ring.

When a journalist tried to undermine Cassius Clay's accomplishment, Cassius ignored him, yelling into the crowd, 'I am the greatest! I shook up the world!'

Hannibal realised how Cassius was able to control the situation, despite the way he was treated. Hannibal followed Cassius into his journey and watched him eventually becoming Muhammed Ali. He saw how the champion disregarded those who snubbed him. He watched how Ali warned an opponent who called him by his former name. Hannibal enjoyed watching Ali dismantle that opponent every round.

He would shout at him, 'What's my name? What's my name punk?'

Hannibal again tried to mimic Muhammed Ali's movements, and the way he punched the bags. This time he watched Ali very closely. He kept trying until he was able to improve his technique. Up to this point, he shadowed Ali for many years, but ended up making decent progress. He relished the fact that he was improving, but it was a very difficult skill to master.

This was the point where he decided it was time to move on. But he knew he would not forget Muhammed

Ali. He wondered if there was another form of martial art. One that involved the use of all limbs.

The spirit world then brought him to a slim man, who hailed from a land close to the middle kingdom. He had small eyes, with helmet-looking hair. He wore a yellow outfit, with black stripes on the sides. Hannibal was curious enough to ask him, 'Who are you?'

The man responded passionately, 'My name is Bruce Lee.' He walked towards him with confidence. 'I take it you are here to learn true martial arts?'

Hannibal was curious to see what he had to learn from Bruce Lee and he nodded in approval. Hannibal was taken to a large hall, which was a different looking gym. There he was subjected to harsh training, and endurance exercises. Soon, exercises turned into specific movement sequences. Bruce explained that this would teach him timing, concentration, balance and coordination. Once he had mastered the movements, the martial artist demonstrated what they looked like in a fighting scenario – but they were hard to replicate in a real situation. The training was slow and gradual. Hannibal spent ten years being taught the principles and mindset of utilising the body in a lethal way. Although the primary objective was for self-defence. Hannibal practised using every limb and joint in his body. Bruce was impressed with Hannibal's quick wit, creativity and resilience to adapting to change and the way he learnt so quickly. He was still very hesitant so Bruce Lee told him,

'Don't think too much, just do it.'

Hannibal was still stiff in his movements and in his strikes.

Bruce reminded him saying, 'Water can adopt any shape. When you place water into a bottle, it becomes the bottle. When you place water into a cup, it becomes the cup. Be like water, my friend.'

Finally, Hannibal was able to understand the basics, but he still had a long way to master this new martial art. He and Bruce Lee then parted ways, bowing to one another.

Along his way into discovering the wonders of the spirit realm, he wanted to see the dancing Avars. Once the spirit realm took him there, he noticed that their clothes looked different. They had a modern touch to them, while still retaining some medieval features. They were dancing to that fast-paced music, which he liked so much. It was a pleasant sight he wanted to revisit . Once he grew bored of the festivities, he moved on.

Hannibal wanted to see what plays looked like in the modern age. He found himself in a modern chamber that looked like an amphitheatre, but enclosed, with well-cushioned red seats. He watched a play called *Macbeth*. He liked the medieval re-enactment, despite him being in a modern age. He appreciated the fact that humans in the future always like to revisit the past. They were keeping the old memories alive, through art and theatre. He watched the play over and over. He noticed the name William Shakespeare being brought up every time. This piqued his curiosity enough to want to meet the author and poet.

The spirit realm took him to the spirit of William Shakespeare. Hannibal found himself inside the poet's study, which was a giant library of scripts and books. The man wore funny looking clothes. Shakespeare was reciting a new poem he was working on. Hannibal interrupted him, asking who he was.

'I am William Shakespeare, the father of modern English. Playwright, author, poet and actor,' the spirit dramatically replied.

Hannibal asked him about the *Macbeth* play. Shakespeare explained some of the main themes like foreshadowing, political intrigue, ambition, murder, guilt, betrayal, greed and one's mortal coil. Hannibal was particularly interested in foreshadowing. After the spirit finished explaining the play, Hannibal asked him about the play he had been reciting earlier. Shakespeare told him it was the biography of a Roman dictator named Gaius Julius Caesar. He explained that he was working on the scene where Caesar gets stabbed by the conspirators. Hannibal's sour expression turned into surprise and shock, from the unexpected revelation. Hearing the words 'stabbed by the conspirators' made the world around him feel like it had been suspended for a moment. He recalled being told that a poet will help him find his stranger. But it felt so sudden, because he wasn't expecting coincidence to help him find the second half of his quest. Shakespeare was enthusiastically explaining the build up to the scene, but Hannibal was too consumed by his own thoughts. He interrupted the man asking him, 'Where did it happen?'

'Ah... It happened at the Senate.'

Hannibal left him to his recitation and moved on. He had finally found the one he had been looking for from the very beginning. This moment made all the prior suffering worth it.

Hannibal continued to wander about in the spirit realm. He came across a burning Athens, being looted by Spartans. He watched the violence from a precipice overlooking the city. He decided to sit on the edge, gazing down at the chaos. Moments later, he felt the presence of someone sit beside him. When he looked over, he saw a man wearing a toga, reminding him of Plato. He asked the stranger, 'Why is there so much violence? A never-ending cycle.'

'Man lives to satisfy his gluttony, greed, as well as serving his self-interest. This is where nature's punishment follows,' spoke the wise man.

Hannibal liked what he heard, following up with another question, 'Who are you?'

'It matters not who I am, for I am a simple man.'

'Do you know a Gaius Julius Caesar?'

'We can find out,' casually replied the man.

Hannibal was bewildered by the vague answer. He saw the spirit realm take them to the amphitheatre at Epidaurus. The cloud descended over the theatre, revealing the tale,

The story began with a young man fleeing Rome. He was marked for death by the dictator, Sulla. On his way back to Rome, he was captured by pirates. He tormented his captors, refusing to obey their instructions. Once he was released, he promised them to return, with a mighty vengeance. When he captured them, he had them crucified, slitting their throats, as a show of leniency for having treated him well. His endeavours took him to Hispania, where he became a Praetor. Seeing this part made Hannibal's blood boil. The story followed the Spartacus rebellion. Gaius was absent from Rome; he was helping quell another rebellion in Hispania. This made Hannibal even more uncomfortable, reminding him of his past life. Caesar was able to become consul, after forming an alliance between; himself, Pompeii and Crassus, being aptly named, the triumvirate. One member of the triumvirate, ventured into Parthia, meetings his end, at the hands of the Parthian army, in Carrhae. Caesar embarked on his own campaign, earning many triumphs in Gaul. He eventually decided to venture further, sailing to Britannia. Hannibal was shocked to learn about this because that is where he found the Hourglass. It didn't even occur to him then, that it was Caesar who was there, when he found the relic by chance. When Caesar returned to Rome, he crossed the Rubicon River, igniting a civil war between him and Pompeii. The civil war ended, with Caesar emerging victorious, once he had subdued the Pompeii loyalists. After many years of ruling alone as dictator, many feared he would become king, bringing back the monarchy. The story came to an end, when he saw Caesar enter the Pompeii theatre. It was the final hearing of the senate before he left for the Parthia campaign. That is when Hannibal decided to leave the story.

Hannibal asked the man, 'What could be more shocking, than learning a confronting truth?'

'The future is more shocking than the rest of history combined.'

Hannibal did not understand what he meant.

The old man instructed him, 'Look.'

They looked into the cloud again. Hannibal saw the great war. He saw weapons that produced strange flashes of light and made terrifying sounds. He saw thousands upon thousands of troops, charging into their deaths, across no man's land. Both sides were entrenched on opposite sides, fighting a deadly stalemate. He had never seen warfare, on such a horrific scale. Violence and fatalities, plaguing both sides. The brutal nature of war had gone too far, and he was seeing weapons never used before. Chemical warfare, mechanised death, planes dropping death from above, indiscriminately destroying everything below them. The disproportional nature of war had far surpassed anything he previously thought was possible. This sight was so terrifying that he forced himself to close his eyes, breathing slowly trying to un-see the horror. When he opened his eyes again, the horror faded away. When he looked into the cloud again, he saw the Second World War. Everything looked different, but the people were the same. However, this time, no one was using trenches any more. The weapons and machinery had changed, but their effect was more potent and devastating. He saw the onslaught of the blitzkrieg, and the terrible sight of the bombers, wreaking havoc on the cities below them. He saw how the sailors struggled amid horrific conditions. They drowned as they jumped ship, amid the frenzy. He could not stomach the sight of troops stuck inside the steel coffins called tanks, which turned into an inferno when destroyed. The final scene was that of a city being levelled to the ground in the blink of an eye. His eyes were fixed on the aftermath of the city being turned into a graveyard. He had no words to describe what he saw. In his eyes, mankind was repugnant, and doomed to repeat the cycle of destruction. Seeing so many vile things, brought him back to the words of the Spider Queen. When there would come a time, where he would question humanity and the world with it.

He was at a loss for words. He asked the wise man again, 'Why is it that they never learn?'

'I know now that I know nothing, for nothing makes sense anymore, because it never did.'

'What do you mean?' Hannibal asked, feeling even more confused.

'No matter how much you think you know; you will find that you don't know everything.'

The old man left Hannibal to his thoughts. Another man whom Hannibal recognised sat beside him. Hannibal gleefully exclaimed, 'I was not expecting to see you here!' He was thrilled by Plato's unexpected appearance.

'I too am glad we meet again,' replied Plato, with a big smile on his face.

'Who was the man I was speaking with?' he asked, suspecting the man to be another Sage.

'You were speaking with the greatest thinker in antiquity, and possibly all of history, Socrates,' he proudly told Hannibal.

'Why are you here, old friend?'

'Do you have questions? If you do, now is the time to ask.'

They were back at the sight of Athens being plundered. Hannibal looked down, thinking about the Herald. He recalled the Spider Queen mentioning the elemental objects. He then looked up, observing the violence, devouring the city. He asked Plato,

'What are the elemental objects?'

While observing the chaos, Plato responded,

'There are two types of elemental objects. The morphing dusts and the precious stones. There are six dusts, each allowing one to manipulate and summon the many forces of nature. Green allows one to command and weaponise the land-based vegetation. Red allows one to create land based natural disasters. White gives one the power to unleash wind and ocean-based disasters. Black dust summons fog and smoke. Purple dust places one in a temporary state of sleep. And finally, blue, which is the most powerful dust of all. This allows one to halt time and space around them. Then there are the stones. The orb allows one to control gravity, while the purple ruby can cause earthquakes. One of them can be found in the heart of Africa, guarded by the lost Medjai, in the Congo rainforest. The other is found in Latin America, but the riddle to find it is in England, guarded by the most powerful witch.'

Hannibal asked the Sage another question.

'Are there other powers to the Herald? Ones I know not of?'

'There are different aspects to the Herald's powers. There are the immediate powers, ones you already are familiar with. Then there are separate powers, such as venturing into the spirit realm, without using a relic. The Herald can use the elemental objects, without them having any effect on him. The most difficult aspect of the Herald's powers are the ones based on levels of mastery. Like the Herald's grip. The Herald's grip comprises the following: overall physical strength, the ability to ward off magic, and breaking illusions. The rest you already know what they do. Finally, the ability to summon and use the black hole pocket. This is a space entity, which devours everything in close proximity to it.'

'Where might I find the morphing dusts?'

'You will find them by travelling through the spirit realm, among the native tribes. Also, by being granted them as a gift, but that is difficult, unless you know who can grant them.'

Hannibal smiled at the prospect of finding the objects. Whilst gazing into the distance, he fantasised over what it would be like, to use the elemental objects. Hannibal thought about the relics. He asked Plato,

'Is there more to gathering relics, or do they serve no purpose, collectively?'

'Yes, there is more to them than meets the eye. Possessing five or more relics, excluding the Hourglass, makes one a master of time. The master of time, is someone who possess the Hourglass. Being a master of time allows one to slow or momentarily halt time. There are many benefits to possessing the Hourglass. Like creating a time zone or time lock, to block time travel and teleportation or casting someone into a different time period. You can also neutralise the powers of the Herald. Bear in mind that the Hourglass takes precedence over all relics combined. The destruction of the Hourglass can bring about the world's annihilation.'

Hannibal's happy expression turned into a gloomy look, as he realised what this meant for his future. Plato was able to sense Hannibal's sombre mood. He also felt that Hannibal's morbid side was delighted by this revelation.

After a deep breath, followed by a sigh, Hannibal expressed his concern stating,

'I am not sure what to make of it all. It sounds wonderful when you explain it so plainly, yet I fear there is more to the Herald.'

Plato smiled, glad to see Hannibal's mind at work, 'Correct. Using the Herald's abilities is a double-edged sword. They are so powerful, that they drain the strength of the host, every time an ability is used, that is after the host had surpassed a threshold, which can be a small threshold. Once the host reaches their threshold, the host gets punished for using an ability. When the host dies, the Herald is unleashed, to wreak havoc upon the world, dismantling it piece by piece.'

Hannibal's defeated look was evident, realising what his predicament was. He asked Plato, 'What happens when the host dies?'

'They are suspended over Hades, until they can no longer hold on, eventually falling in Hades and suffering there forever.'

Hannibal found this disturbing, which made him wonder, 'When someone dies, can they be recalled?'

'Yes. The only way for someone to die without being recalled is to be claimed by the Reaper.'

He remembered being told this, but found himself asking the questions, to confirm what he already knew. Hannibal took in another deep breath. Feeling a great burden after having learned so much disturbing knowledge, he asked the Sage, 'How can the Herald be destroyed?'

'Only an entity can do so. And if it ever were to be released, having the world on the verge of annihilation, the restoration of the world will undo the problem. But if the world was to really stand a chance against the beast, they would need to band together, with the help of the Hourglass.'

'Will we ever meet again?'

'I am afraid not.' Plato stood up. 'For all it was worth, you are still a bright man, facing uncertainty, and I believe you will do the right thing. Be that as it may, this is where we part ways. I wish you good fortune.' Plato left him, following in his mentor's steps.

Once Plato was out of view, Hannibal left the precipice. It was a reminder of a reality he was used to seeing, many times throughout his journey. That is how he saw the world, and it pained him to see it such a way. He wanted to leave the spirit realm, because he did not enjoy much of what he saw. This is when he spotted a light in the distance, so he started walking towards it. He wanted to go to his final destination, Rome. He was glad to be rid of his labours. Relief began to set in, because he never believed he would ever make it this far. On his way to Rome, the spirit realm suddenly turned harmonious. The sandstorm was replaced with clouds and a path was paved for him, leading him back to Rome. He found solace in the quiet of the realm, with the storm being lifted for his final steps of his journey. In the distance, he was able to hear Eleanor of Brittany chanting. The closer he came, the louder her voice grew. Reaching the Eternal City was surprisingly quick.

Once he left the spirit realm, he arrived at a day of celebration. It was an hour before the ides of March. He noticed many statesmen entering the Senate Hall. He knew this was the moment he was waiting for. He began shaking with excitement. He could not believe it was happening before his very eyes. Once they all made their way inside, Hannibal waited outside the chamber. After a short while, which felt like hours, he was able to come to terms with wanting to face his killer. His mind was racing with thoughts. He summoned the pinch of blue dust, holding tightly onto it. Right as he was about to walk into the last hearing of the Senate, he heard a loud voice shouting, 'What are you doing? This is violence!'

He quickly made his way inside the chamber. He saw the conspirators quickly rushing him. The man was able to fend them off long enough for Hannibal to blow the morphing dust in their direction. Everyone froze. It even felt like the air was frozen because it wasn't moving freely. He saw the conspirators surrounding Caesar, right before he was stabbed to death. He slowly made his way to Gaius, to see the man behind the legend. Once he was finally face to face with the man who had inspired him to enter the Alternate Realm, he had mixed feelings. On one hand he felt an immeasurable rage. On the other hand, he felt a great relief, mixed with respect and admiration, after having learned his story.

'Hail Caesar!' he said smiling at him. 'We meet at last. This was all I heard, on my way here. I must say, you truly are a man of the people.'

He began circling around the chamber, looking at the faces of the conspirators, while addressing him.

'Dictator for life, they called you. Despised by the Senate. Fear by your enemies, but with the admiration of the people at your back. Despite personally loathing you, I admire your work. Even Alexander the Great did not have the obedience of his men, when he reached the Hyphasis. I'd imagine your men would follow you into the bowels of hell, if you ordered them to.'

When he had finally had enough of looking at the conspirators, he faced Caesar one last time. Caesar was frozen by the dust, but he was coherent. His perplexed look mixed with horror, indicated to Hannibal that he did not remember him.

'After all this time, I am finally faced with the one who made all of this possible. But of course, I take it that you do no remember who I am. But again, why should you?' Hannibal decided to explain. 'You took something of mine, back in Hispania, which I was able to retrieve during your Britannia expedition.'

Julius frowned, trying to recall the memory; the incidents were familiar to him. He began looking at the conspirators. When he looked at the man to his right, he was shocked to see who it was. He voiced his disappointment,

'Even you, Brutus?'

This had distracted him from Hannibal, who had smiled at the revelation.

'It's funny how the justice of the universe works. I've heard some call it Karma. Whatever it may be, I am grateful for the forces that brought me here.'

'Why this violence?' wondered Caesar, with disappointment having never left his face.

'I asked myself the same question: why? I am glad you too have experienced betrayal. Because that is how it felt when you had me sentenced to death. I found that betrayal cuts deeper than any blade can. How could I have trusted you? Not realising that an ambitious man like you, treads on the skulls of others to climb to the top. But you failed to note the fact that no matter how untouchable you may think you are, actions have consequences. I no longer care for consequences, because one way or another, I have realised a single truth that will end all consequences. But that is a problem for another time. I wish there was a way to preserve you, to prolong your suffering. Unfortunately, I must move on.' He slowly reached out, grabbing Brutus' dagger, he told Caesar, 'This is where we part ways, and where it all ends.'

He then passionately stabbed Caesar, having finally had the satisfaction of completing his own personal quest, putting an end to his curse. He then put the blade back in the hand of Brutus, right before the effects of the blue dust began to wear off. He moved out of the way, to watch the conspirators resume their charge at Caesar. Hannibal watched as each of them plunged their dagger into Caesar's body. When Caesar's corpse was left bloody, marking his death, Hannibal was pulled into the black void. After a long absence, he was reunited with the Spider Queen. She applauded Hannibal, presenting him with the Herald, who was intently staring at him like a hound. He was a ghost-like smoke seemingly hooded figure, shaped like the Grimm Reaper.

'Well done, Hannibal. Your journey of a thousand miles has come to an end. I had complete faith in you, despite the many troubles you've had along the way. Your new self will help you accomplish your new goal; you will now have restored hope to destroy anything your heart desires.'

Having succumbed to his dark urges, with a great sense of despair, he no longer cared for what was right. Once he had a taste of violence and vengeance, he wanted more of it. She knew then that she had totally won him over to the dark side. He was now a broken man, who would be reshaped by the Herald.

Hannibal walked towards the Herald, who was mirroring his actions. When he was face to face with the strange entity, he looked at the Herald's glowing blue eyes, and the strange smoke-like shape it had. He reached out to it, and it reached out to him. Once they locked arms, Hannibal began the transformation. Surprisingly, it was not as painful as he thought it would be. After the brief ordeal, he found himself on his hands and knees, facing the ground. He was able to see a reflection of his new self, which looked different. His eyes were now glowing blue, as though he were a spirit. His flesh had turned to smoke, no longer a human body. He slowly stood up, looking at his hands. They were smoke shaped like hands, but it felt strange for him to not see flesh. He felt different, on the inside, as though he no longer had organs. Emotionally, he felt exhilarated, elated and powerful, more than his past human self. It felt like this was a better, more powerful version of himself. It was difficult to describe, even for him. The Spider Queen gave him a black hole pocket, a final gift for becoming the Herald.

She told him, 'The scene of the failed crime is the best place for you to face your stranger, to put an end to any looming doubts, once and for all.'

He was taken out of the void, into the Colosseum. She then disappeared, with her voice echoing the words, 'You are now the Herald awakened, do what you do best!'

When he looked up, at the other side of the arena, he saw the Stranger emerging from the shadows. Just like the last time, it was during the night. He was still wearing the hood over his head, covering his face. Hannibal decided to address him a final time. The Stranger approached him slowly, allowing for Hannibal to speak.

'I am glad to be here, which is strange, yet oddly satisfying. I realised all this time that the best way to face my fears, was to never hesitate. I may not have conquered all my fears, but with you out of the way, I can be a new me.' He sighed, before stating, 'Why was I afraid of my own shadow?' After briefly dwelling on that thought, he told him, 'Doesn't matter, this is where it ends for you.'

The Stranger began to grow in size, hoping to intimidate him, but instead, it made Hannibal smile. In response, Hannibal matched his size, in a show of force. He then summoned his green aura. Hannibal eagerly dashed at the Stranger, punching him in the jaw. The blow was so strong that it knocked the Stranger down. He allowed him to get back up. The Stranger saw Hannibal summon a bronze staff, which was glowing in his hands. Hannibal then waited for the Stranger to rush him again. He responded with a decisive strike to the chest, which the Stranger was unable to stop. When he did so, the power of the blow made him fly across the arena, violently smashing into the wall. The impact of the hit made the Stranger crawl away in pain. Hannibal was now the one on his trail. He began pacing towards him quickly. He began shouting at him,

'Stand up! Stand up! You think you can get away from me?'

His voice had completely changed, marking his full transformation. His voice had deepened, sounding ominous. It sounded like a spirit released from the depths of hell, the kind that was unleashed to wreak havoc upon the world. The Stranger stood up, and leapt at Hannibal, hoping to repel him. Hannibal swiftly responded by brutally kicking him back down. He then mounted the

Stranger's chest. He had pinned him to the ground. He ripped off the hood, to uncover his identity. He was shocked by the unexpected revelation. The Stranger was him. Nevertheless, Hannibal did not show the Stranger an ounce of mercy. He began violently pounding his head, with his fists, into the ground. He then broke off a piece of the wall, pulverising his skull with it. He had decisively defeated the Stranger once and for all. When he emerged over the Stranger's limp corpse, he heard the Aurora declare:

'The Herald has awakened.'

When he looked to the sky, he saw the Aurora slithering away, like a snake. It was making way for the daylight approaching. After dawn, he was walking through the city. He wanted to witness the fall of Rome. He heard about it many times, but he never actually saw the collapse. He time travelled to the year when Rome was sacked. Hannibal slowly made his way to the north gate. He wanted to let the barbarians in, to watch the city being plundered—just like Athens. On his way there, he saw that the barbarians had already breached the gate. A hail of arrows was launched in his direction. All the arrows missed his vital organs but one. When he looked down at the arrow, he noticed that it came from a longbow. The arrow had struck his heart. He thought he was dying. When he looked around him, he wasn't able to see the Grimm Reaper. The moment felt strange because he wasn't dying. He had already experienced what it was like, to be at a knife's edge away from death. But he felt something different. As though he was being sucked into a different dimension. Tired of the world, he decided to surrender to the moment. He was weary of running from his fate. He gently went down on his knees, waiting for his attacker to reveal themselves. When he looked up, he was able to make out a tall woman, with orange hair.

It can't be! he thought. He looked on with intense disbelief, 'It was you!' he remarked, with horror etched onto his face.

His eyes did not fail him. The woman he saw was Boudica. She was slowly approaching him, with her sword in hand. During that moment, he wanted to die from the great the grief he now felt. He thought that this part of his life was over, but he became aware that this was his consequence waiting to happen. This was the result of changing Boudica's fate. The rogue had come back to hunt him down. Unfortunately for Boudica, being caught up in the moment, she too forgot that he had marked her when he gave her the Hourglass. She was not aware that she could not harm him. When her arrow hit him, this put him permanently out of her reach. When she tried to decapitate him, the sword harmlessly sliced through him, as if he were a puff of smoke.

'No!' she shouted in disappointment.

His body was now stuck in a transition between life and death. He began to fade away, out of reality, and into the graveyard.

The moment was filled with disappointment for them both. It was broken by the Aurora's foreshadowing, 'We shall unearth what has been lost!'